Unavowed

Chapte

According to Verne it was ₍

assertion was an uncontested truth I wouldn't have more to ₍

tell.

That Friday evening six of us - nurses and doctors -

had come straight from the local hospital. We were each

skilled in our own specialization and often worked together on

patients or projects. Some colleagues chaffed us for being

obsessive about our chosen profession and we did spend an

inordinate amount of time studying the most recent

developments in our separate fields. Games drew us together

through a shared trait: curiosity.

Verne, the seventh player, was a businessman who

dealt primarily in land. He arrived in our city about three years

earlier and had remained longer than he normally did in one

place. Paradoxically, he was a buyer of land with itchy feet.

We met through our mutual interest in games that were

predominantly contingent on tactics and strategy, but involved a small element of luck. Perhaps it was the attraction to our group that held him in our city longer than was his custom.

The seven of us were part of a larger network of players; our smaller group was hard-core and half-jokingly referred to ourselves as "The Cabal" because, we said, a force pulled us together to test our imagination and creativity by hatching our own games. My spacious townhouse, dubbed "The Shrine," was declared the venue where we would test new games; because of its proximity to the hospital we could easily gather after work. That night, I supplied a light supper with no alcohol as we wanted to stay as alert as possible for the contest.

Verne was the first to present a game that he'd invented to "The Cabal" as we sat cross-legged around my low circular table. He posted a sheet of white paper, about two by four feet on an easel close to the table, visible to all. The title "Genesis" with a very brief explanation of "How to Play" was followed by the subheading, "Rules". The rest of the page was blank. Sarcastic comments such as, "Well, that must have taken you hours, Verne," greeted his presentation. However, when he laid the board on the table and unfolded it quadrant by quadrant, the jibes ceased while we admired the artwork decorating the nine square foot surface. It was a masterpiece. Every inch was intricately designed with colours denoting paths and themes running in various directions through a landscape depicting mountains, rivers and cities - the product of intense thought. There were landing spots designated as positions for pieces representing the players as they moved about the board. Those landing spots were as brilliantly illustrated as every other part of the board and the design on the players' pieces matched the pattern on the board. He must have incurred significant cost to have had the board so intricately manufactured.

Terry, the psychiatrist, spoke first: "Whoever said it, was right. This must have taken you hours. Thank you, Verne."

Verne smiled and said, "Behold 'Genesis'. One of a kind. Are you ready to play?"

Enthusiasm erupted from the group; Verne took over. "It's a journey," he said, "of your own making. In life we're born into a whole lot of rules, but in 'Genesis' we start with nothing. We'll write the rules up with this black marker pen on the blank sheet over there. We may start with nothing, but nothing's ruled out. You have to be clear that any move or rule you make could come back to bite you. Your decisions will stay with you. Your identity could change in and out of the game - because of the game. The aim of my 'Genesis' is to learn something about yourself and those playing with you. It's a spinoff in many games; in this one, it's the purpose."

Verne produced a pair of dice, a set of playing cards and another pack of his own design, well crafted with the same artistic motifs as those on the board. He placed the two packs in their designated spots, dropped a soft suede bag next to his leg and said, "We may need this later." With a broad smile, he added, "We start with luck: highest number goes first. Nothing unusual about that. But you could eliminate everyone else before we start. Then there'd be no game. What are you going to do?"

Within twenty minutes we were engrossed. I looked around the table at my friends' intense expressions. They were desperately trying to acquire various assets ranging from tracts of land to water rights or mines or shares in various corporations to name a few, available in the game. However, as individual players had attached arbitrary value to perceived assets, their efforts appeared indiscriminate.

Then Randy, the cardiac nurse, landed on a spot labelled "Cultural Identity." We looked to Verne for an explanation of its significance. "Choose a culture or religion that you understand even if you don't live by those rules at the moment," he suggested. "You have to know enough about it, or be prepared to find out about it, so that you can justify any moves you make from now on. To move on, you have to surrender some of those assets you've been collecting so carefully.

"You can opt for freedom. But then you have to define freedom and that definition will stand for everyone in the game. But, if you do that, freedom means that you have to be able to justify moves on your own terms. You can't fall back on any existing moral criteria given by some group or other - like Christianity for example. Some people find it hard to function without given rules. They can't just make up their own as they go along. Remember that you may have to make sacrifices for your choice later in the game, so you'd better be sure that you can stick to it."

Verne emptied items from the black suede bag onto the floor that he'd placed next to his leg. Randy said, "I will choose," his hand rifled through a copy of the Bible, a ring of royal office and several other emblems of culture, "the turban. I am going to wear it like my father has all his life - and his father before him."

The grave expression on Randy's face as he wound the turban around his head garnered our respect. We nodded appreciation for his dexterity in tying traditional knots. Randy walked up to the white sheet, looked at the rule, "Respect all who earn it." He picked up a marker and drew a line through the last three words. The game continued and grew in intensity.

Shortly before midnight, by consensus, we agreed to halt the game. Verne said that it was a good juncture because it could be seen as the end, or we could continue at another time.

We stood slowly, suddenly aware of the stiffness in our legs from sitting in one position for hours and stretched for relief. My hefty six and a quarter foot body is not designed for sitting on the floor, but from the inception of the group, "The Cabal" thought that it would be the best way to immerse ourselves in the spirit of our games. Verne simply leaned backwards without moving his legs, his athletic body outlined through his tailor-fitted shirt. He tilted his shaven head to encompass the whole group and said, "So, is 'Genesis' worthy of the Cabal? What's your verdict?"

Sarah, the brain surgeon, broke the moment of silence: "I think I speak for us all. We're in awe, Verne. You're an artist. A genius. At times while we were playing, I felt like the ground shifted under my feet."

"Thanks," said Verne with genuine humility.

"Well, you're wasted in business. Hey, what's that on your shirt - another 'Genesis' motif? Talk about going all out. What is it?" asked Sarah.

Verne laughed "My business is flexible and allows for creative thought. I don't like being hemmed in. So, business gives me freedom to explore ideas. Any new business brings restrictions. I'm not prepared to sacrifice my freedom to come and go as I choose right now. Compared to you, I have the luxury of time. And this little guy on my shirt is me searching for the right questions and challenges to put into the game."

"Is the game finished?" asked Sally, the orthopaedic surgeon. "It took me into another realm. I'll be thinking about it the whole of next week. I hope we'll play again. Some of the moves have changed the way I see each of us - and our group as a whole. At the same time, I'm feeling kind of uneasy."

Verne turned to me and said, "Doctor Ross Martindale, you're a haematologist; you know how things flow. Are you also feeling troubled?" Everyone laughed and Verne continued, "It's up to us whether it's finished for now. It doesn't have to end. If you think of something that you'd like added you can ask the Chronicler to make a note. Ross, you chose that role."

"Is it work?" I said in mock horror, throwing the back of my hand to my forehead.

Everyone laughed and I thought no more of it.

Mandy, the psychiatric ward nurse, made the decision for all of us, "Well, I'm exhausted and I have to resist the temptation to carry on with the game now. There's something addictive about it. I feel ensnared. It would be easy to play on, but we must give Ross his house back."

I declined their offer to help me tidy up and there wasn't much to be done.

Sally frowned and returned to the conversation about the game, "I feel like I have a premonition. Like we're missing something. Weird. Randy, you can take that turban off now. I'm giving you a ride home. Let's go."

Randy turned to us all and said, "I'll never take it off. I shall wear it forever and, if you don't mind, Verne, I'd like to keep this one as a reminder of my pledge. I also have a new pride in my full given name, Rangseetal."

As they gathered at the front door slipping on their shoes, he added to his declaration that he would always remember my lounge with the large circular table, the aroma of delicious food and fine artwork on the walls as "The Shrine" where he rediscovered something very special, something personal. A note of seriousness underlay the jocular conversation as the group, except for Verne, left my house.

Verne remained behind to help me to clear up. I appreciated his offer though I had declined earlier and I was fully aware that a long, deep conversation would follow which I also welcomed; I depended upon our meandering dialogue to take me out of my specialist's tunnel from time to time to dilute my obsession with work. "Genesis" had washed away the fatigue of the day and I wasn't due for a shift at the hospital till Sunday evening.

Verne and I often had winding conversations. I recall one in particular as we ambled along the bank of the North Saskatchewan River that ran through our city. He described how he grew up in a seaport and sometimes felt he was in communication with the ocean. I found it a bit of a stretch when he tried to convince me that he couldn't remember whether he'd first heard a special story of distant lands from his parents, a sailor or directly from the waves lapping on the sand while he sat on the volcanic rocks next to the Atlantic. You could challenge Verne on the facts, but he'd just laugh and say, "I'm sticking with that."

That Friday evening, while he was stacking the dishwasher, Verne started with seemingly innocent questions: "Ross, do you think that God is up there playing dice with the universe and moving cards around on the board to dictate our journey? Or, do you think there's a Devil-figure playing deep below your basement, roaring with laughter at our illusion of choice?" But Verne wanted more and asked, "Or does each one of us humans have a pinch of arrogance to believe that a supra-human being might actually care a tiny bit about our comings and goings? You know, Dr. Martindale, you'd call it hubris because you like classical stuff."

"I'm not rising to your bait, Verne. You're thinking about Randy, Rangseetal, choosing the turban? I wonder how long that will last?" I said.

"Right. He's stuck with it for a while, if he wants to keep playing 'Genesis'. I didn't land on that spot; if I did, I don't know what I would have done. You landed there. Why did you choose freedom, no set boundaries? You knew the conditions and now, according to the contract of the game, you have to keep an open mind about anything that comes your way, no matter how peculiar, unless you can justify brushing it aside. But you don't even know what that strange thing will be. When it happens, you'll have a hard time ignoring it."

"Do you think that Rangseetal is taking the easy path? Opting for a life of multiple choice answers?" I asked as I glanced around the room that we had tidied in less than twenty minutes.

Verne replied, "I don't know. Do you think that the game ends for Rangseetal, or the rest of us for that matter, at your front door? Could tonight's game change us permanently or temporarily or not at all? Perhaps a glass of wine will stimulate the creative juices to help us through that one."

"Great idea."

Walking over to the fridge, I recall thinking that, as a scientist, I should find my "Genesis" challenge of the coming days or the impending chat with Verne pretty straightforward:

haematologists are familiar with biology and chemistry. "All mysteries usually have rational explanations," I said, as I reached down into the fridge door for an open bottle of Chardonnay from Beaune in Burgundy. I poured two glasses, and joined Verne in the lounge where he was relaxing on the couch. I handed him the glass and sat ready to engage in tough dialogue.

Verne appraised the wine. He examined the colour, its reaction on the surface of the glass, the bouquet and finally, relishing the first sip, he said, "Ross, this is superb...and expensive," and diverted, to make me an accomplice, "We understand each other. We appreciate the finer things in life." As he spoke, he waved his hand around my lounge, gesturing to the original artwork on the walls and then with a sweep of his hand stroked the table we had recently played on, "And this? It's no ordinary piece of furniture."

Verne created an image of himself as nonchalant and ultra cool; but he was also extremely well informed about many things. His behaviour was far from random; he could justify his own actions with precision to support a personal commitment to his decisions. He always planted topics firmly in a context - a pond that starts clear and innocuous, but inevitably turns into a bog.

I smiled and admitted, "It's a polished cross-section of ancient oak from an English forest. The tree lived its full cycle and was removed to make furniture."

"Extraordinary," said Verne, "But I'd expect something like that from you. How much is the insurance?" he jested.

"There's no point," I answered.

"I know. So, does all this stuff you have, give you that sense of freedom? So much so that you feel you don't have to rely on 'The Turban' or any other set of rules? Is that why you think that you can opt for 'Freedom' in and out of the game?"

"I'm not that free," I laughed, "I'm lucky to be free from university loans. Maybe one day I'll be that wealthy but, right now, my freedom comes out of my work. I'm a doctor, a scientist. Questions about the universe are grounded in evidence. I see life and death every day."

"I hope your work doesn't get in the way."

"What do you mean? You're in a different boat. But no less comfortable. You own land all over the place."

Verne's answer, "Like you, not enough yet. Land could be my freedom one day. I aim to own a piece on every continent and any significant island. If I can do that, I will be able to buy into any country or culture I choose, never mind what anyone else thinks. But to answer the question about you, your work shouldn't trap you into a way of thinking and let it define who you are."

I contradicted him silently, thinking that you can't purchase a place in another culture. You have to grow into it, absorb all the customs; you have to live it. I preferred to remain culture-neutral, free from the trappings of restrictive ideas generated by traditions handed down and practiced for what I considered then to be nostalgic reasons.

Verne seemed to read my mind and pushed his point with perfect timing. He said, "Doctor Martindale, you probably think that you are absolutely free from any cultural or religious fuss or rules," he said, swinging his bare feet onto my Persian rug and padded over to the floor to ceiling bookcase behind the table. In mock-admiration he proclaimed, "My, Doctor Martindale, what an impressive array of books you have." From my chair, I simply raised my eyebrows. "Current medical books," he said and turned his head to gauge my reaction. "current, I stress. A fine collection of nineteenth-century novels and modern novels. A few books by contemporary thinkers - mainly American. And what's this, Doctor? A collection of many - most of Shakespeare's works?"

"Your point?"

"A splendid collection for a culturally free man of the twenty-first century."

"Most are just stories. What are you getting at, Verne?"

"Anyway, next to Shakespeare is a pppperfect place for me to leave 'Genesis' for a couple of days. I'll pick it up next time I'm around if you don't mind."

Verne drained his glass with a victory flourish. I reacted and said, "Stories shape who we are."

But he was ready and answered, "It's more than that. We have to be ready for a particular story at a particular time in our lives." Adroitly, he tacked it onto our own situation by saying that Rangseetal only made the decision that night because he was primed for a radical change in his path through life. I'm pretty sure that Verne knew that his next allusion, "The readiness is all, Martindale," furtively found a chink in my protective veneer.

He knew that he'd found an opening as he walked towards the front door and added, "Ross, are you ready to make all your decisions based entirely on your personal moral framework? Or are you going to rely on other moralities or stories that you've gleaned over the years? Will it be pure science? Or is it going to be a mixture: a blob of science and a dab of fiction? Or will it be the other way around?"

As I opened the door, I laughed to hide my irritation at not having a ready answer. We stepped out into the warm summer night air and stood looking east down the road to see the sun already lightening the sky. I experienced the comfort of hometown familiarity, the place I was born and where I had grown up. The long summer days, distinct seasons, the straight roads. When I verbalised my thoughts on the positive aspects of the city, he reminded me of the extreme winters.

"The harsh winters are part of who we are, Verne."

"That's the joke around here. Do we know who you truly are? Do we really know what is beneath this paved, black tarmac in the 'City of Champions'? Are we a prairie city, for example or are we just the 'Gateway City'? Have we stolen someone else's being and disguised it with our identity?"

He had a knack for directing seemingly innocent statements into the quagmire as I mentioned earlier. My response, "What are you talking about, Verne? That's nonsense. Of course we're a prairie city. And, you're just flipping conventional wisdom on its head about stealing someone's identity," simply gave him the opening he was waiting for. I still had to learn to suppress my knee-jerk reactions with Verne if I didn't really want an answer. Of course, deep down, I enjoy his probing snippets.

"Not everyone would agree with you about the certainty of this being a prairie city, Ross," he said. Then, buffing the road with his sandal, he added, "What would be here today if your ancestors hadn't come along and laid down these Roman-type roads - grid format? The same thing happened in

England years ago and in every colony after that. Would this exact spot be prairies or forest? The sun that will soon rise in the east wouldn't be fractured by the buildings in front of us. As I scrape my foot on the road, what can you smell?"

"Not much. Mainly the exhaust of the last car that went past. And what do you know about the Romans in England?"

"Exactly. And not much," he laughed. "After all, I'm only passing through. But I didn't notice any history books on your shelves. Do you read any?"

"I have," I answered, "I get the general idea of history, but I prefer to focus on what's happening today."

"The general idea sometimes leaves out the local people and your own specific story." Verne left it at that and went on to explain how, in the process of creating "Genesis", he had experienced a feeling like no other; as if he had been transported to a magical world. His ultimate aim was to build a game that forced players to transition between the real world and the world of the game even after it had come to an end. He asked me whether playing "Genesis" that night had led me to question our society's rules and laws more deeply. He insisted that ambiguities are normal and that I should open my mind to them. He disclosed that he felt that he had picked up a message while playing: one that had reminded him of the importance of finding plots of land around the world. He confessed that my mention of England tacked onto that message had aroused something deep in his soul. He concluded with, "Anyway, I don't expect anyone else to live by my rules; I just want to be very clear about them for myself. I hate feeling tied down. More than ever, I want to take a walk on the wild side for a while.

"Look after my game," he said, and headed east down the road. From where I stood, I saw the night sky growing lighter, fragmented between the divisions of the city blocks. Verne reached the corner, paused, turned, and walked back slowly. He halted two paces away from me and said, "Is it irresponsible to want to live free...have 'land-tickets' all over the world so I can come and go as I please?"

"I'm not going to impose my rules on you. You don't even have to know what they are. But I'll let you into a secret - I have bought a plot of land nearby. When I've built on it, I'll decide whether I'll keep two houses at the same time." We smiled in understanding. Once again, Verne walked off at a brisk pace.

I turned and walked towards my front door and reassured myself that my life was clearcut. A slight shiver from the cool of the early morning air jiggled my body like a shake of dice in a cup. For a fleeting second, recalling Sarah's words, I thought that I felt a slight shift of the ground under my feet.

I closed my front door in an attempt to shut out Verne's conversation. The tidy kitchen and lounge area satisfied my sense of orderliness, but the emptiness of the house jarred slightly. As I climbed the stairs to my bedroom, I reminded myself that "Genesis" was simply a board game, but roughly a month later the game sent me a message that I couldn't ignore. It would mark the start of a topsy-turvy time of my life. Right then I was drained by my conversation with Verne. I lay down on my bed and dropped off to sleep.

****

I woke the next morning with a vague recollection of dreams permeated by ocean waves whispering secrets and subterranean rumblings ripping up roads, disrupting my peace and home. A daze governed my waking, my breakfast and discovery of Verne's computer USB stick jammed between the cushions of the chair he sat on when we were chatting the night before. I knew that it was his before I read the handwritten label, "Genesis Rules" because the stick itself was marvelously etched with "Genesis" motifs like the rest of his board game. Typical Verne ambiguity, I thought to myself about the wording. I put it on the table and made a mental note to return it to him after work one day in the week ahead.

Wednesday morning I finally remembered to take the stick with me to work with the intention of dropping by Verne's townhouse on the way home. The hospital is walking distance from my house. I try not to drive to work: a nod to my personal responsibility for daily exercise and to reducing my carbon footprint.

When I reached Verne's house, I found his front door ajar. I knocked and called out before stepping inside. There was a vacuum about the place and, in response to my salutations, Jack, the landlord, popped his head over the upstairs railing and greeted me. I expressed my surprise to see him inside Verne's house.

He quickly reassured me that it was legitimate by saying, "Hullo Ross. It's good to see you again. You missed Verne by a day. He left yesterday. So I'm just cleaning up. Not much to do of course."

"When will he be back?" I asked.

"He doesn't have any dates in mind. He's such a good person to do business with, eh. Gave me three months rent to cover any losses that may come my way, you know. To be honest, I don't know where he's gone. He seemed real determined to leave. Didn't know where he was going, though. At least he didn't say."

Jack is a well-known owner-builder around the neighbourhood and always friendly. He continued, "You know what Verne's like. Just packed his stuff into his backpack and headed down the road. Could've just got as far as Starbucks or maybe all the way to Timbuctoo, eh."

I laughed at his description and replied, "There's no stopping Verne when he gets something into his head. It's a bit annoying though. I'd have thought that he'd at least say goodbye. I could've returned his stick."

"Oh yeah, he did say you might be by and left a message for ya, ya know."

"Well?"

"He said, you should bring it to him. And you'd know what it is, eh."

"Of course," I said, trying to conceal my amazement with a smile. I shifted to practical questions, "Has he left a forwarding address? What about his furniture?"

"Well, he couldn't say where he'd be, ya know. A lot of this furniture's mine, eh. Verne said I could keep the rest. He seemed to get his whole life into his backpack. Said that's how he travels. As I said, he's a great person to deal with. No penny-pinching from him, eh. To be honest, you don't find many like him anymore."

"I wonder how he could leave his business here so easily?"

"I know that he bought some land recently on the outskirts of town. Won't be worth much for a few years yet. He can leave it for a while. I guess he's out to look for more prospects somewhere else," Jack replied.

I scanned the house with my eyes and couldn't see any proof that Verne had ever been there. "It's truly amazing," I mused half to myself, half to Jack, "there are lots of backpackers traveling the world these days, but none can stuff their whole life in a single bag quite like Verne. He gives new meaning to traveling light."

I realised that there was little point hanging around; Verne was not coming back. I said goodbye to Jack and left, arguing with myself. He could have said 'cheers'. Does he really think that I'm going to up and join him just to return a computer stick? He's nuts. I'll never understand him.

Inside my annoyance, I sensed a kernel of sadness as it dawned on me that I might never see Verne again. Conversations with him took me away from the stresses of my work. His troubling questions and suggestions introduced me to ideas and possibilities that provided distraction from my demanding work environment. Verne's departure meant that I would have to find other strategies to question normal daily reality. There was no alternative but to accept the way that he rolled. His speedy, clean departure reminded me of an enigmatic aspect of his personality: he lived his life in a series of chapters and that one was closed; the protagonist moved on as you turned the pages.

Chapter Two

Ten days later, I had just finished work when I received a text, "Hullo mate." It was Verne

"Hi," I replied and waited for an apology.

"Surprised by my snap decision to leave? Magic, haha."

"I shouldn't have blinked."

"Sarcasm doesn't suit you. LOL. Would've been worse to drag it out."

It was pointless to quibble with Verne, so I asked, "Where on earth are you?"

"On the outskirts of London. Centre of the world. Buzz of business all around me."

"Made any deals yet?"

"Nope. Distracted by a weird feeling. Something pulling me. Relentless."

I pictured Verne's shaven head with a thoughtful expression in his eyes. I knew that I should wait patiently for him to expand.

Thirty minutes later he texted, "Profoundly different feeling here." Another text, "For me, that is." And, "Country is familiar and exciting at the same time. A mixture of calm and exhilaration."

I replied: "Your antennae are too sensitive. Most of us just enjoy that city for what it is. Don't get carried away."

The next day Verne caught me off guard, texting, "Hey Ross, are you going to bring my property over?"

My thumbs twitched to retort, "I'm responsible. I don't jump at every whim," but I'd learned that sarcasm doesn't suit me, so I deleted it and instead answered, "Don't be ridiculous."

It didn't satisfy him. "You should get your blood flowing. Anyway, when you change your mind, I'm in Cornwall." He added, "I'm in a game of Hunt the Thimble."

I knew the conversation could be endless so I shut it down with, "Good luck, I guess."

Two weeks passed without further word from Verne. Devoured by what I thought to be my indispensable work, I forgot about him. One evening I was clearing papers on my desk and uncovered Verne's USB. I picked it up, twirled it around in my fingers, and then decisively plugged it into my computer. As expected, "The Rules of Genesis" came up as a title. I knew that a blank sheet would follow so I flicked off the monitor and headed upstairs to bed.

At five thirty the next morning, I routinely went to check my email and noted that I'd left Verne's stick in the computer port. I turned on the monitor to be confronted with very definite directions. Under the "Genesis" heading, it read, "If you are the 'Chronicler', hit the 'next' button."

I smiled, thought, how ridiculous, and clicked the mouse. My sardonic smile evaporated as I read the instruction that followed, "With immediate effect, you have the responsibility of keeping an accurate and detailed record of your life as it unfolds, including interactions with strangers and messages from friends."

I dropped my head into my hands and laughed in frustration. Verne was aware of my predisposition to satisfy my friends' requests and stick to rules. I had chosen the "Chronicler" piece and it was part of the game.

With uncanny timing, Verne sent an email to my Inbox which began with his familiar, *"Hullo Mate"* and went directly to the point.

Have you ever felt pulled to a place for no particular reason?

I've been in Cornwall for two weeks and can't explain why I came here. Feels like I've been dragged by a magnet. You asked about business deals: they don't interest me as much as usual. It's the locals who are fascinating - such characters. I'm a newbie, yet I feel connected to them like close friends or even family. I still want to own land all over the world because that way I'll have many havens. That's real independence. Weird: almost as if my feet are stuck in the soil, and the ground here won't let them go. If I can buy the right property here in Cornwall soon, I will be free to choose to continue with my global land quest. Till then, I'm here.

It's easy to walk around Penzance where I'm staying for a few days. Though high tourist season is over, the narrow streets are bustling with happy locals. They enjoy their town and its history that seeps from the walls of old buildings like the "Turks Head Pub." I mean old. It's supposed to have been there since the thirteenth century.

Talk about essence: Cornwall has enveloped me and I want to know more about the stuff you can't touch. OK so you think "Turks Head" is old. Yesterday, I took a taxi five kilometres west to Chysauster (pronounced Che-zoi-ster by the locals). It's the site of a restored iron age village, complete with a "Fogou" (pronounced "Foogoo") which archeologists think may have served as a coven for mystic ceremonies or a refuge in case of attack. No one's sure.

On the way there the driver came out with "Myth, magic, history and legend swirl around 'ere in Cornwall." He said that mixture is "what feeds him," and that if he ever left this place, he'd "die of thirst or starve. I don't have to go around the world searching for something that's right 'ere in front of me nose."

He meant it metaphorically, I know, but I get it - maybe because I do know that my ancestors came from around these parts only three or four generations ago. I've lost touch with family, but the locals hereabouts really could be my cousins. The taxi driver's question, "By the way, laddie, what are you looking for?" confused me. I thought my hunt for land was my clear goal, but I couldn't tell the taxi driver. But is it just expensive stockpiling in case of trouble in one place or another? What do you think?

I encountered Chysauster and I'm shaken. I'm not exaggerating when I say I was transformed in that village that's been uninhabited for 2000 years. I'm the same person, with the same basic thoughts, but I see things at a different frequency. *Since Chysauster, even stones and rocks shimmer with life. Before, they were lifeless parts of the landscape. Now they whisper to me to "Dig deeper!" We've talked about hearing voices from the sea, but now it's more personal. My Chysauster experience has fanned psychic embers inside me.*

I can hear you laughing and saying "madness"; I say, "magic", but don't worry, I'm not going around talking to others about it because I'd probably be put away. You and I have had some deep conversations so you're really the only person I can tell right now. If I can find a way to put the whole story back together, I'll share it with you. Better still, you come out here to feel it for yourself.

I hope that you'll store this stuff somewhere.

Cheers mate

Verne

I gulped the last of my morning coffee and glanced at the time on my computer. Cynicism towards Verne's stories and time pressure sparked a flippant reply to him about waiting for the next chapter in his Cornwall saga. I eased my conscience by saving Verne's email with a brief explanation onto his USB stick under the day's date, completed my morning routine and left for work.

As I passed through the hospital entrance, my responsibility to serve my patients swept all other thoughts from my mind. I returned home exhausted, ate a small meal and collapsed into bed to sleep enough to face the next day.

Apart from work and occasional games evenings with friends, I had no interests. The Chronicler role to record my uncomplicated life filled a vacuum; it was becoming a systematic act. I noted my activity on the USB: *morning again; coffee and email to start my regimen; notice the Inbox contains a new message from Verne:*

Hullo again Mate

I know you'll be surprised by this - I even shocked myself as I wouldn't normally spend time writing stuff like this. I couldn't sleep thinking about what happened to me at Chysauster and, with no one to talk to, I wrote it down. Recently you called me a Romantic. Maybe there's a scrap of truth to that. If I were one of those old Nature poets, I'd call my piece "Reverie" or something like that. I think that I might have had a vision. Maybe I should just admit myself into the cuckoo's nest. Anyway, if you do read the attachment, you should be a tad tight - as they say around here - to put yourself in the right frame of mind.

Chysauster gave me the feeling of walking back into an ancient time. The archeological teams that worked on the project have done a brilliant job of recreating the village where inhabitants practiced mixed farming, maybe even tin and copper mining to trade with Romans based at St. Michael's Mount off Penzance. There's a boundary wall around the village and archeologists have speculated that humans probably inhabited wooden shelters at Chysauster long before the construction of stone houses.

Google or tourist brochures provide lots of information. They'll give you a good sense of the place, but I'm going to take you with me where technology can't go. Brace yourself for my outlandish Chysauster experience.

Cheers mate

Verne

I copied Verne's email onto the stick and added the following synopsis of my reaction:

I suppress my curiosity. If I open the attachment before work, I'll be distracted for the whole day. Verne is unpredictable and his stories unsettle my conventional view of the world. He can transition easily from one place to the next: from a meditation mat to the racetrack in seconds. I prefer a constant steady speed in a reliable vehicle. Verne is ready to hack his way through a jungle; I stick to the clear open road where stumbling blocks are visible a mile ahead. I add "Read Verne's story" to my calendar (otherwise clear for the evening) and I will head out the front door on time for work.

I was amused by the novel habit of recording my day on the stick so, before reading Verne's impressions of Chysauster, I jotted down a personal note on the USB stick: *This evening I walked home from the hospital at a brisk pace, poured myself a glass of wine and sat down at my computer . I am prepared to read Verne's attachment. I've added it to the record verbatim.*

Chapter Three

"Encounter at Chysauster"

The taxi driver's words, "Myth, magic, history and legend" chimed in my mind as I stepped onto Chysauster land with utmost respect for the past. Awed, I stood surveying the outlines of the ten houses, marveled at the durability of the more than ten foot thick stone walls and noticed the way that grassy, natural vegetation had been allowed to grow over them. Visitors are welcome, but this place is not set up as an exhibit for tourists: no orderly, organised museum-type displays. There are a few boards outside the houses with scant explanation of the way that the stone walls above head height were so built so sturdily without any type of cement. More information is available on Google or in brochures. A lot is left to the imagination.

Chysauster's atmosphere soaked through my pores and then, to my amazement, I heard voices, soft at first. I scanned the area to look for other visitors: I was alone. It was as if I was interrupting a conversation until I realised that I was the subject of that discussion. I heard: "This one shows reverence. Bring him in." Incredibly, the bodiless voices said, "Welcome to our village, to our homes. Take your fill. See it through your eye. Through your eye, through your eye. See all."

I gave my head a shake, trying to disregard the voices as a product of my overactive imagination. I have heard sounds in Nature, from the sea. For the first time I heard them from the land and the stone walls of the buildings; they were persistent, distinct, directed towards me on a personal level, and I did not dismiss them.

In baffled wonderment, I strolled up the gentle slope toward the highest point in the village to orientate myself and Chysauster in a wider context. The Autumn weather was unseasonably warm; however, when I felt the breeze penetrate my jersey, I wondered what the ancient inhabitants wore to withstand colder temperatures and how they would conduct their lives on such a day. At the top of the hillock, in every direction, I was confronted by a dazzle of natural colours: greens, browns, yellows, reds, blues and flecks of white splashed on fields, copses, sea; foamy white horses, sky and clouds stretched as far as the eye could see. I could have been the only person on the planet at that moment, the central point of the same circular panorama of strategic advantage that an ancient villager would have commandeered thousands of years ago. Villagers would have been able to scan their crops and animals or gain an early warning of an enemy approaching. What kind of conversation would I have with such a villager?

I looked at the ground beneath my feet and realised that under the sod, somewhere around the walls, lie the bones of the dead villagers, occasionally aroused by tourists' footsteps. What were those voices telling me when I arrived? What stories were they trying to pass on to me? As I walked down the slope towards the wall of the nearest house, I could not divorce myself from the niggling thought that I might be descended from the inhabitants of this village or at least one like it; that some small trace of these people may be incorporated in my DNA or blood.

I was starting to see through my eye into the landscape of my mind. My romantic being was stretching out to the wall of the house in front of me about three feet above my head, grasping *for a story that would bind me more deeply to Chysauster, to Cornwall and to the surrounding land. With a brush of my hand, I connected with the grey stone pillar marking the doorway of the remains of the house in front of me and I let my imagination lead my footsteps along what would have been a road or path to the edge of the village. I sat down on a grassy mound with a sweeping view in front of me similar to the one that I had appreciated a few feet higher up the slope. My seat could have been part of the perimetre wall back when Chysauster was a vibrant village.*

My inward eye took over and the wall became more distinct. In the middle distance a man appeared, standing on the wall seemingly unaware of me. In my mind's eye, the tall, proud, upright figure wore loose flowing clothes, like a robe or caftan and his long grey hair spread over his broad shoulders. Even at a distance I could see that, though he was no longer young, his tanned, aquiline features indicated that he was a man of distinction. His bearing and steady stare into the distance to the east depicted his firm resolve. With a quiet chuckle, I told myself that he closely resembled one of the ancient villagers.

I was about to call out to him when I was distracted by the sound of clanging metal disrupting the tranquility of the scene. I turned to see what held the man's attention: it was a group of about a hundred advancing in our direction, too far away to determine detail, except for the sunlight constantly glinting off shiny objects. They were moving up the hill quickly and, as they came closer, they appeared to be dressed in Roman uniform, carrying weapons - spears, swords and shields. My first thought was that I was lucky enough to be watching a reenactment of some historic scene by a few obsessive historians. Or, maybe this was a film scene. I looked around for cameras, but there were none. This emulated a real live event: Roman soldiers dressed and armed as they would have been 2000 years ago were launching an attack on Chysauster. I tried to call out to the figure on the wall, but my voice was trapped inside my mouth. All attempts to gain his attention were futile. When the group of Romans was within one hundred metres I could hear the military commands.

Above the clanking of the armour, I discerned the cries and

yells of the troops in Latin (which I could suddenly

understand). As the soldiers roared, "Barbarians. Barbarians.

Kill the barbarians," I searched the walls and grounds for an

enemy. The solitary, dignified figure on the wall stood defiantly

waiting for the soldiers. I was less than fifty metres away.

There was no escape.

The man on the wall calmly raised his hand in greeting or

command to stop. A soldier at the front of the squad with a

reddish plume on his helmet lifted his hand in similar fashion

and the soldiers came to an abrupt halt. They remained,

crouched like athletes at the start of a marathon, weapons at

the ready, muscles tense, waiting for the command to attack. I

expected to witness carnage and be the next victim, but

everyone seemed to ignore me as if I were invisible. The

plumed soldier and the villager on the wall stared at each

other for about a minute. Then, with sword at the ready, the

Roman advanced cautiously as if a hidden enemy might leap over the wall.

Callous murder seemed inevitable and, with tension at fever pitch, the Roman mere feet from his victim, the figure on the wall spread his arms in a gesture of welcome. At that moment there was a movement some distance back from the wall around the nearest house and another figure, or shadow (I'll never be sure), glided towards the fogou. The Roman seemed to crash into an invisible physical barrier; he was transfixed for a few seconds. It was either a reaction to the gesture by the man on the wall or a response to the fleeting shape I had glimpsed behind the wall. The Roman stopped to reconsider his action. He turned his attention back to the man on the wall. The two men exchanged hand signals and the villager invited the Roman to join him on the wall. After a few more gestures and words, the Roman turned to his troops, bellowed a command and, muttering, the soldiers relaxed and lowered their weapons. The villager on the wall responded by calling to people inside the wall and within minutes others emerged from the houses or the fogou and carried dishes of food over the wall to the soldiers. The two leaders walked away from the group in a serious conversation involving many hand actions. Frequently, the Roman glanced back towards the group, but with more interest in the villagers than his own men. He seemed to be searching for something or someone.

The Roman officer turned towards his men, raised his hand to the side of his mouth to project his voice and called out an order to a specific soldier who lifted his curled trumpet to his lips to signal to the soldiers.

A car horn jolted me back to the present and the scene dissolved as suddenly as it had begun. I reprimanded my over-active imagination for straying and reminded myself that I had limited time to explore the historic site.

Verne's engrossing account had dragged me closer to the computer screen and I leaned back to stretch out the tension between my shoulder blades induced by the tiring day at the hospital or the remarkable story from Chysauster. I did laugh and "Madness" was on the tip of my tongue, but I withheld my judgement and admitted to myself that the ancient place sounded interesting. I decided to read on, mostly because I had nothing else to do that evening, not even a good book to read, and Verne's story was entertaining. He had provided a natural break for his readers and I walked to the kitchen to refill my glass before continuing with the story. It started with a Verne-type sub-heading:

Making a Chysauster Memory

As I walked into the village away from the perimeter wall, my earlier yearning to talk to the ancient inhabitants intensified. Nonsense, I thought to myself. However, though my hallucination of the Roman scene had dissolved, the stones around me seemed more animated and penetrable.

I meandered through the remains of ancient human habitation; the walls and doorways of many of the homes are still visible. I wondered how I had been able to reimagine such a vivid

scene that could have taken place thousands of years ago.
Then it struck me that this piece of land is not simply a pile of
rocks, remnants of ancient buildings, ruins. It is the indelible
mark of a bygone community. Was I following the advice of
the voices at the entrance? Was I hearing through my ear and
seeing through my eye? Chysauster became a translucent
window stimulating my imagination to see into the distant past,
to glimpse more than the tangible residue of stones and
artefacts. It was as if the spirits of the ancient villagers still
hovered around, conducting their business in the peaceful
haven and, in exchange, perhaps, the revenant presence
gained a peek at modernity through visitors like me.

Hunger pangs reminded me that I was still part of the
corporeal world as I reached the entrance to the fogou. The
sun and the shadows signaled that it was well past noon. I had
been absorbed in the micro world of Chysauster for hours and
had lost track of time. Though ravenous, I controlled my
craving and ate my sandwiches slowly with occasional
draughts of water while reflecting on the ruins around me and

my vision. At the end of the meal, I felt like a dessert. A berry bush grew right next to the mysterious fogou entrance, tempting me with its fruit which could have been mistaken for raspberries. I risked a sample and, feeling no ill effects, I gorged. In fact I soon felt mentally elated, though physically lethargic. There were no other visitors around that day, so I closed my eyes to restore my energy before heading back to Penzance.

When I opened them a few minutes later a stranger was leaning against the mound covering the fogou as if he was guarding the entrance. He spoke in an uncommon dialect. It was an unrecognisable version of a Cornish dialect, but like my earlier comprehension of Latin, I was able to understand him fully. He wore similar clothes to the figure on the wall: a long coat down to his mid calves, fitting loosely around his neck with wide sleeves. His silvery hair and beard were long and, at approximately six foot, he stood at the same height. In that way he seemed very familiar, but from a distance, earlier, I hadn't been able to clearly discern the features of the figure on the wall. This man's face seemed to have been chiseled from the rocks but, though hard and grooved like granite, humour played around the corners of his mouth and in his blue eyes. I had to suppress a romantic notion that a wizard had suddenly appeared before me.

I looked over at him from my comfortable resting place and, determined to seem unflustered by the fact that he may have been watching me for some time, I greeted him with a relaxed, "Hullo Mate."

"Well hullo there and welcome," he replied. "I've been waiting for some time to talk with you."

"How long?" I asked.

Instead of answering my question, he said, "Have you enjoyed exploring our small world here?" (I think that he said "world", but it might have been something else).

He continued, "I'm delighted that you could stay for a meal. Most people come in and walk about our place as quickly as they can to tick it off their list. They don't have much real interest any more. I saw you communing with things around you, responding with all your senses."

"Thank you. Yes. I've been to other historical places, but here I feel like I've discovered something very special. Like I've been looking into a mirror: one that's placed a long way away and I'm a small speck in it; a fragment in the whole picture that is unfolding while I watch. Maybe it's the quiet solitude. I'm Verne, by the way."

He introduced himself as "Cador," and surmised, "Oh, you probably felt alone till now. It's not always this way. In fact, while you were resting, there was a bustle here. People going about their business. You would have enjoyed watching them."

"Bugger. I didn't realise that I'd been asleep. How long was it? Embarrassing. I should get moving before closing time."

"Relax. I've made arrangements for you to stay as long as you like. There'll be no outsiders or visitors till late tomorrow morning. You're probably rested now so we can talk."

"Cador, is that how you pronounce it? You say there were others here; I'm surprised I didn't hear them. I'm a light sleeper and usually wake up even at soft sounds."

"Close enough" he smiled at my attempt at his name, "Well, you've come a long way," he said, nodding towards my backpack.

"And my accent. But I've been around these parts for a few weeks now. I shouldn't be that tired."

"Maybe it's not just fatigue," he mused, "I've occasionally seen this reaction before in a visitor. Do you feel that you blend in *easily here? Do you sleep comfortably wherever you go or just when you're close to home?"*

"I'm actually far from home. I usually adapt easily, but it's different here. It's as if I've latched on to a leisurely pace. I've picked up on a slower inner rhythm and feel more in tune or integrated. Why do you say I'm close to home?"

Cador sat down next to the entrance to the fogou with his back against its embankment and our eyes met on the level. "I picked you out when you arrived." I was getting used to him ignoring my questions. He patted the entrance to the fogou and added, "Do you feel a connection to this place that goes deeper than these things you can touch?"

I realised that Cador had quickly focused my thinking. I was fascinated by the structures and the fact that they were still so solid and permanent. With a bit more archeological repair, they would stand proud in the landscape - the handprint of men and women who once walked these hills. Again, I could hear their voices. I couldn't formulate a reply incorporating those thoughts; all I could do in response to Cador's question was nod my head in acknowledgement. In an uncanny way, he tracked into my earlier thoughts as he responded: "Does it cross your mind that you might be related to some of the people who have lived here?"

At first I struggled to understand how he could know what had been going on inside my head, but quickly I accepted his comments and questions. I admitted that those ideas had been whirling around in my mind; that it was as likely a spot as any on earth to be the home of my ancient ancestors. Cador seemed encouraged by my answer and took me down another avenue of thought as he continued, "This piece of land is your heritage; here you are on a different side of the argument. This land is sacrosanct - for you."

"What argument?" I laughed and said that for many this would just be a pile of stones and a waste of precious time, but his reply showed me that he was listening carefully and hadn't forgotten my earlier words.

He leaned towards me from the fogou wall intent on conveying something that he thought was very important, but even now is still not clear to me. He said, "Distance from home's always a hard thing to measure. You'll find that you don't have to justify being here in any way. You're not an intruder and no one will intrude on you."

I scrabbled with my fingers under the grass, picked up a handful of soil and let it run through my fingers and confessed that, "I do feel grounded here, like never before."

"Here, all this is part of you; here you have nothing to prove. The understanding will grow. We can talk now while the others are asleep. They always send me out to deal with difficult situations. I usually resolve them without too much fuss." I pointed at my own chest, thinking that I was the problem, but a smile played on Cador's lips as he continued with what seemed like calculated flippancy, "He came back, you know."

With prescience reflected by the angle of his chin and a single, slow, deliberate nod, he clearly anticipated my "Who?" and his answer was perfectly timed to throw me off balance. "The Roman., then, seeing that I was stunned, he prodded, "the one you saw me talking to on the wall."

It was a moment of disclosure. Cador confirmed my hunch that he was the man on the wall. It was terrifying to realise that he had entered my imagination and knew of my innermost thoughts. He let the idea settle in my mind and walked over to the berry bush next to the entrance to the fogou.

"You've had a few of these," he said, "There are always raucous parties when we eat them. You should try a few more. They'll help you over the hump."

I suppressed my scream to tell me who he really is; for him to go away and leave me in peace. A calm replaced the terror and instead of rejecting the invitation to eat the fruit, I moved towards Cador and the bush to share in the feast with him. He was right there in front of me; as substantial as you and I.

His chuckle was engaging and he added, "These berries will help us to understand each other better. The full moon tonight will light our way and we can take things further...if you want to."

I hesitated to trust Cador, but at the same time he seemed to understand things about me that I have been wrestling with for a long time. I was enjoying his company, so I stuffed my mouth with one more helping of berries and said, "OK, so who was that Roman? Why did he return?"

"He came back for a woman. You saw their first interaction at the wall."

"The officer was distracted by something behind you and it bothered him even after the soldiers and villagers mingled."

"It's a long story and like all good stories there's much to understand about Carenza and the Roman. We should walk over to the wall so that the tale will penetrate your senses."

"Carenza? The figure who ran behind the wall?" I asked.

Cador simply nodded with a genuine smile of appreciation.

I was intrigued by Verne's story and at the same time slightly concerned that he had either lost touch with reality or was stringing me a line and he would reveal some joke at the end. I couldn't resist the itch to find out, so I broke with my rule of only two glasses of wine on a work night. I replenished my glass and continued with Verne's narrative.

Chapter Four

Carenza

The path to the wall is short and direct. While walking, Cador said, "You may think that you've heard this story before, because it keeps coming back, or bits and pieces are wedged in other tales. This one's unique to our part of the world and Carenza is our country's lass. At any rate, I haven't told it to anyone."

By that stage I'd grown receptive to a myth or legend, especially told by someone who had local knowledge. What harm could there be in listening to a story? As Cador described the events of long ago, I felt as if I was passing through a new frontier leading back to an unexplored past, like a traveler who would hear things unknown to anyone else in our time. I told Cador that I would try not to interrupt him, so he began.

"Carenza is the most glorious woman ever seen in these parts - almost as if she was not born from human parents, but

created by Nature. The sun glints off her golden hair and shines out of it at the same time. Breathing her name is like the first notes of a song and her speech tinkles with the tunes of Nature. I see from your expression that you'd like to meet her, but I warn you, there's more. Her body is perfectly formed; each muscle ripples beneath the surface of her unblemished, tanned skin. A refreshing aroma of the sea hangs about her as if the ocean bathes her daily. Don't let your emotions run away with you, Verne. She is bewitching. She is out of reach for any man in this village and they know it; yet she can command anyone to do her bidding. As an outsider, and a conqueror, the Roman was unaware of her power and mystique. He only saw a beautiful woman; he was entranced.

I don't know Carenza's origins. She has been among us for many years, yet she comes and goes as she pleases. The first time I saw her she arrived in our village unannounced. I found her sitting on this wall with a peaceful expression on her face contemplating the fields, gazing out to the sea in the distance.

I was much younger then and struck by her beauty. Her invitation to sit next to her was more of a command than a suggestion; it felt exactly what I intended to do anyway. That is her allure. Whether she is talking to men, women or children, she tunes into their thoughts and merely guides them in tandem with their own intentions, almost affirming their purpose and at the same time taking control. She can be very dangerous.

The Roman arrived with all his bravado, authority and military leadership experience. His mental resilience matched his physical durability, strength and power. He was comfortable commanding men and his troops seldom questioned his orders. I had the sense that he was a ferocious, skilful warrior, though I never saw him in combat. Carenza is flexible and accommodating; the Roman was rigid, meticulous and demanding.

You probably wonder why I stood on this wall unarmed when the Roman soldiers were approaching. I know that you are as puzzled as I, that you were there at that moment. Thinking with great intensity in unison may, on rare occasions, warp time. We can't alter the reality of that moment.

Of course I was scared and had absolutely no idea who was approaching or what would happen. Nevertheless, it's our job and responsibility as leaders to make decisions that protect the whole community. It's cowardly for us leaders to summon people to fight the enemy or throw weapons at them when we can defuse the problem by negotiation. Those Romans didn't usually have the patience for discussion because they felt that they were stronger than everyone else. Leaders should always try to develop policies and strategies that save lives, not waste them in childish, useless battle. But that's another matter.

It turned out that my brave stand on the wall was a sideshow for the real drama that took place behind me. Timing is everything. As the Roman officer was walking forward, he caught sight of Carenza. I often try to imagine what he saw in *that moment: Carenza in full flight, leaping like an antelope with her golden hair loosened, darting from the house to the fogou. I'll never know whether she planned it, but the Roman's myopic worldview broadened in an instant; his single-minded purpose of conquest melted at the sight of the semi-divine Carenza. I didn't know what had happened, but his hesitation signaled to me in the moment that something had snatched his attention. His resolve was diluted, allowing me to reach a settlement without a battle. Carenza caused the Roman to falter in his stride and glimpse a different possibility in his life which would include her. Though I was praised for negotiating a peace, Carenza was the real hero. She'll never divulge whether her streak in full view was intentional, and that secretiveness is part of her attraction.*

From that very first glance, they were completely entranced by each other; their souls were prisoners in each other's bodies and they actually glowed in each other's presence. The attraction for each other emanated from a mutual respect for their unique, contrasting, exceptional qualities. A true complement. *They tried to hide their emotions in every way they could because they feared reprisals from their own people. They even pretended to be angry with each other. It didn't fool me.*

The Romans were only here for a few days and in that short time Carenza and the Roman sealed their love for each other. I overheard their conversation one evening. The Roman said, "I cannot neglect my duty to Rome and must return even though it will crush my soul to leave you." His speech was already softer than when he arrived and Carenza replied with her gentle confidence, "That may be, but you will return from this Rome place or thing because you will find your real happiness here with me."

Her words revealed that she understood his internal conflict and she was simply telling him what he already knew. While he was away Carenza squinted into the horizon daily waiting for his return. She was not distressed in any way because she had no doubt that he would come back to her as soon as he could, but her life was on hold until then.

Carenza carried on with the occupations only she could perform. Each evening the children would gather around her for storytime. Sometimes the adults would try to sneak in, but she'd send them off to their houses because she said grown-ups would break the spell and only children believe in magic. She let me listen because of my special role in the village. Her stories were always about people who had lived here or nearby and carried out heroic deeds for the good of all. There were tales of great battles, fights with dragons and monsters. At the end of each story the village or community was always the winner. When she told these bedtime stories, Carenza could time the conclusion exactly right so that the children in the circle would be tired, ready for bed, but not too tired to make their own way to the safety of their parents. Even the children thought that they had made their own decision, though Carenza had put the thought of sleep in their minds and sent them off home.

She was right about the Roman. He must have completed his military service because he would never have broken trust with Rome, but Carenza is irresistible. I was side by side with her here on the wall when the Roman approached from the base of the hill for the second time. His hair was longer and he had exchanged his soldier's uniform for locally made clothes like ours. The only memento of his military career that he carried was his sword which he kept out of sight most of the time and never again used it in anger. What struck me as most noteworthy was that he never spoke of his army days. It was as if he had been reborn and for him, his past was a memory of another person's life. Small changes were apparent, yet profound: I'd be able to identify him anywhere with his unique bearing, but he walked at a slower pace with a looser step and as he got closer I could see that his face was less troubled.

He waved to us on the wall and I couldn't help recalling his first threatening arrival at the head of a squad of soldiers ready to tear down everything in their path. Carenza stood immobile, clearly radiating joy, but ensuring that the Roman had to walk to her and she also knew that I have to approve of all who enter our village. I raised my left hand to him in greeting and indicating to Carenza that he was welcome. He leapt onto the wall and they embraced for a long while. Then, turning to me, he clasped my arm just below my elbow as we had at the end of our first encounter and several times while he was bivouacked with us. We had earned each other's trust.

Carenza took him straight to her house along this same road we are walking on now. The Roman wanted to pave it soon after he returned, but most of us rejected that idea as we thought it was a waste of time to cover the earth between our houses for the sake of appearances. That was one big difference between the Roman and many of us. Here is the house. It's still in pretty good shape. You can see that we build so that we remain connected to the earth, the land and all things natural. We build with materials that we find hereabouts and make use of what is available. We let the water run into our houses through channels along the ground. Feel these walls. They'll be here for all our descendents. Touch them, they're not going to fall over. Sniff them. We use rocks we find herabouts. It doesn't change the smell of the place. We let grass and moss grow on them so that we're one with the world. We live in the world, not on it.

The Roman wanted to convey the water above our heads and carve the stones for no real purpose other than to look at them just outside the house or even inside. Pretty soon some of the younger people in our village wanted them too and started to argue about the size of their houses and who had the most number of useless stones in the shape of heads and human bodies in their houses. There was a division in our village. The other big difference was that the Roman measured everything. He even measured the length of the day and tried to get us all to go to bed and wake up at the same time regardless of how we felt that morning. You can imagine how excited most people were about that. He spent a lot of time writing things down and keeping records of how many stones went into building a wall and events that took place in his life. Details.

He even wanted to specify how much love he should

apportion Carenza. That is where she drew the line and

started to break down his remaining rigid barriers.

Carenza was generous with her love for the Roman and all

living things. She would not set limits or a boundary on her

feelings for others, especially her Roman and the two sons

they had together. He worshiped different gods from us -

stone gods inside his house. He placed fruit or harvest in front

of small stone images of them. Ridiculous really. For a few

days Carenza sat with him while he muttered sentences of

thanks to the statues. Then one morning Carenza took her

Roman by his hand and led him to the eastern wall to watch

the sun rise with a full view of the fields and the sea. I was at

my usual spot on the wall so I saw them - just over there. She

placed herself between him and the rising sun and I heard her

say to him, "Behold, the morning and everything it offers you

today. Give thanks without limits." He stared at her for a

moment, smiled the most relaxed and broadest smile I have

ever seen on his face because he suddenly knew that he had everything he wanted and would ever need. He never turned to the statues in his house again. He came to understand that stones, especially the larger ones, are sacred and we should not tamper with their form or let their spirit escape from them.

The Roman would have recorded their story and what happened afterwards. We, at Chysauster, don't write things like this down, We tell and retell the story from memory to focus on the essence. Telling the stories to our children keeps the tales and people alive in our minds, in our souls so that our children's children's children can remember us and the heroes of our land. For some reason, this story faded and hasn't been told till now.

Shortly after that Carenza and the Roman packed a few belongings, prepared their sons for a journey and left, stating that they would not return. I was extremely sad and so were the people of our village. That was the first time that someone had decided to leave our village, saying they would not come back. As I told you earlier, Carenza had often come and gone from our village and each time she returned the aromatic ocean seemed to follow her. She had an urgent need to leave from time to time. On this occasion she indicated that it would be permanent. They had resolved to establish something new together. No one has occupied their house since. There is no substitute for Carenza.

After they departed, I organised a group of villagers to take his stone gods out to the fields and crush them so that they could never be recognised again. If we left them around the village it wouldn't have been long before someone collected them together to try to get others to follow new ideas that had already proven alien to our land. So, the Roman and Carenza have largely been forgotten by most people around here. With this story, I have resurrected them in you."

Cador stood up and stared at the entrance to Carenza's house. The sadness hadn't left him. I broke the silence, asking, "Why does that story tug at my insides, Cador? It happened so long ago, yet I'm shattered by the outcome, like it's important to me now. I want to know what happened to them. Why do I feel like I have to do something about it?"

"I would also like to know where they have ended up. The thing about Carenza, Verne, is that no matter how many times she departed and returned to the village before that, she never seemed to get any older. She was always the same exhilarating, glorious woman. If you were to meet her now, you would be as entranced as I was all those years ago on the wall. Verne, why did you come here anyway?"

"Cador, I want to buy land all over the world. To be able to call myself truly independent in any part of the world."

"You sound like the Roman when he first came trying to take our land."

I smiled at the comparison and had to admit to myself that if I could have bought a piece of Chysauster right then, I would have at any price. In fact, for me, all the land I own would be worth a small piece of this village, the crucible of the story of Carenza. I would have given up my world-wide ambition for a tiny patch of Chysauster land. I asked, "By the way, Cador, you said that you have to approve of all who enter the village. Did you have to approve of me?"

Cador returned my smile and, as if reading my mind, winked and said, "Insiders are satisfied to dwell here physically and spiritually.This land's not for sale, Verne. Besides, you wouldn't know what to do with it. You would want others to see it, to visit. You would want to profit from it."

The thought had crossed my mind. I tried to make excuses that Cador dismissed without a reply. Instead he latched onto one of them: "You say you wish that you could be part of this piece of land, this story. That won't happen by owning it. You have to live it."

This exchange had become too weird, even for me and, even more than when I first arrived in Cornwall, I felt as if my feet were sticking in the soil; that it was hard to lift them. A desperate anxiety to escape flowed through my body. I thanked Cador for his time and the story and said that I would be on my way. He laughed, "How do you think that you are going to leave now? You won't get anyone to come out here at this time of night. Spend what's left of the night in Carenza's house. You may get your wish to become part of our world if only for a moment. Don't worry, I've made arrangements with everyone for you to sleep here."

I laughed nervously at first, then I chuckled when it suddenly struck me that Cador must be an actor who dresses the part of one of the people of the period to let visitors experience life as it was when the place was inhabited. He'd certainly succeeded with me. I thought that he deserved special thanks, so I said, "You are amazing. You do a brilliant job. I would like to pay you,..," raising my eyebrows, I waited for him to reveal his real name, but he doggedly maintained his role, so I resorted to "...Cador."

"That's right," he said pointing to a space marked by the remains of a wall inside the house, "I don't know what you mean by pay, but that's the guest room. You should sleep in the family area. Carenza would have liked you to do that. They won't be back."

Though I wasn't prepared to sleep exposed to the cold Cornwall night air, I had little choice because Cador was right, I couldn't find my way back to Penzance at that time of night. Carenza's house was the safest refuge. Besides, I've been in rougher situations. So, despite a minor anxiety about the legality of spending the night in a heritage site, I entered the house and spread my mat as I have in so many places and slipped into a deep sleep for about four hours.

When I woke the next morning, the sun hadn't risen; however, despite the short sleep, I was completely rested and revived. I had the sensation that I was emerging from a cocoon, ready to face new challenges. I scanned the village for Cador, but he was nowhere to be seen and I supposed that he had gone home to rest before his next shift as a guide at Chysauster.

When I left through the reception area, the lady preparing the office for the day looked startled to see me departing, not arriving. I assumed that she was a new shift and hadn't communicated with those who made arrangements with Cador for my stayover. I complimented her on the quality of the guides. She started to contradict me, but let it go. The discordance of that little exchange at the ticket office still plays around inside my head and I can't help wondering whether I've been spending too much time on my own and if that conversation inside Chysauster with Cador actually took place or it was a substitute for real company.

I finished reading and sat back in amazement. There was no catch to Verne's story which made me wonder whether he was fantasizing. Admittedly, I was starting to enjoy the routine of storing my day's thoughts, activities and Verne's messages on the USB stick. I'd decided to write in diary format in a style that showed I had reflected upon my day to day happenings which seemed trivial in contrast to Verne's reports. It occurred to me that, if I wanted to reread the Chysauster account, it was easily accessible. An email from Verne interrupted my thoughts and enterprise:

Hullo Mate

In case you're wondering whether I'm still on an even keel, have no fear. I mainly wanted to try to explain to myself what happened and, if others read it, they may report having had similar experiences in different places around the world.

As I'm traveling through this English peninsula of myth and legend, I'm starting to understand that "Myth and Legend" are the essential magic of the place. Mysterious happenings are a little more credible when you're exploring a site like Chysauster. I'm privileged to be the first in eons to have heard the Carenza Story.

I hope that you enjoyed my first attempt to capture a weird moment. You should come to Cornwall to experience things for yourself.

Cheers mate

Verne

Verne was trying to reassure me of his sanity with that latest message, but in fact he left me more disturbed because he was treating Cador as if he were talking about one of our mutual friends. I added it to the USB together with my reaction. It was time to shut off the computer and get some sleep. After one more day of work this week, I will be meeting with my builder to plan the construction of a new house.

Chapter Five

I brushed aside Verne's romantic notions and kept my focus on practical issues like work and building my future. The next day passed at the usual frantic pace of a busy hospital and the weekend began. On Saturday morning I prepared for that meeting with my builder, Jeff Clement; Verne's and Cador's comments about the Chysauster ruins encroached on my thoughts. Building with spirit had a nice ring. It nurtured a niggling notion to leave a house that would capture my essence after I have departed from this world. I paid less attention to the details regarding the other characters whom Verne had mentioned because building my house was uppermost in my mind. Cador's remarks lingered and the thought remained with me that, eons after they had died, those people in Verne's tale continue to inhabit the ruined walls as an afterimage to stimulate his vivid imagination.

Although Verne and I had common interests, I was able to separate our paths and expectations: he had accrued a buffer of wealth and assets; I was in the process of consolidating a financial foundation by building a second home which I thought would be a solid investment. I saw myself as a hard-working, successful, stable citizen who contributed to the community and was well rewarded for my efforts. I was meeting my goals. Verne seemed a bit irresponsible and cavalier in his approach to life. He avoided real commitment which was evident in the way that he collected land in various parts of the world as options in case of trouble in any one place.

It was during this phase of private self-praise, that my life took a peculiar turn or detour and events accelerated so fast that, if I hadn't established the habit of keeping a note of them on the USB stick, I would have forgotten most of what happened over the next few weeks. I had developed the lazy habit of leaving the USB plugged into my computer port. Dutifully, I stuck to my task as "Chronicler" each day.

My site meeting with Jeff to discuss the blueprints for my new house marked a change in direction in my life. Science is my natural frame of reference and that meeting was like an experiment in spontaneous combustion that set molecules in a motion which seemed random at the time.

Jeff Clement was energetic, with decades of experience in the building trade. He was a confident man in early middle-age who generally wore blue denim jeans with his loose fitting, round-necked t-shirt untucked and, of course, the ubiquitous baseball cap. After greeting him and scrutinising the broad plans that we had revised in his office during a previous meeting, Jeff guided me around the property to show me where the lines for the foundation and basement would fall. Then we perched on the tailgate of his truck to speculate about various possibilities for the house.

I felt that my money gave me the prerogative to talk about any aspect of the coming operation. Sitting there together in the sunshine, seemed like an appropriate opportunity to make my attitude clear to Jeff, so with little thought, I said, "You know this is my second property and house. I want to make sure you understand that I'm not doing this only for profit. I want this house to be exceptional; one that people will admire for its integrity."

Jeff's long pause reinforced my smug feeling that I had said something weighty, until his response brought me down to earth. "How many builders did you interview before you chose me, Ross?"

"I can't recall, five, ten," I replied.

"And what was their key point?"

Once again, I was a bit thrown by his calm manner and that he seemed to be ignoring my wish. I gave a flippant answer along the lines of, "Stuff about end dates, project length, earliest start date. I'm not entirely sure."

"And me? What was my priority?" asked Jeff.

"You said something about finding the best time of the year for materials to bond with the ground or what materials would endure best in this climate. Things along those lines."

"So, you don't really know what you're talking about do you, Doc. Tell you what: you chose me because you thought that I'd do the best job. That better be the reason. Not the cheapest job. So, I won't ask you about your trade secrets and you don't ask me too much about mine. Right."

"OK, I was trying to let you know how…"

"I know what you want, right. Why do you think we meet to talk about the plans and here on site so you can have a bit of an idea, right." Jeff raised his voice, "If you don't pay attention, you're not going to learn much. I use the best. No shortcuts. No cheap materials. Right. If you are looking to cut the cost, let's be quite clear here and now. Tell you what: you can find yourself another builder."

"Jeff," I said, "I want a really solid house that will last. But I own the land and the land has to work for me."

He slid off the tailgate, planted his feet in front of me, his lean, wiry frame almost vibrating, "This is stoopid. It's never going to work. Tell you what: find another builder. One who will do it your way. I'm done."

He rolled up the plan, pulled his keys from his pocket and started walking towards the door of his truck. I have learned in my practice to let people erupt till their anger subsides otherwise they think that you are trying to evade the issue, but I almost mistimed it. It was my turn to shout - I knew that I had to interrupt his course and if he got behind the wheel there was no turning back.

"I want you to build a keeper. You're the best for sure. You're in charge here."

He stopped and turned. I continued more quietly: "Jeff, I want you to build me a home that my grandchildren will see and live in. Maybe even their children."

He smiled, relaxed slightly and said, "I'm sorry. I just get tired of people with a bit of money telling me what to do, thinking they know what's best. If you mean what you said about me being in charge, I won't disappoint you."

"I mean it. I just want to learn."

"OK, tell you what: I'll break my rule and tell you a few trade secrets. I'm not running the other guys down, mind."

I nodded agreement and he sat down again on the tailgate.

"They're not really secrets because it all complies with the regulations, right. Nothing's been fully tested, certainly not by me. Only time will really tell. You'll see the decay when those responsible are dead and gone. Anyway, some of the stuff that they use will grow mould from the inside out. You won't know till it's too late then all hell breaks loose. No one's breaking any rules. Sometimes builders don't even know that they're dropping standards because they don't research. I test my stuff as best I can myself and watch how it weathers in all conditions. The way I do it costs more and I'm sorry if I went off pop just now, but it drives me crazy. Building's a hard competitive game and I take a chance not using the cheaper stuff."

"I'm not in a rush right now and I can afford the best. It sounds cocky, I know."

Jeff looked me in the eye and said, "Good. Because I am serious that if you want to do it the easy way you'd best find a different builder. Right. I'm the enemy of sloppy. My house will give you shelter and peace of mind. I want to give my customers a real home – one they can depend on all their lives, even their children's lives."

"That's what I'm looking for."

He shook my hand and, with authenticity rare today, he uttered an extraordinary pledge: "Tell you what: like you said, I guarantee you a house that your children's grandchildren will be proud of. Or, if it's pulled down as houses so often are these days, I promise you that the materials I use will still be in such perfect condition that they could be used for another house. I hope it outlasts both of us; that when it is demolished and I can't prove it to you, my ghost will be there saving the building stuff."

We both chuckled at the funny image, but I added, "I don't want a haunted house. We'd better keep that to ourselves." Jeff drove off in his truck. At least we ended on a more realistic note because everyone knows that older houses are razed to make way for modern homes here on a regular, systematic basis. We've developed ways to make our walls perfectly smooth inside. They satisfy our sense of propriety, but it's highly unlikely that anyone will be walking around these ruins in two thousand years time, searching for clues about us.

I took a folding chair from the trunk of my car, placed it on my empty land between the other houses, sat down to think about the clash with Jeff and regain my equilibrium. I'd probably judged him too quickly: humour was one of the many layers of his personality. I was glad that I had engaged "the enemy of sloppy" to build my house and set high expectations for himself and others. It would be a challenge to work with him, but the end product would probably be excellent quality.

In my calmer state of mind, I wondered whether Verne and Cador would approve of Jeff's promise and standards. Of course, I knew that the two in Cornwall were discussing something deeper that I didn't fully understand, but it did strike me as coincidental that Jeff made a joke about his ghost after I had read Verne's email describing his sense of the long dead villagers at Chysauster. I smiled to myself at the thought of trying to convey my impressions to Verne; if he was present, he would certainly throw in a story or a question to shift the ground and shake my confidence.

I was adjusting my thoughts to the Verne-effect, when a figure emerged from the shadow of a neighbouring house. He sauntered along pushing a shopping cart that rattled on the pavement and paused in front of me. We gazed at each other in mutual wonderment. I must have been an incongruous sight, seated on a fold-out chair, in the middle of a vacant lot between the established houses. He was also extraordinary. Like those who survive off others' waste, he carried items that he had collected in a cart - empty drink cans worth a few cents and old clothes. His characteristics triggered my doctor's instinct to scrutinise detail: a few days of beard growth, a bit grimy on the surface, nails not as dirty as his hands and the mud on his clothes was superficial, less ingrained into the material than would be the case with continued hard wear. The cuffs of his jacket were relatively clean. Though dirty, his hands were not as calloused or cracked as they should be if exposed to the elements without respite. I had quickly spotted the clues separating him from the normal. I was good at my job.

A small modern digital bluetooth speaker with crystal clear sound playing from his cell phone was an interesting addition. I had noticed other bottle collectors with cell phones, but a more techie setup like this one broke the stereotype. He struck up a conversation.

"Askuvie," as he introduced himself, was not visibly old, young or middle aged. In fact, it was hard to determine his age - even within a decade. I asked him about his unusual name. Suppressing a smile, he said that he had found that it was the easiest way to get around his real name: it was an abbreviation of one that was too complicated for most people.

My pride aroused by the dismissal, he held my attention and we continued to chat. The longer we talked, the more contradictions emerged in his character to match the physical disparities I have mentioned. He was slow to answer, sometimes pondering for several minutes before responding to ordinary questions. I started with, "Askuvie, do you collect bottles all year round?"

Several lines of Carol King's "Tapestry" filled the silence before he answered, "Only when it serves the purpose."

"Surely the purpose is to make a few dollars? You can't save enough to take breaks?"

"That would be telling, but no, it's only a part of who I am. I also stay on this land partly with intention, because I cannot leave it - unconditionally."

"Mysterious," I replied, curious and a bit on edge. Then with renewed confidence, "So, your real name's a secret and you're restricted to this area? Should I be nervous?"

"Depends on your capacity," he replied, unable to conceal a smile which revealed a set of perfectly aligned, white teeth.

Another taunt; I nibbled the bait, "Capacity?"

"Capacity for veracity," came back with patience.

Slightly irritated, I couldn't resist; I wanted to know more about Askuvie and struck at the bait, "What do you mean by 'this land' and where do you live?"

Uninvited, he stepped across a line dividing the pavement from my property. His encroachment bothered me, but not enough to feel threatening. I like to think that I have skills to detect nuances in people's speech, facial expressions and body language: Askuvie was playing me. He evaded my question with, "Not on the street, but more about that later. Let's talk about you. Has anyone built on this piece of land before?"

"Not technically. I'm building a skinny house. Infill, as they call it."

Without any hesitancy in his step, Askuvie walked right up to my chair and squatted comfortably next to me to gaze in the same direction. His next question seemed normal for him, "OK, so whose footsteps have tracked across here?"

"That's a weird question. The people who lived here, the neighbours. Maybe children at play."

"So, recreational footsteps?"

"Huh?"

"Footsteps of games: shallow footprints. Will you be covering over footsteps of survival, of struggle...of intensity?"

"You've lost me."

"Do you think there may be more serious footsteps of hardship, maybe at a deeper level?"

"I don't really know what you mean. Perhaps you're going to tell me."

"Again, that depends upon your capacity," he laughed, "but I don't talk about this in the open. You'd have to come to my place. Then I'd know that you have decided to take this further."

Askuvie gave me his street address which he called his "point of connection", and that if I did choose to visit I would probably find him in the garden where he spent most of his time. He added that it was where he felt attached and nourished; where he did all he could to replenish the land in return for its bounty. He promised that if I ventured over to his spot, we would continue the conversation. I understood from

Askuvie's wry smile that he knew that he had all but landed me, and that he would dictate the course of events.

Askuvie eyed some larger bushes on my property and asked if he could conceal his cart and bottles there. I consented, as building was only scheduled to start months later and he assured me that he would pick them up on his next round. He stood up, stashed the cart, thanked me and with weird words, "Let's not grow much older before we meet again," he walked off toward the east, covering enormous ground with each stride. His lengthened shadow ranged in front of him, claiming and releasing the land he traversed, like an agent of his more substantial self.

I kept that encounter to myself at the time because I wasn't able to place Askuvie in my well defined world of acquaintances; he, his shadow and his bluetooth speaker, had slipped through a crevice he'd discovered into what I considered to be my stable world. Besides, I felt that he had entrusted me with secret knowledge of his abnormal existence which wasn't my prerogative to divulge.

I derived a sense of purpose from rendering a high level of care to all my patients during the routine, busy work week that followed. In conjunction with a few of my talented colleagues, I was able to claim partial credit for solving a couple of particularly vexing cases and alleviating those patients' suffering. It gave me satisfaction.

Despite the exhaustion of a frenetic week, I found myself wondering what Verne was doing in Cornwall. Askuvie's invitation to visit him at home also taunted me: he had presented it as a challenge and there was no mistaking his provocative attitude. Askuvie had aroused my curiosity and I wanted to know his real name.

Chapter Six

Since Verne's departure, my colleagues and I hadn't been able to coordinate our schedules and enthusiasm for games evenings had dwindled. Consequently, by noon on the Saturday following my meeting with Askuvie, my chores were complete. I decided that if I walked to my new property I could detour via the address that Askuvie had given me. I half expected it was a ruse as it was in an expensive area; there was a chance that he was a charlatan. I reasoned that it would extend my walk and at least be good exercise. Autumn leaves were losing their cheering effect and, though the midday sun was warm, I carried a coat because one notices a distinct chill in the evening air at that time of the year - Nature giving notice that colder weather is on the way.

I arrived at the address Askuvie had provided to discover an old house, obscured by a bough of a gnarled tree like a muscular arm concealing the steps and front door from sight from the road as if conspiring to provide a natural defence. However, as I walked closer it became apparent that it was an illusion, like so many other deceptive aspects of Askuvie's property. The siding was cracked beyond repair, the roof years past expiry date, judging by the curled and missing shingles; the steps leading up to the front door shouted, "Step on me and be hurt." Without exaggeration, the house looked like it would tumble down if I leaned on it. A handwritten sign hanging on the front door evoked a smile, "Visitors Welcome

Only When Summoned": another crease in Askuvie's personality - intriguing and repelling at the same time.

I remembered Askuvie's direction that I'd probably find him in the back garden, so I ducked under the branch and walked along the side of the ramshackle house following an unpaved, barely noticeable, narrow path which came to an abrupt end at a dense, untrimmed cedar hedge higher than my head. A stone pillar or marker seemed to be incorporated into the further end of the hedge. If Askuvie's land did extend behind the hedge, it was uncultivated. I rebuked myself for wasting my time in believing such an implausible character and was about to leave when Askuvie appeared soundlessly next to the pillar. I mean appeared: it was not as if he moved into position, rather his form darkened where he stood, which may have been a trick of the light playing between the trees.

With a genuine smile, he invited me to "C'mon in." He separated himself from the pillar and each took on a more definite shape. Patting the pillar, he added, "You do know about inukshuks, don't you?" I braced myself to enter the dilapidated dwelling, but was further surprised when, instead, turning in the opposite direction, he pushed through an obscured opening in the cedar hedge into a wild wonderland. Initially the space seemed like a neglected garden. Typical of older houses in that neighbourhood, the building covered far less of the property than modern houses do.

As my eyes adjusted to the dimmer light inside the bower, the arrangement of the dwelling place became more evident. The whole area was shaded by trees which, together with shrubs and bushes, concealed it and its inhabitants from the roadway; the foliage muffled any street noise from the quiet neighbourhood.

Askuvie lit a small lamp made of soapstone which emitted enough heat to warm the enclosure as well as sufficient light. He observed my fascination and softly said, "There was trade here, cultural and intellectual exchange before the settlers arrived. It was not always direct, but all things are connected; items and ideas were passed along so that the evidence, like this lamp, sometimes puzzles the experts these days. When it doesn't fit their scheme of things, they ignore it or bury it. This lamp comes from the people in the north where the winters are even longer and colder than here."

He gestured for me to sit on the ground and passed me a blanket with his now familiar wry smile (which replaced words). Whether it was the effect of the lamp or that the enclave was insulated by the hedge, I couldn't tell, but I didn't need the blanket for warmth. As I sat down, I was aware of Askuvie carefully observing my every move and expression. The environment seemed to discourage the usual small talk normal between those who do not know each other well; niceties were not necessary. We sat quietly for several minutes without the awkwardness that sometimes cramps new relationships. When I had taken in some of the features of the garden, Askuvie in an almost formal way said, "Welcome to my sanctuary. I hope that you are comfortable and will frequently spend time here."

"Thank you, Askuvie," I replied, trying to seem as nonchalant as possible. He was aware of my surprise. How could he not have been?

"So," with a slightly wider smile than usual, he continued, "You must be a bit disconcerted by my arrangement. I live outside as much as I can and use the house for storage and growing vegetables, especially in winter months. It's there if I need it in extreme conditions. I know that it's unconventional, but dispensing with the unnecessary works for me."

"The holes in the roof must help with irrigation," I said and I was relieved that he laughed.

The aroma of food cooking pulled my attention to a small three legged pot warming on embers. Responding to my glance, Askuvie offered me lunch. I accepted. He produced ceramic bowls and, opening the pot, exclaimed, "Just about ready…I think we can enjoy this now. I was expecting you to arrive soon."

I was learning to suppress my reaction to his surprising comments and accept that, with time, I might understand his intuition. The meal was an exceptional vegetable broth, flavoured with herbs I did not recognise. "All grown myself," he added. The food stimulated our conversation and Askuvie said, "If we are going to be friends, we must be able to ask questions without restriction...I'm sure you have a few right now. Holding back will only make things awkward. Be prepared that we may come to the answers more slowly than your questions flow."

Encouraged, I hesitantly began, "Thanks for the meal. It's delicious." He nodded. "And, this...camp is remarkable..ingenious. It feels like we're away from the city, like we're on our own. Let's start with the concrete: why this?" I said, gesturing around with my hand.

"I'm living on the land. I don't have many visitors, except the occasional invited guest." After a brief pause, Askuvie continued, "There is nothing better than sleeping outside and enjoying the fresh air - though it's a bit polluted. My bed is over there In the corner and you'd be surprised how warm this place can be."

I looked over to see a raised portion of the ground with stakes suspending a material that gave the appearance of a camp bed which Askuvie claimed was less spartan than a hammock and that he had never experienced ill effects from sleeping on it. While we ate the meal without any rush we continued to get to know each other. Askuvie asked many questions regarding my work, but most of all, he seemed interested in my origins, my parents and grandparents.

In response to his questions I told him that several generations ago, my ancestors came out to the eastern part of this country from Europe, but I couldn't really trace all the strands to his satisfaction and he pushed me with a twist of his own, saying, "C'mon doctor: you're a haematologist. You should know more about your bloodline." I laughed, but could only relate recent family history: my grandparents had come to the city from a prairie farm, my father set up in business which was successful enough to allow me the luxury of studying medicine. I'd practiced and specialized for a decade now and I'm very satisfied with my choice of career - though a bit stressed at times. I ended with the notion that I'd often been encouraged by my parents to emphasize that I was the first doctor in the family.

With a unique blend of taunting and playful respect, Askuvie commented, "As far as you know," and then suggested, "So, right now, you don't know of all the ancestral strains that have gone into your creation." It wasn't a question, but he followed it with one that I have considered and reconsidered since: "Would you like to know the answer to that?"

"It hasn't bothered me in the past."

"Bothered?"

"Well, why would it matter now?"

"That will be up to you. Depends if you're interested in how the past has brought you here." Then, almost speaking to himself very quietly, mused, "Is it your work that troubles you?"

"No, why would it?"

"Maybe it gets in the way of your passion."

"Work is my passion. What else would be of equal interest to me?"

"I don't know yet. We may discover that. Where would you like to end? Not in your profession. In life?"

"It's too soon to say."

"Right now, maybe. But with patience, it may come to you."

I brushed that comment aside and we turned back to Askuvie. He answered questions with a great deal of thought - a bit out of the normal speech pattern. When I asked him about his name, his response was deliberate. In the dappled light that played on all surfaces, he looked at me intensely with eyes that searched for something that he expected to find. It was as if he was reading me; looking for information. Then, seeming to reach a conclusion, with concern, he cautioned, "If I tell you this one piece about me, we will establish great trust and agreement. No matter how you react to what I am going to tell you, it cannot be shared with others until the time is right."

Askuvie's eyes seemed to penetrate my conscience and, sitting in the middle of his bower, we nodded our total understanding. It was one of those rare bonds of trust: I didn't realise until later that I was being allowed a glimpse into dimensions of a hidden world. From then on, Askuvie would decide when it was suitable for me to see something new and he even seemed to shape my emotions towards each novel experience. I had to trust his judgement.

That day in Askuvie's sanctuary with the shadows of the leaves and branches playing over the ground and my body, I became aware of an alternative perspective; a compelling, yet misty reality that sought to erode my sanity. Without further avoidance, Askuvie revealed how much can be incorporated in a name with the words, "My complete name is Askuwheteau which means 'He keeps watch' and that is what I do here. I have a university education - a minor part of my being, my state, my destiny. Like everyone, my life is complex. Askuvie is much easier for most people in all ways."

"What do you mean by 'keeps watch?' Are you a kind of sentinel?"

"That's a good word for it. Probably the closest you'll hear." After a pause, with a twinkle in his voice and eye, "It doesn't take much high school humour to play with my name after the first three letters: A, space, S, K... then you choose: E, W, or for the intellectual wannabees, a semantic play with V, I, E in French, or V, I, E...add a W; Or A, S, K...then a space and U and whatever you like after that."

"That's a lot of possibilities," I said. "There's humour, life and diversity built right into your nickname."

"We have to laugh at ourselves. I think that I may have to help you with that. But identity adjustment is a profound thing. Do you want to be someone else?"

"Not right now. But who knows? You may show me a different angle. Seriously, as a start, Askuvie, or would you prefer Askuwheteau, what do you guard?"

With his usual smile, Askuwheteau replied that I would know when to use the full name; inside his sanctuary was an example. As I looked around I started to grasp the genius behind his "place" which was almost self-sustaining. That natural space met most of his needs. Maybe it seemed wonderful to me because we are so used to our modern world of consumer convenience, or because we are severed from the natural world. The longer I sat in that enclave with Askuwheteau, the more it seemed natural, and the world outside, the land of make-believe. Askuwheteau spoke softly to increase my comfort inside his haven and adjust my perspective to better understand what he was telling me.

"The meaning of my name is nuanced. Not so much guard as 'watch', to protect, to monitor, to report or record." A shadow of sadness flashed across his face as he expanded, "There's no direct translation for 'Askuwheteau' but 'sentinel' resonates. I track things that happen; I contact people who care deeply about the land. You looked receptive."

Askuwheteau continued, "You asked what I do. I keep a watch on the health of the land around here. This piece of land is a gauge. It helps me in my task of compiling information for those who know how to use it best."

I looked around his sanctuary with some scepticism and summoned all my self-control not to sound cynical, patronising - keep any hint of derision out of my voice - when I said, "Are you self-appointed or is there some sort of organization involved?"

Without any sign of offence Askuwheteau calmly expanded that, "This piece of land has been in my family, either directly or indirectly for hundreds of years, perhaps over a thousand years. When larger agreements were made, then broken, we manoeuvred to keep this particular ground untrammelled, unsullied. Do you think that I could have learned how to establish this self-sufficient arbour from books? Could a haven like this be established in one lifetime? The knowledge is transmitted, treasured from generation to generation." Then after a lengthy pause, he answered, "No...I am not self-appointed. This is a 'designation', with the emphasis on 'design'. Of course I have a choice. I can walk away, but the expectations are higher than you can imagine. I'm not generally supervised by anyone in the community, but I am accountable."

My doubt grew into full-blown incredulity, judging his story to be a gross exaggeration. Askuwheteau responded to my raised eyebrows and anticipated my next question and answered, "I'm telling you this because the future is more uncertain than it has ever been and you are the right person to engage at this point. I detect a darkness, a shadow, partly through my sources and also through some intuition. And I'm telling you because you are already familiar with the dangers. You responded in a profound way when Jeff told you about the mould in buildings; the thought has remained with you till now."

"How did you know," I began, "You were watching us...of course? Jeff built for you too?"

Askuwheteau shook his head, "I don't build in that way, but I pay attention. It doesn't matter how I came by it. What remains important is your reaction." By this stage I thought that I had intuited Askuwheteau's origins, but he continued, "Despite what you have told me, you will find that you have a personal response to the land that is not totally clear... yet.

"You have enough to think about for now. We will talk at another time. It's getting late and I have to prepare for the night." With a chuckle, he added, "I can't just turn off the lights and lock the door."

I left the shelter of Askuwheteau's garden and postponed the visit to my own property. With my thoughts in a tangle, I wondered whether ordinary things would ever make sense again. Askuvie's unconventional existence and his suggestions, scuttled by the irony of his own humour - sometimes self-deprecating - swirled around in my mind. It struck me how precariously we perched on the surface of the earth with very shallow roots holding us in one place. I wondered whether our mental stability is somehow dependent upon a connection with the ground. For some inexplicable reason, Cador's words, "We live in the world, not on it," came back to me.

Inside my house, I noticed that my computer displayed several unread emails. However, it was after midnight. The emails could wait so I went to bed and quickly fell into a sleep punctuated by scenes of Askuvie, swearing me to silence about his secrets. Askuwheteau had made me privy to a closely guarded truth, as if I had undergone an initiation ceremony and entered a new realm. While my essential being remained unaltered, his questions and revelations had ushered me into terrain barred to most people.

Chapter Seven

Sunday morning, coffee in hand, I approached my computer. Verne's name was at the top of the Inbox, but I dealt with the other messages requiring brief responses before opening his email. I wanted to enjoy Verne's without the nagging distraction of having to attend to anything else. As usual, his flippant greeting belied more serious content. Dutifully, I saved his email and its attachment to the USB stick. I will share his revelation with you.

Hullo Mate

I have been exploring this Cornish peninsula for many days now, never tiring of the dramatic variations of its topography: craggy cliffs and billowing oceans that have inspired the stories of these parts. Ambition to accrue plots of land around the globe still urges me back to work: buy a good spot here and move on; counter to that, I have never heard the voice of a landscape chorus so loudly in my mind. Consequently, I'm torn between reverting to the practical aspects of life or continuing to explore this romantic Celtic environment a little while longer. It's not just the amazing features of the fascinating villages, even the tourist traps like St. Ives and Lands End, or the antique buildings such as the birthplace of

King Arthur, that intrigue me. Cornwall's nooks and crevices

conceal forgotten myths and secrets yet to be revealed to

those who are persistent and receptive. Chysauster, above all

places in this peninsula, ignites my imagination and it was

there that small fissures divulged unexpected treasures and

understanding. Like my first piece, I have written the

attachment in a form that may be of interest to others in the

future, though I have not discussed the content with anyone

else as they may question my sanity. I want your opinion first.

Cheers mate

Verne

Returning to Chysauster

At Chysauster a thin, nearly transparent, curtain hangs

between the past and our present world: a threshold. I have

developed a deep respect for the people of ancient times and

the care that they took with everything. As Cador explained to

me during my first visit, they built with the rocks scattered around them which don't release toxic gases like our buildings do as they age.

This time when I arrived at Chysauster and purchased a ticket at the kiosk, I asked the lady there which guides were working that day. She answered as cheerily as could be, "Sorry, luv, we don't have guides here. There are guidebooks and maps in the corner."

"Well, maybe he's not a guide," I said, "Does the actor fellow who dresses up to tell visitors about life in the village come here regularly? I don't know what you'd call him."

"Don't know anyone like that and I've been here years," she replied. I was about to ask about Carenza's and the Roman's house, but my first question had raised her guard so I checked the tourist literature for anything new and, finding none, sauntered out into the village. I thought that I'd start at the perimeter and spiral inwards.

Reaching the houses I was struck again by their solid structure - their resilience against two thousand years of weather and human interference. I marveled at how they have retained their shape, and wondered whether there is some magic glue binding them. A few tourists seemed to be moving too quickly past the wonders of a bygone age. I overheard one urging her friends to "hurry along through the silly ruins because the seafood in St Ives is the best you'll ever taste." I was relieved when I was alone with the stones once again. By that stage I was back at the 'Roman house' where I spent the night on my last visit. I sat for a few minutes examining a doorway and then, as no one else was around I picked up a stick and scraped away some dirt from the joints between two large stones, curious to see what held them together. These were the stones that were shaped - a Roman innovation of the time, according to Cador - and it seemed like mud or sand had collected between them over the years. In the process, I flicked out something other than grit onto the ground. I picked it up and cleaned off the mud to expose a tiny metal object which appeared to be an intricately made, circular gold earring in the shape of a horned sheep-like head. I looked around for someone with whom to share this marvelous find. Then I put it in perspective, realizing that it was more likely left there by some bored kids who had stuck it away in revenge on their parents for dragging them around what would have probably been, for them, a crumbling mausoleum. I was alone, so I resolved that I'd hand it in when I left. I popped it into the front pocket of my backpack for easy retrieval.

I felt a bit hungry so I decided to see whether that berry bush crop was still available. I also realised that I was not exactly at the centre of the village, but the berry bush, twenty metres away, was the middle - I'd gyrated to where I'd met Cador. I felt a bit lethargic and needed a boost of energy, so I helped myself to the berries again and I must admit that I was rather disappointed that Cador was not there to entertain me with more of his personal, 'stage version', of Chysauster. After the snack I was still drowsy because I'd been up since five that morning and, like my last visit, I must have dozed off in the late autumn sunshine. I think that it was only for a few moments. When I opened my heavy eyelids with difficulty I was convinced that a shadowy figure was pulling at the zip of the front pocket of my backpack that I'd left a few metres away. He muttered something like, "Open up. What is this? He only has one. He won't know what to do." I can't guarantee it, but the fleeting figure that disappeared around the hill over the tunnel, resembled Cador. Perhaps it was my sense of guilt at prodding between the stones, or wishful thinking that Cador would materialise, or the wild berries, but it was disturbing that someone - even Cador - was rummaging through my bag. I checked the front zip and there was indeed a piece of cloth jamming it; however, it was easy enough to dislodge. Someone familiar with zips should have been able to open it with ease.

Disconcerted by the incident, I became impatient to depart and, as there was no one in the shop or office at the time to receive the jewelry, I kept the trinket. I know that it's a crime to remove anything from historic sites, but it is so small it hardly warranted the time and explanation to some bureaucrat who would treat my story with disbelief and might even decide to prosecute me in the name of diligence. Twinges of guilt did follow me along the road away from Chysauster.

However, a more powerful force came into play as I recalled the words of the character fiddling with the zip on my backpack: "He only has one....He won't know what to do." True on both counts. So I turned around and headed back inside to search for the other earring and find some direction. After all, it was early afternoon.

I returned to the Roman's house and examined the stone parts of the structure more carefully. I scratched tentatively now more mindful of all the implications and tried to discover a second earring. Of course there was nothing. I also knew that this would probably be my last visit to the village, so I decided to have one last look around at my favourite spots before continuing on my journey. Back at the entrance to the fougou where I had chatted with Cador, I took the earring out of my backpack and placed it on a flat stone and wondered what

Cador could tell me about it if he were there. Did it indeed come from ancient times or it was merely a modern trinket?

I speculated for a while about the habits of the ancient inhabitants and what they would have thought of a Roman in their village - whether they could have fully accepted him. I started to think of everything about him that would have been different from the villagers: his hairstyle, the way that he carved stones, his hygiene habits. He must have thought that he was bringing something better to those in Chysauster. I half-closed my eyes to meditate on the Roman: what he would have looked like, make him more flesh and blood, but I couldn't even give him a name or facial expressions, let alone have insight into his personality. In my mind he would always be "The Roman"; I couldn't visualise him any more clearly than I can imagine how other people see me. Perhaps that was what he was to those in Chysauster: a foreigner, slightly imperious, occasionally disdainful of Cador's people and their customs, totally in love with Carenza.

"He wasn't physically different; it was how he saw the world." I was startled by Cador who had somehow silently approached and entered my stream of thought with precisely the right words. His intrusion should have been eerie, but seemed natural.

Dressed in the same costume he wore previously, he took a seat near me. Though surprised, we were on the same page and I went straight to it: "Cador!. What exactly do you do here? Why do you hang around?"

"Good day to you," he answered with a smile, "I do what I have to, Verne. Mainly I try to make sure that people don't oversimplify things. I guard against that easy view of the world that disagreements can always be settled - a huge mistake. Usually the most powerful have that outlook, but things are never resolved with force. They remain volatile, especially when a stronger one tries to suppress and restrain the weaker. The powerful talk about victory, but beneath the surface the conflict ferments, like the mead we brew and perhaps that's the best example. The Roman always wanted to be in control. He watered down the mead. Can you think of anything more ridiculous - spoil delicious mead with extra water? You can't get rid of the mead by adding water. If you want water, don't spoil it with mead - even in small proportions - the water's perfect as it is. Just as the presence of the mead will always bother someone who wants a pure drink, the defeated will always niggle conquerors who want formulaic solutions to problems. Well that's how the Roman did all things - except fighting. He thought that he could solve all problems by measuring exact proportions into a mixture.

The day he arrived at the head of his squad was an exception because he acted on impulse, instinct. Would you like to know what we talked about that day through rough language and signals?"

Of course I wanted to hear more detail. Cador is so good at telling stories that sometimes it seems that he was actually there two thousand years ago when those unrecorded events

*took place. It was as if he was resuscitating a lost oral history.
At least, he must have researched the period really well
because he definitely brought it alive. I snatched the
opportunity: "How did you know I was thinking about the
Roman, Cador? I've been wanting to hear more about that first
encounter and the building with stones since my last visit."*

*"Easy guess. What else is there to think about around here?
Except perhaps your own part in the story! Anyway, that's
something for you to discover."*

*He went back to that pivotal day. "You will recall that as the
Romans advanced up the slope, our Roman walked ahead of
the rest of the soldiers and I raised my hand. It was in
greeting, not a threat or command. It surprised them, including
our Roman and he signaled for his soldiers to halt. They did,
but I could feel the tension. Their ingrained impulse and
training was to charge; it was almost irrepressible and I half
expected them to ignore the command. I understood then that
their way was to destroy and plunder all in front of them*

without mercy. I couldn't figure out why our Roman had paused, but I knew that I had to use the moment. Somehow I placed a doubt in his mind: What if the thing you wanted most in the world was here in the village? What if you killed that one, most precious thing that would make your life complete? It was a complex thought to convey through rudimentary words and hand signals, but it worked. I didn't know at that point that his distraction was Carenza and the thought was already seated in his mind. I offered him food which he had to take with both hands. He wanted more for his soldiers and that gave me leave to call on the villagers to bring out some for his soldiers. He probably wanted a second glance at Carenza."

"I saw all that happen, Cador."

"I know."

"But how did you sustain the truce when the soldiers were so impatient?"

"Timing. Carenza's dash had given us an opportunity and the history of our world changed in a moment. A vicious peace held while the Romans camped outside. They weren't really satisfied and were very critical of their leader. I heard comments like 'Our captain's heart reneges all temper," and, "May as well be buried in this wasteland." But the Roman and I managed to prevail with both parties (some villagers wanted to sneak into the Roman camp and night and murder them while they slept) and we all survived. What's more, our Roman could return with dignity. Sometimes very powerful groups think that they can completely exterminate those they consider vermin, but if even one other remains with one memory of former beauty, the conquerors can never rest easy in the subdued land. Nor can their descendants. That was not the case here. I did hear of catastrophe in other parts of the country, not far away, which is one reason why I think that Carenza and her Roman would never be able to flourish outside our village."

"That's extraordinary, Cador! Why do you think that the situation here stayed calm? When did you realise that Carenza and the Roman were in love?"

Cador was quick to respond, "The second part was easy. I told you last time, they couldn't hide it - from me anyway. As to the cooperation between our peoples: there's never one reason or a single answer," he paused for a long while, "I've pondered this over the years and, as I said earlier, it is my responsibility to ensure that people consider the complexities involved in matters. I overheard comments amongst our villagers too, about the Roman, some criticising Carenza, others damning me and my path, but that is part of being chief. Carenza was popular, adored by all the village (despite her choice in that case). I also knew that our villagers were preoccupied with the need to harvest and wanted the Romans gone. Possibly by me taking on the responsibility, in my action of making an agreement with the Roman, not fighting, the two of us were able to keep everything intact. A big part was that our Roman was completely honourable - I could trust him and as long as he could control his soldiers I could ensure that life in our village continued on a smooth path, on the charted way. Trust had a lot to do with it." Then after a few seconds pause, "Our Roman...his deep emotion… like mine...is for the best...for his people…for their well-being. He knew that his soldiers could easily have destroyed us and our village, so did I, but he chose a path of placation, a path that most of his kind have not trodden. It was when he saw Carenza that the blaze of love overwhelmed the fire of battle. He was changed forever. As I said, many of his soldiers scorned his choices. With that alteration to his identity, I thought that I'd never see him again when he left...that he'd never survive without the illusion of the purity of battle. I don't know how he managed to carry out his duty with those forces crashing inside his being. He must be very strong."

"That's a marked contrast with today," I said, "People don't seem to perceive any good in their opponents these days."

He didn't respond to my comment. Instead, he switched to a matter that was bothering him, "I see you have the earring on the stone there. What are you going to do with it?"

Again, I was astounded. Had he been stalking me? Presumably I hadn't recognised him without his costume and he had changed while I was relaxing. Anyway, Cador had reminded me of my find and dilemma; that I'd probably declare it on my way out.

"Don't do that. You've identified the wrong problem," said Cador, "Keep it as a reminder of our village and our friendship. They'll never miss it, Besides, the owner isn't here anymore. After a while, the real solution will be clear to you."

We were walking down the slope toward the exit and I couldn't suppress my incredulity when I asked how he knew such a thing. He answered with a chuckle, "You'll know her when you meet. I've something to do back up the hill. Go well," and he raised his hand in a salute or farewell wave, turned around and disappeared from sight over the hill.

As I left through the tourist exit into the modern day, It didn't take much self-persuasion to keep the earring as I thought that they would probably just throw it away or it would end up in the gift shop as some fake relic because the markings were unique and it may have some inherent value being made of gold. I'm not much of an expert on fashion and jewelry, so I took Cador's suggestion and left it in my backpack with a twinge of guilt. Cador must have seen some mischievous tourist or kid hide it between the rocks. Despite that, I admit, hanging on to it still bothers me a bit.

Verne

As I finished reading, another email from Verne arrived:

Hey mate,

If I'm rambling or boring, just put the attachments aside for some other time. I write them partially so that I will remember what happened on my trip in some detail and partly because I want to share these experiences with anyone who might read them. Perhaps I'll even convince you to join me for a couple of weeks. In the meantime, as I said at the start, I'd appreciate your opinion. At any rate, you'll know what to do with them.

I think that I shall hang around in Cornwall for a while. There's still a lot to discover.

Verne

Verne's email expanded his Chysauster story and intensified the mysterious aspect of my already extraordinary weekend. I was annoyed that Verne had construed my reaction to the Chronicler role so accurately and he was able to predict that I would "know what to do with them." How could he know that I was following through with the ridiculous facet of the game?

I refilled my coffee cup. My usual pleasure of a leisurely Sunday breakfast and reading the Saturday papers was smothered by my curiosity to peer into the convoluted tunnels Askuvie and Verne had opened. As soon as I crawled into them, I realised that I had to reassess my own life.

Chapter Eight

My next shift at the hospital was not till Monday morning. With an uncluttered Sunday in front of me, enjoying the Fall sun warming my living room, in the middle of the comfort of my middle class existence, I reflected on how my life that had been impacted by the queer events of the last few days - actually weeks. It had started with "Genesis," followed by Verne's departure, texts and emails and then meeting Askuwheteau.

I decided to take stock of my life. I jotted down the targets I had set and met, starting with the ineluctable facts: not old, not young; old enough to have a bit of perspective; met my parents' expectations; respected in my chosen career; spend a lot of time furthering that career; compete with others in that career; occasionally have fun with friends or colleagues - usually from my work environment; no special relationship likely to develop into an eternal bond (why am I even using words like that all of a sudden?); moderately fit (at least healthy); mainly content; enough money in the bank to live comfortably and build a house while still living in the one I already own.

I paused and gazed out the window at a magnificent tree, spectacular in its golden, autumn colours. I wrote one word: "Wow." And stared at the next two on the paper, "So what?" It was as if someone else had written them. After about five minutes of numbed silence, at the bottom of the page, I scrawled, "Damn 'Genesis'. Damn Verne. Damn Askuwheteau."

Hopeful that physical exercise and breaking out of the confines of my house would counter the spiral of bathos, I shrugged on my favourite lightweight coat and went out for a walk around the neighbourhood. The flood of oxygen to my brain brought some stability, or at least less self-critical thoughts. Walking, sucking in the cool mouldy-leaf-scented air,

I realised that my thoughts were not simplifying, they were layering. My personal history had been determined by a blend of imposed goals and things that were very important to me.

I found myself in a bizarre dialogue with myself: Success has given me some freedom. That very success also circumscribes my future and my planning: I'm a doctor; build a house to show the world how well I've done. That's my choice. Askuvie is much freer. He does as he wishes, lives outside and is in tune with the seasons of the year. He lives independently. But he's not free; he's bound in ways he chooses not to disclose. I'm also independent. But are either of us free? He said something about being obliged to stay on the land and that it is part of who he is. Perhaps even he is limited in his choices. Has he chosen a kind of wild freedom that has its own rules? It's beyond my comprehension, so unrelated to my reality; I should avoid it altogether. What about Verne? He's not cluttered or bogged down by things around him. Without doffing his hat, he simply cut loose and left, traveling without baggage or guiding Northern Star, untrammeled, a truly free agent. I could do what Verne did, but

I have responsibilities. I can't just follow an instinct, a whim, an inner voice. I can't merely copy him. That's not my freedom; I have to find my own path. I've been measuring and celebrating my progress in terms of beacons prescribed by convention. Maturity involves lining up my own measures of achievement. I have to search inside myself to find markers; not ones stuffed with other people's values. It's difficult to identify my own beacons of achievement. Or isolate my own past.

As my internal argument quietened, I found myself gravitating towards Askuwheteau's place with a faint hope that he might offer some answers, or at least an opinion, on Verne's experiences. Askuwheteau could swap multiple lenses in front of his eyes to interpret the world; I used one lens ground from my medical background - and those books on my shelves. I was confident that Askuwheteau would value Verne's stories; that a conversation with him would expand my limited boundaries.

Chapter Nine

As I approached Askuwheteau's place I saw him striding towards it in his typical fashion from the opposite direction, enjoying the morning air. Layered leaves lying thick on the ground parted in front of him and he blended with them as naturally as the surrounding naked trees.

"Good morning Askuwheteau," I said, detecting a note of deference in my voice - perhaps an effect of using his full name.

He smiled a welcome and beckoned me into his sanctuary. This time, I ignored the house and entered through the dividing hedge. Immediately I felt a serenity that I had forgotten possible. Inside his arcane bower for a second time, I had learned to suspend my disbelief. Once again, we sat on the ground on blankets. In a respectful, but natural manner. Askuwheteau offered me water bubbling through a small stone opening about a foot above the ground in the corner and disappeared into a stone hole immediately below. At the first sip I felt the delicious liquid course through the meridians of my body. I had never tasted water like it. My reaction must have been evident because Askuwheteau anticipated and answered my question: "The water comes from the river and is purified through the stones which flavour and fortify it. The nutrients in this water will satisfy you in unexpected ways" Cutting my next question short, he continued, "You weren't ready for it on your first visit and didn't see the supply because I can divert it. The water will give you energy and you won't be hungry for some time."

"I'm a doctor," I laughed, "I'm suspicious of unofficial water supplies."

"Don't worry. I'm the living proof it's clean," chuckled Askuwheteau. "There is an old system that brings the water all the way up from the river, giving the nutrients time to settle. It's as pure as any water you'll ever drink. Remember, I'm an engineer and I know about chemistry. Before you take the next sip, enjoy the aroma - it changes with the seasons."

I raised the glass to my nose and the bouquet included Aspens, Chokecherries and other local autumnal vegetation which flavoured the next mouthful.

Askuwheteau straightened his back, looked directly into my face and said, "You have come burdened with deep questions and we agreed that we would be completely open with each other."

"Askuwheteau, you told me that you are connected to this piece of land and that you cannot leave, that you have a specific role to play here." He nodded as I continued, "That you have chosen this lifestyle."

He corrected me: "Chosen yes, but with respect, deep respect for the past and the expectations of my predecessors. But that is about me, doctor. You aren't here for that. You are far too troubled. You want to know something about yourself. We can talk about me later when you are settled. Just as I, and the people I represent, can't expect anyone else to change or surrender, neither can you. You have to win your own freedom. How you interact with others and perform your own duty or whatever you want to call it, determines the nature of your own liberty - if that is what you choose. I have freely chosen a path that restricts my choices."

"So, you're not really free?"

"It depends how you see it. I've chosen freely to accept my destiny and everything that goes with it."

"Ha," I said, "destiny implies inevitability."

"Maybe, but I did say I'd chosen to accept it. Now, shall we first deal with your search for purpose. Before we get started, consider how free that stream of water is. Does it depend upon my actions? Or will it find a path of its own despite my interference? Don't answer, just think about it."

I'd given up trying to understand fully what Askuwheteau meant or how he was able to read my mind; so, rather, after a long silence of reflecting why I had come, knowing, as I said, that he saw the world through multiple lenses, I admitted that I couldn't rest; that my grand life seemed to lack something. Askuwheteau avoided saying what we both knew - that he did not hold the answers to my mental tumult.

Instead, he pointed to the large new houses close by. "Why do you think that people build these?

"It's comfortable for their families and they have the means. Basically, because they can, and they enjoy them," I answered.

"Who decides when comfortable becomes sumptuous, extravagant; when does enjoyment cross over to wasteful...maybe even selfish?" I couldn't answer. Askuwheteau sensed my discomfort and said, "Let's change our view. Let's look at the houses - and mine - from the street so we can see them side by side."

We pushed through the hedge, crossed the street and stood facing Askuwheteau's house between the several other newly built houses that a couple of decades earlier would have been categorized as mansions. About two minutes passed. Without turning to look at me Askuwheteau said, "Doctor Martindale, what do you see?"

Inexplicably, my conversation with Verne in my living room after the games evening came to my mind and I recalled his comment about my library. I answered, "Culture. Modern day culture."

Askuwheteau nodded repeatedly during another lengthy silence and turned to me with a twinkle in his eyes that turned to sadness as he asked, "And what about my home?"

I started to answer, but thought that it would embarrass him, so stopped and realised that I was uncomfortable because my answer would reveal my prejudice. Askuwheteau laughed and slapped me on my back. It relieved the tension and he answered his own question: "My house is a statement." In response to my furrowed brow, he added, "It says, don't take things for granted."

I stared at him and said, "Some may say, here's a cheap knock-me-down where I can make a big profit."

"You're right too. And that's where words are so important in culture. You know the term, 'take possession,' in the housing game?"

"Of course."

"Well, those words are as empty as the cavernous bunkers these people have built for themselves."

"It's just a legal term, a phrase to keep people on the same page when they're moving."

"I see it as more than that. But you've probably never had your land taken from you. Neither you nor your ancestors.

You don't even know who they were past a couple of generations."

"What difference does my own history make?"

"Nothing much on its own, but the phrase 'take possession,' exposes a belief that the owners have a permanent hold on the land or property." He paused for a while and added, "At any time, someone can come along and declare a change in the rules and take it away."

"I know that," I said, "but I don't think about it."

"Because it hasn't happened to you or those who gave you your family's memory." Askuwheteau paused for a while, staring at his house and continued, "My old house makes a statement at a deeper level. It disturbs my neighbours' complacency."

"You're right there," I said, "they probably consider it a mess which makes them pretty irritated, even angry."

Askuwheteau laughed and said, "Do you know that while this house has stood here, the houses on either side have each been replaced twice? Why do you think they do that? Why don't the new owners just make modifications to the existing houses?"

"You have to move with the times. Keeps the neighbourhood desirable."

"There's more to it, Ross. Look at my dwelling. It blends with the infinity of Nature. The others clash with Nature. They're trying to impose something finite on the flow of life. I think they're trying to resist the inevitable that awaits us all. My house integrates with the flow. It also disrupts the neighbours' confidence - false confidence. It contradicts the fresh new look of their houses and keeps telling them that things rot and die."

I couldn't resist laughing and said, "That's another way to see dilapidated."

Askuwheteau just smiled and said that it would take time, and eventually I'd be able to appreciate things in multiple ways. We left it at that.

As we pushed our way through the hedge back into Askuwheteau's bower he attacked the topic from another angle. "I'm sure you've heard people around here say that the crows and magpies have taken over the area," he said and waited for my confirmation. I nodded and he continued, "If those same people would wander down into the river valley, pause and listen, they'd be delighted by sparrows, woodpeckers tapping on the bark of dead trees, even the occasional eagle. They coexist."

"What's that got to do with the houses, Askuwheteau?"

"People stop looking after a cursory glance. They miss all that's going on in the mix. Wild things don't threaten our cities from the outside any more. In the end though, the mould from the inside will suffocate those who are struggling in vain to stop the change living in their shiny new houses. Deep down, they're uncertain. They sense the slow contamination. They blame others for the decay, but it's really at the heart of the construction of their own houses."

"They just want a nice place to live and they can afford it," I said.

"You can't buy freedom. Trying to possess land or property is the ultimate mistake, the ultimate illusion."

"Is that what Jeff was talking about? Is that why you know?"

"That's part of the answer. Jeff is motivated by different reasons which he doesn't fully understand about himself. Jeff…" Askuwheteau decided against further information, "…Doctor, you'll have to give it time. You'll find your home when the time is right; you'll know it. That's closer to the question you really came to ask."

"I'm not sure what the question is that I came to ask. We are spinning around it, close to the nub. What will home look like?"

"I can't give you a visual," he said. "You know, when you play a game and the rules are a bit fuzzy and you haven't worked out your strategy, but you know instinctively that a move is the right one?"

My mind jumped back to Verne's "Genesis" for a brief moment as Askuwheteau paused to let his point sink in and continued: "Use your senses: listen carefully and watch people's actions around their houses; it may sound intrusive, but smell the inside of their houses. They call places 'home', but their actions don't match their words. They buy and sell them happily, especially when they think they're making a profit or getting something more swanky to rank them higher in the pecking order of their friends. Sometimes there's a bit of a pull when they move; some emotion is attached, not necessarily sadness. They use one word for two separate entities: a shelter and the absolute centre of home. For me, the one is an element of the other, for me it's all one. The unaccommodated can still be at home. When you experience home it gets inside you, through your skin, into your bones, you'll battle for it in a different way. It won't be for sale."

We'd been sitting and talking intensely for a long time and Askuwheteau got to his feet. I asked, "Is that what you have here? You told me that you were assigned to stay here. Are you keeping watch on this land?"

"It's not that easy. The stakes are high. I told you that I sense a darkness. I know, that sounds like a movie or fairy story, overly dramatic. We keep control over this small lot. It's not just about the piece of ground; it's what's below and what comes out of it. At some point I'll have to make a significant sacrifice. I'll have to weigh that sacrifice in the balance if I have a choice."

"Aren't there others who will support you? You talk about 'our' and 'we'? Where are they?"

"I know that it sounds secretive and mysterious, but there's nothing unnatural about it. Most of those who should be part of this stage have been ripped away. It's not just that they are severed from their physical home."

"Can I help? Can't we do something about this?"

"No, doctor, this is a conundrum. You can't fight my struggles - our struggles; the best you can do is not oppose them. The underdogs have to liberate themselves. You can fight relentlessly to build a better world where more people can be immersed in their homes, but that will involve a sacrifice that endowed people are not prepared to make yet."

"What's the difference, Askuwheteau?"

"That way, you're leading your group to the negotiation, not fighting against something. You remain loyal to those who deserve your loyalty. You, joining the march of the underdog, is insignificant in comparison. Though the goal is the same, you are promoting the process through different means. That way either group, or groups, keep the authenticity of their struggles. If there's a direct head-on clash there's too much destruction on both sides. One weak group struggling for survival, doesn't negate the continuing struggle of the strong group. Groups aren't normally suicidal; they don't have a group death wish."

"Nothing new in the idea that groups will naturally, instinctively, hold on to power, it has to be taken from them," I said, adding conventional thought to the conversation, but it felt like a subversive comment.

"That's why strong, rational, calm and compromising leaders have to do the negotiation first and foremost. They have to be able to rise above petty squabbles, jealousy, envy, covetousness, to see a vision of a better world. Only then and after the talks, can they lead their nation, village or whatever their group is, to an authentic lasting solution. People have to walk into a better world. Anything else is transient."

"So where do you fit into this picture, Askuvie?" deliberately using his nickname name .

"With difficulty, and that's what's so exhausting...doc.," he retorted with equal intention, "Everyone seems to want the same material things, but all those parameters have been decided along alien rules for a long, long time. Imagine a sports league where the strongest teams write the rules of the league; where the weakest teams never have home game advantage and the league rules emphasize their weaknesses.

"It's a hackneyed analogy, but we were kicked out of our own sandbox by the bully and then the teacher came along and forced the bully to share." Askuwheteau looked at me with deep agony in his eyes, "Share our own sandbox? Can you see the irony? The outcome maintains the inequality. The power is hidden in the relationship by those making the rules."

"I don't know what to say. Nothing I do can help? Is that what you meant by 'don't oppose' your struggles?"

"Close, but you can't get off that easily. Here's first prize: Give up your house, your land and ask my permission to live there. Of course that sounds inconceivable, but it goes further. I'll wear an orange t-shirt to urge people to help me understand my shallow, myopic view of the world and accept you with more sympathy. You give up all the stories that have helped you to make sense of the world. Try to form new perceptions using my stories. The other way round is patronising and the liberal movement makes assumptions about my ambitions."

"This doesn't fit the way I've looked at things; it sounds hopeless."

Akuwheteau jumped in quickly, "You mean the way we all fit into your comfortable view! No, of course it doesn't because you always see yourselves as in control, even when you're giving and helping. Don't take it personally. It's just that you can't change that perspective - and what's to be gained by making yourself weaker anyway?" Then he added, "We're the hosts, not you. But we were so gracious that we tried to do things your way and still do. It's a mistake."

"That's so contrary, Askuwheteau. It's almost like an industry has emerged from self-deprecation. I can't grasp these circles within spirals. I need time to understand you."

"It's a process, Ross. It'll come. First you have to discover what really drives your way of seeing the world - not possessions, You have to rediscover the oldest, deepest ideas. And leaders have to know that too. But I've been discourteous. You visited me to unload your troubled mind."

"How did you know? I came out this morning to tell you about a friend of mine, Verne, traveling around Cornwall, England. So much of what we've been talking about comes together in Verne. He obsessively buys land all over the place. You also said that I should understand my own stories first. Well, he's been emailing me about his travels. They're a bit out of the ordinary and I feel awkward telling someone else. I know that you won't scoff at it. Is it something about that 'capacity for veracity?'."

Askuwheteau replied that his sanctuary was a safe and wonderful place to tell and hear stories. He added that he was delighted that I had graduated to that different form of communication rather than constantly interrogating him and trying to analyse everything he said. I laughed, although I didn't really understand the implication. He insisted that I have another glass of water to keep up my energy and "Bring some colour to the tale."

I recounted in as much detail as I could recall, trying to be true to Verne's accounts. "It started with a game he invented," I said. Askuwheteau sat comfortably on a blanket opposite me, his eyes never leaving my face and occasionally reacting with a knowing smile at some of Cador's insights and the occasional chuckle when I revealed some of my own reactions.

"So, you lost me. Who's your friend, Cador or Verne?" he said with a deadpan expression when I finished. He was partially joking and I laughed at his humour, then prodded, "Why do you ask that Askuwheteau, what's beneath it?"

"That's why you're different, doctor. You're not just one of the smartest doctors around these parts, you also detect the layers: Cador and Verne exist hierarchically in your mind, yet you've introduced them to me in equal terms even if you didn't intend it." With a claw-like gesture of his left hand, he said, "They have equal substance for me. If you like, they are both fictional characters in your story as you tell it to me. Or they could both be real and live because you say they do. I believe you either way. What else can I do?"

"The distinction between the two is crystal clear in my mind."

"Maybe that's because you're so analytical - scientific - and it's your story," he laughed. "Anyway, now I can explain that fundamental shift that I mentioned earlier. Give up your story and adopt mine and see if you are as secure in your understanding of the world through my story. That is the change you have to make. But you're not ready for it. First you have to be really strong in your own story; really understand it from all angles before you can branch out. When you do that, you will draw strength and sustenance from it. You might then be able to believe my story like I do yours?"

"If you told it to me, I might."

"Maybe I have. You are just in the wrong position to see it. Not yet at the centre."

"What do you mean by that? Tell it to me simply."

Changing to a squatting position, Askuwheteau picked up a stick, drew a circle on the ground and said, "OK. Maybe this will explain everything we've been talking about. What do you see when you get on a plane and fly out of this city?"

"First the outskirts of the city...then fields, farmed fields. Wheat. Canola."

He made markings toward the periphery of the circle to represent the items I had mentioned. He asked, "And then..?"

"Depends on the direction. South, more fields, other directions, fields, mountains, hills, forests..I don't know. What does it matter?"

"Where is this city when you have a terrific... a deific view?"

"In the middle of nowhere...yup...in the middle of a whole lot of farmers' fields and mountains and...wilderness."

Once again he sketched representations of those things and drew a second much smaller circle that intersected with the first, pointed to the centre of the second circle and said, "For me, Ross...for me, and some like me, this is the middle. Outside this circle is my Nowhere - which includes a large part of your circle. This is the centre of our world."

"Right. But where's my centre?"

"I would say your centre is in the middle of the first circle."

Fleetingly, you and I together may be at the middle of this intersection which feels good. But it can be better."

"What do the circles represent."

"Everything that goes to making who you are, Ross. So you know best what goes into yours. There are many other smaller ones like mine that intersect with your large one and may even overlap with each other."

"How can things be better than the two of us in this intersection?"

"No one knows yet. There will be rearrangements of the circles as time passes.. The circles are not only two-dimensional; they gyrate downwards. Right now Verne is exploring the spirals of your circle with exciting discoveries."

"What can I do, Askuwheteau?"

"Examine your own circle inside out, upside down. Change circles when the time is right. Verne's new perspective of your circle and the stories that he's heard and told you have thrown you off balance?"

I nodded and Askuwheteau continued, "It's not just about your circle, Ross. Some people may see any rearrangement of the circles as cataclysmic. If they become concentric circles and there are no intersections, who decides on the rules for the outermost circle? The whole? Or are they already in that pattern?"

"That's so much to take in. You make it look so basic, but it's really complicated."

"Ross, it's another one of those things you should just think about. Don't try to come to a fixed understanding. Put it on the back-burner, as the old folks say."

"It'll be far back. I'm in the middle of difficult cases at the hospital? I should go home to get ready for work tomorrow."

"Give it time, doctor. New ideas take lots of time. Eventually you will have to move into another circle to look at things from the centre and the outside. Or at least to a completely different point in your own circle. That may help."

"Thanks for the chat. One thing I am sure about is that I'll be back to carry on this conversation, if that's OK with you?" I smiled sincerely.

"It's OK, doctor. That's why I don't fit in easily with any group; maybe only a small circle of hopefuls. The others are always wary and vindictive." Then, as an afterthought or clue that would resonate, "Can you see now why I am reluctant to live inside the house?"

I nodded with a question, "Compromise? Complicity?"

He continued, "It's a pity you're not my neighbour. You are an exception. You get a large part of it. You understand how I am obliged to remain true to the past; to build a unique future where we will all be recognised as genuine. I can't surrender to the threats."

Standing next to the Inukshuk, I asked, "How do you know when you're in the centre of your circle - at home?"

"Ross, when you're in the middle, there are no shadows. It's so bright that it's startling."

"That's it?"

"And, when I am in the middle," Ross, "...my centre...things are stable. Nothing is spinning around me. I am at peace with the world. That's it."

We shook hands, turned to go our separate ways and, with calculated spontaneity, he said over his shoulder, "Hey Doc, do you ever get the feeling that you don't quite fit with your science-type friends at the hospital even though you're one of the best? Sooner than you think, you may find that there are some things that you need repair."

"Hey, Askuvie, do you want me to be a loner and lose sleep? We laughed and waved goodnight.

I took a long route home to try to settle the thoughts whirling around in my mind. I'd left my house with the hope of making sense of things; I'd only succeeded in cultivating a broader sweep of questions. Late autumn winds and weather had carried new perspectives, disturbing my serene ignorance. At the same time I entertained the possibility that I was merely anxious about getting older and my life was a bit one-dimensional - not much to it besides my profession. Perhaps that admission was faint clarity.

When I returned home, I did my best to capture my version of the details of Askuwheteau's insights on the USB. I tacked my response to Verne's question to the end of his email: *"My short answer is tenuous. It's definitely not a dismissal. Sometimes we meet people who show us a completely new vision of life. It takes time, experience and effort to understand what they are offering."*

I visited Askuwheteau several times after that and we continued to explore those ideas he revealed to me that Sunday, though I felt that Askuwheteau had more to offer me than I, him. Fall is short in this part of the world and before the temperatures dropped below zero, Askuwheteau had prepared his dwelling for winter. Details aside, it was much colder in his place than inside modern houses with the heating cranked high, but the temperature inside his sanctuary was bearable. I couldn't really grasp how he managed it. With very little inorganic material he insulated the living space against the incursions of the cold weather; however, prejudice permeates the thickest skin.

Chapter Ten

I hadn't visited Askuwheteau for over a week when I noticed a letter in the local newspaper in which the writer complained about his neighbour who, he thought, was unable or unwilling to maintain his own property. The author's reference to an overgrown hedge, the impenetrable view of the back garden and the dilapidated house described Askuwheteau's land. Thinly disguised racist comments like, "If the owner cannot comply with the standards of this neighbourhood, he should move to a place where his lifestyle is more acceptable," had dodged the editor's scissors.

Askuwheteau's analogy with "home games" surfaced in my thoughts. For several days, a flurry of letters appeared and I scanned each one to search for examples of underlying rules. A few declared how people in that neighbourhood take great pride in cultivating their gardens for all to enjoy as they pass by. One suggested that someone should invite, and pay for, the "miscreant" to enter the best garden competition to encourage him to take more care of his property. I was in the hospital cafeteria and had to stifle a laugh at the intrinsic irony that Askuwheteau was the "Sentinel," nurturing the land. But to see that you had to look through a different lens.

Interestingly, none of the authors mentioned meeting Askuwheteau, so their prejudice was based on a vague sense that whoever lived there lacked western values. Their main concern was appearances and that what they considered to be his neglect, would lead to a devaluation of property in the neighbourhood.

It wasn't long before the "Backyard Battle" entered the realm of the columnist - the domain of the somewhat informed opinion. The clash between neighbours became the topic of conversation amongst the groups I worked with at the hospital. About a week after the newspaper furore had started I joined a few friends and colleagues at a table in the cafeteria. We had worked together in some desperate situations where patients' lives were at stake and have seen each other with our guards down. We tended to share our opinions openly with each other. Some were members of the "Cabal". Conversation turned to the controversial newspaper letters.

"Signs are he's First Nations," Sally, the orthopaedic surgeon, said. "A couple of letters have described his looks and also report traditional stone objects around his property."

"I thought no one had talked with him," I said.

"It's not certain," Sally replied, "anyway, one letter says that he has a degree from the U."

"How would anyone know all that? Noone's met him," said someone from the far end of the table.

Sally said, "Well, whatever. None of that has helped. Why can't he just keep his house and garden in a reasonable state? I'm sure that his neighbours are totally reasonable people. Reasonable is all people want for goodness sake."

"You're right, Sally," chimed in brain surgeon, Sarah, "it's a great neighbourhood and the people who live there aren't bigots. They are liberal and open to all sorts. I mean, imagine having to look at that mess every time you go outside in your own yard! It'd drive me crazy."

Someone entered the conversation with another perspective. I think it may have been Rangseetal who said, "The first letter said you can't see the backyard. Anyway, you know the so-called modern Western society hasn't been the best role model. What have Europeans and their descendants done to the land? All others have learned from us is destruction of the land and violence. We took this land without a second thought for anyone or anything living here."

Sally reacted, "Jeese. That's ridiculous. You would say that. I don't know what's happened to you. Put on an orange t-shirt and go hug a tree. Apologise for breathing to the tree and anyone who'll listen to you. Think it through more carefully. It's got nothing to do with this situation." The others at the table laughed and the lone voice was silenced.

I muttered inaudibly, "Maybe we should give the dispossessed what they deserve?" In Sally's and others' minds, we'd given too much already.

Encouraged, raising her voice, Sarah continued, "To be honest, I would do the same as that neighbour. We all have to live in this area together and we can expect certain standards. Believe me, I'd have something to say if he was my neighbour."

From the other end of the table, came a voice of apparent reason, "This is Canada, after all, not some ghetto. Thank goodness we have laws that keep all this in place and we don't have to deal with it ourselves. Who is this guy anyway? Has anyone here spoken to him?"

I didn't respond and preferred to keep my knowledge to myself because I found the tide of conviction overwhelming. Despite my time spent with Askuwheteau, I was ill-equipped to counter the ignorance, either through weakness or sound knowledge.

Sally, who had been following the issue closely, emerged as the table "authority" on the matter, said, "Yup, the newspapers have been trying to speak with the guy, but he won't let them on his property. Who knows, we may have a pervert in our midst, or some crazy who'll go postal without warning. To be honest, I'd be nervous living next to someone like that."

"Think about it," piped up the other end of the table again, "What would happen to the value of your property living next to someone like that if it all went unchecked." A few muttered concurrences reflected support for the disenchanted neighbour.

"I'm not one for stereotyping, you know," concluded Sarah, "but he's been given all the chances, this guy. And he can't be poor, living in our neighbourhood…" not really able to finish her thought, but knowing that the usual sequiturs from others would carry more weight than her unspoken words.

And they did; her words inflated in the others' mouths: "…I mean, how much can people keep giving? There have to be limits and standards" as well as other similar comments followed in quick succession.

This was more vicious than the friendly rivalry of our games evening. My friends were not interested in the facts - the truth which I kept inside. Whatever verified evidence came to light, they would only find ways to reinforce their own versions of the situation. They had already demolished one attempt to present a contrary point of view. Nothing that I said then would have changed a single opinion.

I was enraged, I couldn't engage in the conversation; I was diametrically opposed to most of the scattered viewpoints and I'm embarrassed to admit that I failed to support the lonely voice at the other end of the table. Inside my mind the jagged edges of my silent argument kept puncturing my colleagues' neat packages of the world, but I simply didn't know how to voice my retort. Our violence in the form of intolerance learned in our civilized institutions oozed all over that lunch table. Those who had benefited more than most from our advanced education system had picked up their invisible scalpels to dissect the deviant, Askuwheteau, who had dared to digress. Judging another, they discarded the basic principles of cutting-edge scientific enquiry they'd learned so diligently in the labs in medical school. They summoned our legal system to fulfil its promise to keep a neat and tidy balance amongst all good citizens. References to mental health, muddled with simplifications of cultural and socio-economic deficiencies, left Askuwheteau lifeless on the lunch table.

Most painful for me was that I made ridiculous assumptions: That I couldn't share the truth with my colleagues because of my loyalty to Askuwheteau; that it was best to keep it to myself; that even acknowledging my friendship would provoke a barrage of questions not mine to answer. Or was I afraid that the professionals around the table would view me as questionable? Would I reveal a weakness in my defence, a character flaw that would discount me from furthering myself in any way? At best I could expect to be vigorously cross-questioned and, if I diverged from popular opinion, I would be swamped by a tidal wave of opinionated statements even though I was the only person around the table who actually knew Askuwheteau.

"This is Canada, after all!" really floored me. This is a land of free speech and association: a beacon of democracy. Yet in this open informal forum I couldn't counter any of the accusations. They moved so quickly from a neglected backyard to a pervert - tried and convicted by the "jury" around the table. They had decided that Askuvie was nothing less than anti-social and a potential danger to the community based on less than flimsy evidence in the form of a few letters of opinion in the newspaper. They were convinced and I was dumbstruck. Askuwheteau's parting words to me of "repair" had acquired prophetic proportions. I felt a desperate urge to break free from the circle of suffocating opinions of my friends and colleagues around the table. My emotion was tinged with guilt because I recognised my own willingness to protect the value of my property even at the cost of others' misery.

Askuwheteau was isolated in this wrangle. The exchange around the table left me with an overwhelming urge to visit and report to him that, even from a distance, he had sent a shudder through our neat and tidy story. So, at the end of my shift, rather than going directly home, I headed towards his place.

Though cold outside, the clear sky and sight of the river flowing along its natural course, cheered my soul until I came in sight of Askuwheteau's property when I was alarmed by flashing blue lights and uniformed police officers swarming around it. Officers with serious expressions intently examined the ground inside a cordon of yellow tape and barricaded the perimeter with their stares. Undeterred, I addressed the closest officer, "Good evening. This seems unusual," not knowing how to open the conversation.

"Not unusual. Sir, please be careful. This is a possible murder scene and members of the public need to keep away."

I was shocked. Perceiving my reaction, the officer paid more attention. "Sir, did you know the occupant?" he asked. When I affirmed that I did, he called over to a female officer, "Inspector, this gentleman is an acquaintance of the victim."

As the word "victim" penetrated my confusion, she looked up from her task and lithely moved over to introduce herself as "Inspector Sanderson." Extending her hand, she said, "I'm coordinating this investigation." Tension surged through my body and emotion must have distorted my face because Inspector Sanderson continued, "I understand that this may be difficult and shocking for you, sir, but I would like to ask you some questions." She escorted me off the street to a chair in the front garden and, after offering me water, went through the formalities of recording my name, address, occupation. I think that she used the routine questions as a vehicle to convey her calm and professional manner. It did help me to relax. Then she asked more directly related questions such as, "How were you associated with the deceased?"

I couldn't process that description of Askuwheteau as "deceased," so I answered, "We are friends."

"How long had you known him?"

"Only about two months. What happened?"

I'm sorry, sir, please be patient. I'll tell you what I can once we are over the formalities. Do you know of any relatives?"

"No, sure, I'm sorry. No he didn't mention any relatives."

"How often did you visit?"

"Maybe ten times and I haven't seen him for a while."

"Ok, sir. The reason I haven't asked you to identify the body yet, is that it's gruesome. But, as we can't locate a relative, do you think that you can perform this service?"

"I'm a doctor," I replied, "There's not much that I haven't seen."

"It's different when you know the person, sir," she cautioned, "You'll find this disturbing."

I thanked her for her concern, but assured her that I could manage and asked her to lead me to the body. She turned to mount the stairs to the front door.

"Aren't we going to the back garden?" I blurted out, feeling that I was giving away secrets.

"No, he was murdered in the house," explained Sanderson, but alert to all signals, she moved me out of the category of "clearly innocent" in her mind, and I was now on her list of people to "ask more questions." Entering the house, I was surprised by its normalcy and my reaction didn't go unnoticed by the astute inspector, "How often have you been in here?" she asked.

My "Never," raised her eyebrows. At the same time I tried to spot some of the things that Askuvie had described about the interior of his house. There was nothing, no evidence at all. It looked like a completely normal, modest house.

"Have you spoken with the neighbour?" I asked, wondering how she would react.

"Yes, when he first came in he made some extremely crass comments like 'Probably killed by his own kind.' Actually it was much worse than that and I had to caution him that I am an officer of the state. Later when he saw the body he changed. Then, outside he said a few odd things like, 'I guess he did make an effort to clean up around here' and 'Not half as bad as I thought.' What do you make of those statements?"

"You do know that they were at war with each other? Have you seen or heard of the newspaper articles going on about the state of his property?"

"I am. But can't really understand what the neighbour was so worked up about."

"Well Askuvie and I always met outside in the back garden."

"What, even in the cold over the last couple of weeks?"

"Yes."

Inspector Sanderson led me to a conventional bedroom where the body lay a few feet from the doorway. "Here's the body. Do you know of any distinguishing marks?" she said.

Askuwheteau's face was completely disfigured and my experience told me immediately that he was the victim of an acid attack or that it had been poured over him after death. Despite my experience in trauma units I couldn't hide my shock and distress. His clothes were basically undamaged and, other than his disfigured face, I determined that it was probably him from the shape of his head and body; he was definitely dressed in Askuwheteau's clothes.

I shook my head in answer. "He's barely recognizable," I said. Why have they done this to him? What did he do to deserve it? Is this what the neighbour meant by 'probably attacked by his own kind'?"

"I suppose so. In an investigation we take note of all comments - even the inappropriate. We try to evaluate the facts in any form. It's not always easy. The first thing we have to do is confirm the victim's identity. Can you recognise the deceased as your friend?"

"I'm pretty sure that it's Askuwheteau. That's his legal name." Instantly I realised that I had acted on Askuwheteau's assurance that I would know when to reveal his full name. I added, "Have you found anything outside in his garden?"

"I've taken a look around. Is there anything in particular you have in mind? Would you be OK walking outside with me to see if it triggers something for you?"

We went through the house to the back door and I was confronted by an open space surrounded by a neatly trimmed cedar hedge, three feet lower than I remembered it. A patch of newly rolled-on lawn and an artistically paved patio provided a platform for some deck chairs conveniently placed to facilitate conversation. I had to sit down. The inspector probably interpreted my behaviour as a shocked reaction in response to being reminded of good memories of my friendship with Askuwheteau and, as with my colleagues, out of loyalty, I concealed the garden's transformation from the inspector. It was stunning and I muttered, "It has changed...a lot...but as you mentioned, inspector, the neighbour was also surprised by how much Askuwheteau had tried to 'clean up around here.' It's extraordinary."

"Thank you, doctor. I know this must have been excruciating for you." With that Inspector Sanderson handed me her card and as sensitively as possible asked whether I was "planning a holiday in the near future" and "where I could be reached." She dispensed with the formalities with such aplomb that it almost sounded like an invitation when she offered her services if I should have any further questions. Perhaps it was.

The initial jolt was wearing off as I walked home through the suburban streets. All leaves had dropped to the ground from the branches of the exposed trees as they prepared for pure survival through the inevitable icy winter. The flow of oxygen through my body, the sight of the trees and muddled reflection sent me back to the nagging questions: What was Askuvie doing inside his house? Why had he stripped the property of all that had been there? He would never have done that. He had implied that it had taken generations to establish - which I never understood. This latest development further revealed my limited understanding of his life.

I'm a doctor: science is heavy in my makeup. I believe what I see and try to test it. I knew that I had sat in Askuwheteau's garden home several times. I also knew that I had just seen a very conventional garden in that same spot without a sign of the old habitation. Is it that easy to erase any trace of a friend from the ground so quickly? That sanctuary had been his home and the conversations begun between us would never be concluded. I was devastated.

Chapter Eleven

The next few hours were a blur. I know that I ate something out of the freezer without inspecting or tasting it. Exhausted: shocked and numbed by Askuwheteau's death and the sight of his corpse; or fragmented by the insensitivity of my colleagues' crass lunchtime comments; unable to even write a single word about this eventful day, I fell asleep. I woke very early with an urgent sense of obligation to record events on the USB. In fact it was such a powerful impulse that I worked at it for over an hour before I realised that I hadn't even made my morning coffee. I interrupted my task, started the brew and reflected on my compulsion to write. I rationalised it easily by reasoning that there was no one to talk to about Askuwheteau's horrific death and Verne's exploits. Askuwheteau was dead and Verne, the only other person who might have offered some explanation of the surreal happenings of the last few weeks, was thousands of miles away, involved in his own fantastic adventure. The computer stick was my solace and confessor. On the other hand, as a scientist and a medical doctor, it was my natural inclination to keep a record of my work.

That morning I took Verne's USB out of my computer, stared at the "Genesis" design and wondered whether some of my friend's mental faculties had given him the slip. I stood up and dropped the USB on my desk next to Inspector Sanderson's business card.

Two hours of writing had passed in a flash and gave me enough equilibrium to drink a second cup of coffee, eat a light breakfast of cereal and prepare to face the day and my jury of colleagues who enjoyed a mattress of opinion untroubled by the stony floor of hard facts.

As expected, at work in the hospital, discussion and argument around the news of Askuvie's death was more intense than the humdrum of latest developments in the world of medical science - or even real politics. Speculation, judgment and an abundance of commentary on the "backyard battle" filled the air whenever work slackened, not waiting for tea or lunch. People around me spoke with conviction, while I, restrained by my conscience, overwhelmed by others' conformity of thought, fell silent. My involvement in the police investigation placed limitations on what I could share and my loyalty to Askuwheteau was a bond I could not break; truth was bursting in the confines of my soul. On the one hand I felt like a pariah amongst my colleagues; on the other, aloof, because I had kept faith with Askuwheteau by withholding information from the police and my coworkers. The concoction of feelings was a source of constant consternation, one which I couldn't shake off during my waking hours. I couldn't dispel the melancholia.

Relief came in an unexpected form. I had been home from work one evening for a short while, trying to relax, and deciding what to eat as food had lost its appeal, when the doorbell rang. I opened the front door to the uniformed figure of Inspector Sanderson which gave me a mixture of surprise and pleasure. Her friendly smile and greeting cheered me immediately. She explained that it was a routine visit and I invited her inside. She declined the offer of tea and came to the point: she usually tried to follow up with people who had experienced the trauma of the murder of family or close friends, compounded by the stress of an interview like the one I had with her a few days earlier. She explained that the investigation was proving more complicated than expected and she was exploring all avenues. Inspector Sanderson's official demeanour could not disguise the fact that she was an exceptional, intuitive police officer and human being, who broke with my conventional notion of members of the police force.

In response to my light-hearted jest about the TV detective series where the cop revisits a suspect because of an implacable voice in his ear, she reassured me that she had categorized me as innocent. She continued, "Doctor, I think that you're up front, but that you were holding back on some information the other day. You may have been in shock or confused."

She had let me avoid admission or denial. I picked up on the pattern and said, "I'm sorry. Is there a specific question you have for me? Is there some way you think that I can help?" I had noticed when she entered removing her cap, that she was younger than I had first gauged, in fact very young to be holding the rank of inspector. Her action was also an indication that the interview would take a while so I suggested that we sit down in the living room. Initially she declined because it would involve removing her boots. I assured her that I didn't mind her boots in my living room and without fuss she consented and we moved inside to sit comfortably.

I took in information that I'd missed at our first meeting. In her boots she was close to my barefoot height. Her black hair was meticulously tied back, exposing her high cheekbones and well defined jawline. Her athletic physique and poise was discernible inside the bulky uniform. I became acutely aware of her piercing blue eyes as she scanned the room and examined me for any tell-tale incongruences. Her eyes conveyed a river of words: they inspired a calmness and comfort while alert to any iota of information I provided or concealed.

"Tell me about your visits to Askuwheteau," she said, "and especially the time that you spent outside in his garden?" The best way to describe her effect on me is to imagine someone inching open a sluice gate and allowing water to trickle onto parched fields. As the water reached the dry soil, plants began to break the surface of the moistened earth.

"There's not much to tell," I answered. "I visited Askuwheteau on several occasions and each time he would offer food and drink and we'd sit and chat about various things."

"How did you meet Askuwheteau?"

"A direct question with a convoluted explanation: I had finished a planning discussion about my new house and he arrived, walking along the road and he just came over and started talking to me."

My answers were tentative, as I still felt bound by the contract with Askuwheteau. I knew that if I told her any of the unusual details, I would uncontrollably divulge all. Despite my skill at communicating discreetly with patients and my intention to filter the story, Inspector Sanderson cut through the facade with a laser: "Doctor, I can't figure out why you are holding back with me. I know that you are. I respect your loyalty to your deceased friend. But as I said earlier, this is a complex investigation which is why I have been freed to conduct it behind the scenes. Apart from a university education, I'm highly trained in interrogation and international relations. I know that it's extremely unusual for a cop to divulge this kind of personal information, but I want you to understand the urgency and importance of this case. Let's make things easier. Call me Sandy - most of my friends and colleagues do. Just think how some patients can hinder your diagnosis of their illness when they hide symptoms. It drives you crazy. Well..."

Sandy was even more adroit than I had suspected. In a few sentences she had presented her credentials without pretension, swaddled me in a cover of confidentiality usually reserved for close companions and sliced through my reserve. She touched my intrinsic admiration for excellence which broke my resistance entirely. I felt an unbounded trust in this woman.

Without any further hesitation,I dropped my guard and prefaced my explanation with, "Inspector...Sandy, I am in a pact not to reveal any of what I am about to tell you; however, in the interests of this investigation.... I'm conflicted." I expanded upon Askuwheteau's colourful character: Askuvie, the bottle-collector; Askuwheteau, the student and engineer; Askuvie the shadowy neighbour; Askuwheteau, my friend; Askuwheteau, the sentinel; and at that point I gave a very scant description of his garden bower and no hint of his deeper purpose.

With barely perceptible nods of her head, she expressed her understanding of the information. Sandy repaid my trust with her own revelation. She reiterated that this was not a regular police matter and that she had been attached to the investigation because of her wide range of knowledge in many topics and her success in the field. In this case she had been studying traditional authority structures that had merged into western society; her research had included those societies that had seemingly completely disappeared. I was starting to comprehend why she was such a high ranking officer at little over thirty years of age.

In response to my information, she said quietly, "Doctor, this is extraordinary. Thank you. I had a feeling there was something more going on here. I suspect you were allowed a glimpse of a circle close to the centre. I don't know why you were chosen, or whether it was purely accidental. Very few have any inkling of the existence of this power structure - regardless of their origins or heritage. There's an ancient wisdom at play here that I've learned to respect and treat with great caution. I think that your exposure could have been purposeful. By the way, I have heard of the kind of garden you have described. You're not losing your mind." She smiled in such a way that I felt affirmed like never before; I wondered what I had to do or say to evoke that smile again.

Although I'd grown more accustomed to alternative ways of seeing things over the past few weeks, knowledge like this that implicated me directly, was a jolt. Askuvie's...Askuwheteau's unconventional way of living had bumped me outside my comfortable frame of reference and my *mise en scene* of the world would never fit in the same way again. Yet, here in my living room, was someone who understood the dislocation and could accompany me through a door of understanding into that world. Maybe.

Sandy continued, "They're not going to come to introduce themselves to you. Don't worry, you're probably not in any danger, except that I can't understand why you were drawn in so close. Doctor Mart...."

"Ross...I hope, I mean, we may be having more meetings about this so 'doctor' is too formal. Who are these people? I never saw myself in danger till you mentioned it now. They sound like a kind of 'Illuminati."

"Thank you... and you may not be far off the mark there. Actually, if they exist, it would be hard to outline their goals. Brilliant leaders know that they cannot confront institutions head on and gain advantage. Often those I've described are not in official state positions, but influence events imperceptibly. They often draw on enormous power from sources far beyond the cognition of average human understanding - whatever that may be."

"And Askuwheteau? Was he one of those?"

"Not yet. He would have been on the outer defenses at that stage in his life. He was very acceptable in the general community in many ways - an engineer - and had been visible in the normal way as he grew up - high school, university, workplace. He was just eccentric. Or so he seemed to everyone."

"I'm feeling a bit uneasy about this whole thing. Can we go over to Akuvie's house to see how things are developing there?

"Do you know that Askuwheteau didn't actually own the house?

"No, it wasn't something we talked about. The land, the soil, the earth, was the important part for him. The ownership wasn't my business. So, it never came up. It never crossed my mind."

'Anyway, the owner has moved back. But, no, I definitely can't be seen anywhere near the house. In fact, officially I'm not on this case any longer. The murder part; the public aspect that is. Reporters are going to be swarming all over this one for a long time - even when other events rouse public excitement. Very few people will know that I am working on it. Neither will the police involved in the official case. Other officers have been assigned to the case and will speak with the media. I'm working on this other dimension of the case that interests our highest chain of command. Actually at a federal level."

I was impressed, a bit bewildered and somewhat disconcerted. "I'd really like to check out the place."

"There's no point. You won't see anything. The house looks like any older city home."

"What about the owner? Is he one of the shady leaders you mentioned?"

"He's not 'one of them.' He follows their subliminal instructions, unaware that he's part of a larger plan. I told you: it's subtle. There's so much circling and backtracking on trails to throw us off the scent that it is virtually impossible to find out an individual's real identity or part in something. As I said, this group is composed of the most intelligent people you will ever meet - and won't - of course. Their way of operating is as much a part of the air you breath, indistinguishable from the gentlest breeze in the trees. Theirs is not the kind of intelligence that you measure on Stanford-Binet tests."

"How should I act? Should I be cautious?"

"There's no point. You won't know if they're watching unless they want you to and then it's to evoke a specific reaction. Just carry on with your normal activities."

"I'm starting to feel a bit uncomfortable. I don't know how to 'carry on' at work when this topic comes up. In a way I'm sorry that I know so much about it. Before the murder the stereotyping was bad enough, now the prejudice is in the open."

"It won't improve. I've been involved in this area for some time now and it's hard to settle down. At least you won't have to confront the kind of rabid outburst I did with Askuwheteau's neighbour on the day of the murder."

"I can imagine. How bad was it? I hear some pretty stupid things at work."

Sandy laughed: "Nothing like this I hope. How about I try to get the tone right. 'What the bloody hell can you expect from someone who lives like an animal? He's no better than a rat. Vermin. In fact, he's like microbes on a rat's body. That's what he is. Him and all his kind just contaminate the world around them and it's not even dog eat dog. It's an infestation. There's just too many useless, dirty animals wandering around pretending to be human beings messing up all that civilized people do to keep the world in a good state. Too many - that's the problem with the world today. Let them all kill each other. Savages. Bloody savages."

"You're a good actor," I said, "I thought someone else was speaking."

"Sorry. Too personal. I'll keep it professional. Somehow, I feel that I have your trust - one hundred percent."

I reciprocated, attributing it to the nature of the case and my sense of isolation in the circumstances. I returned to the topic: "How does that come from someone seemingly well educated in the twenty-first century in an upper socioeconomic bracket? That's beyond appalling? What do you do when you come across that stuff?"

"Money isn't the only predictor, in my experience. I guess he was really angry. Trust me, Ross, I hear that all the time. It's very distressing. We both see some of the darker side of life, but at least your colleagues are better at hiding it."

"I get angry about that neighbour and my colleagues because they think that they own everything and are reluctant to share any part of their home with anyone slightly different. They're ready to flatten anyone who gets in the way of their lifelong ambition to own the biggest and best house."

"You're starting to sound like Askuvie," Sandy replied: "It's not a stretch to see that they do own it all. Anyway, it's hard to tell how they feel. Most of the time. Sometimes they can't control themselves. Of course the neighbour calmed down when he saw that I didn't react in the way he'd hoped. I just stay calm and it usually works to bring down their fever pitch. They usually realize that they're on dangerous ground making these views public, but they hope to uncover fellow reactionaries and when they don't, they know that they have to temper things. But it's out there for sure, Ross."

"I suppose my patients are focused on their health when they come to see me."

We had been sitting for the whole time and Sandy glanced at her watch. She started to move out of the chair, touched the table and, looking at the books on the shelves, said, "You do have an appreciation for history. Another dimension you keep to yourself."

Sandy was standing. We were at the same eye level and I returned her smile and said, "I don't know enough about it, but I am interested."

"Most people like you don't have to deal with that bigoted element most of the time. They're vicious and not as intelligent as they would like you to believe. Most people back away when they encounter that violent intolerance because it's scary. When these idiots come up against people who just calmly stand their ground and dismantle their prejudice, they usually cover up. Of course, they don't change their minds, but at least they hide their feelings."

"That's a good strategy. I used to talk with Askuvie about this, but he never provided direct answers; he always said that it would become apparent to me. How do you keep a positive view of the world knowing this is all around you?"

"Not easily."

I changed topics out of genuine interest: "Can you tell me more about what you actually do?"

Sandy smiled (not the rare one of earlier) as she answered, "It's very experimental and progressive. Basically, I'm left to determine my own schedule, though from time to time I'm connected to an official unit - like I was when I met you. Then they'll find a way to have me pulled out so that I can do my real work."

"What's that?"

Sandy started walking towards the door as she said, "In this case, essentially, collecting information, signs or clues that most people would miss; connecting dots - you're one of them - and putting them together in a context or narrative."

"I'm just a dot?" I laughed. "Why do they need you? This sounds like something sinister. Something that we should worry about."

"Ross, it's not destructive. I work on several levels. Sometimes in uniform, usually in mufti. I spend a fair portion of my time trying to put things together as I said. Community's not just about dealing with emergencies - we have to aim for something better."

"And then?"

"I know that you are totally discreet," she said with a guilty look as she placed her cap on her head as if to signal an end to the informality. "Please think about your time in Askuwheteau's garden home. And.." with a faint smile, "Try to relax. If you do turn out to be more than a dot, I may tell you more."

Sandy had let me keep my dignity with humour. She added, "By the way, I won't be wearing a uniform for a while after today and you may not recognise me next time we meet."

Somehow our conversation had slipped from the original purpose of an official visit to one more relaxed and informal. I wondered whether she had intentionally given me the impression that she had let her guard down to extract more information or, like me, she had responded in the moment.

Chapter Twelve

I couldn't resist walking past Askuvie's house the next day on my way to work; it was one of the routes I had taken since getting to know him. Adjusting my pace, I tried to glean information from the area and I was struck by the benign normality of the scene - a well-kept garden and the once vociferous neighbour raking the leaves on the grass verge. In my mind he remained a potential suspect despite Sandy's explanation of extraordinary events and her covert role. As I reflected upon her exposition, it did seem a bit outlandish. I couldn't help questioning her credibility and my credulity. On one level it sounded like espionage. But who was the enemy? Since her visit, there were moments when I slipped in and out of a dreamlike, like I was skating the perimeter of a surreal world, a dangerous vortex to trap my overstimulated imagination. While Sandy was in my living room her account seemed plausible; when she left, bizarre. Over a few fleeting weeks Verne and Askuvie had pointed the way down paths of loneliness and uncertainty leading out of my workaday life; a work environment in which the harmony had been destroyed by deep-seated differences between colleagues. Under the circumstances, Sandy and her explanation offered relative stability.

That was my state of mind as I passed Askuvie's place and I could not resist the urge to greet the neighbour with as normal a "Good morning" as I could muster.

"Hi," he responded.

"Looks like hard work."

"Oh, no. Not when the result is there for all to see."

"Well, we're expected to keep Nature in its place, I suppose."

His creased brow interfered with his smile and I thought that I might have placed some doubt in his mind as to whether everyone accepted his innocence. At least I understood some of Sandy's comments about how our moods are gently altered; I could have shifted the neighbour's spirit in a different direction with a less compliant answer. It set me wondering as to how accidental our state of mind is. With only one piece of information, in a brief interchange, I had the power to influence a stranger's day. It gave slight credence to Sandy's explanation of what lies behind official decisions. I was on a path of self-doubt into a web of my own making. I had always dismissed conspiracy theories - and still do.

As my confusion and lethargy grew, it became increasingly difficult to summarise all that happened each day. I persevered with my obligation as "Chronicler" to record all on the USB. Besides, it was still my only confidante, especially for my more fantastic thoughts.

Chapter Thirteen

At the hospital I immersed myself in work, delegating very little and over-elaborating on tasks when there was a danger of having time to engage in smalltalk which was peppered with uninformed rumours about the Askuvie murder. I had developed a detachment then, knowing that published news items were merely a distraction and that the end result of all publicised investigation was inevitably inconclusive. Cases are destined to be allowed to gently fade away as another unsolved crime. Sandy's information had left me with a feeling of ambivalence: reassuring, that my sense that complex crimes are often not solved was real; disconcerting, because that might be the result of a deliberate strategy on the part of some powerful force.

One evening after work I decided to walk in the river valley as the temperature was still tolerable with about an hour of daylight remaining. I always wore runners to work, suitable for walking on the well-groomed paths alongside the river. It was there that I saw an athletic figure in running gear loping towards me about a hundred metres away and I moved to the right-hand side of the path to allow the runner to pass on the inside. I gazed out at the river.

The runner stopped and said, "Certainly adds contours to the city blocks, doesn't it, Doctor Martindale?

"Hi Sandy," I replied. "How are you and how's the investigation?"

As she had intimated, I hadn't recognized her out of uniform with her black hair tied back in a pony-tail, but her voice was unmistakable. She was more relaxed than on previous occasions and said, "We really are lucky to have this piece of Nature right in the centre of our city. I'm well but the investigation's a bit slower than I'd hoped. I'm glad that I bumped into you. I've been wanting to ask you a few more questions and this is as good a place as any."

"You should finish your run and come around later."

"Oh no. I've covered about five k's which is enough for today. We can talk. And there's less chance of bugs of the electronic kind out here."

We both laughed and sat down on a nearby bench to watch the river and carry on the conversation.

"I only run in an emergency - if I can't anticipate it first. Look at me. I'm a slower model. Askuvie and the investigation are the talk of the town. At work I wrestle with a mixture of feelings when I hear people talking about it. I'm detached on the outside. Inside, aloof and more informed than those around me, but I realize how little I know. I'm annoyed by people's assumptions."

Sandy rewarded me with one of her special smiles, saying, "You look just fine. Running's an addiction - wish I could kick the habit." With a more serious expression, she continued, "I thought that you might be stressed and I realised that I probably owe you more of an explanation. I'm sorry that I can't tell you the whole story. In fact I might distort things if I go into areas that are not really mine and are still speculation."

"Please don't compromise yourself," I replied. "I'm fascinated, but it all sounds a bit of a stretch."

Despite the surroundings and her running gear, Sandy retained her calm, professional core. "It's hard to know where to start because there are so many aspects. As I told you, I have studied traditional power bases. This may look like a common murder with the normal motives, but there are indications of deeper, complex reasons. I am trying to uncover whether that power base is behind this whole incident."

"Hard to believe of course."

"Of course. Who would believe it? The upper levels of government are taking this seriously and my job is to find out more about it. Ultimately, we would like to work together with them, whoever 'they' may be."

"Is it dangerous? It sounds like a spy story."

Gazing meditatively at the river as if grasping for inspiration, Sandy replied, "I don't know if it's dangerous. It's not a spy story though there are layers of secrecy. It's more like a chess game that started centuries ago and the players are so strategic they won't disclose their endgame till they can be certain of the desired outcome."

"Who do you report to?"

"Directly to Ottawa. I know, it really is hard to believe." She turned to me with one knee on the bench in my direction, "I'm young, but that's part of what's needed to get this done. Also, I'm an unlikely looking character in the role."

"Age is just a number as the older folk say...but it works both ways."

"It's OK, that's part of the cover. Not many would suspect me to be anything other than a regular cop with a bit of ambition."

"Clearly. I understand ambition very well."

"Well that's when I join with the conventional force. Only one or two people know my real function and connections. I don't know why I'm telling you so much. I think that you may have been given a special role and it's only fair that you have some understanding of the complexity you may have already entered."

I answered that, "I do know that the workings of the world are complicated," and I welcomed Sandy's next remark.

"Also, I've been isolated in my work for so long that I need a confidante and you happened to be on the spot and seemed totally trustworthy. I'm taking a chance of course - that you are what you seem to be. It sort of feels like we've been thrown together. So, here it is."

She remained facing me on the bench and invited me into her confidence a little more. "We all have a picture of a conventional system that is somewhat transparent. But it wouldn't be called subterfuge if all the facts were out in the open and it all made complete sense would it?" Once again, I noticed her eyes seemed to change with the environment and the weather; the piercing blue, tinged with the grey of the cloudy day.

"Some people say that about science."

We both smiled, but Sandy took it as a chance to change topics, "Ross, can we talk about the case for a few minutes? Being outside like this may help you recall Askuwheteau's place."

"Of course. Any way I can help. It also helps me unload."

"I like how you can move from work to the personal and back again. You can help. Just relate everything you can recall about Askuwheteau's garden. Free run. Don't worry if you think that you have already told me about it. Any detail."

"OK. Like you said about your job, this is also broaching the world of make-believe. I can't talk about this to others. They'd think that I was crazy. Especially as his garden's no longer there which is even harder for me to believe."

"Just let it flow."

For the next half hour I recreated the natural bower behind Askuvie's house, from the entrance to the fully equipped encampment. Sandy seemed to be able to know when to ask questions about intricacies that I didn't even realise that I'd omitted or even stored in my memory and finally she asked whether I could sketch the garden the way I remembered it. Without hesitation, I surprised myself by picking up a stick like Askuwheteau had done and outlined his place in the sand.

Sandy scrutinised the picture for a few minutes and said, "Thanks Ross. This has been very helpful." She looked at her watch and said, "It's probably enough for now and I'm starting to cool down too much. I'll be on my way. It was so lucky meeting like this." Sandy was stretching her legs in preparation to resume her run when she seemed to have an afterthought. "Perhaps you should make a few notes when you get home so you don't forget what you've told me."

I almost told her about my recording events on the USB stick, but held back, feeling that it was weird - especially as she lacked any knowledge of Verne and "Genesis." I felt a distinct disappointment that she was leaving and we would not walk back to the road together. So, instead of telling her about my routine recording, I offered a weak and vague invitation in response, saying, "Good idea. We could compare notes some time."

"I'll touch base with you soon," she said, picking up on my tone or unspoken feeling.

"To me it still looks like the angry neighbour may have played a role."

Sandy was still stretching and replied, "Not a chance. I'm fine-tuned to personalities and character traits. He hasn't got it in him. I know that he sounded like a hardline right-wing extremist, bent on ridding the world of people who spoil his pristine valley. Those who execute in the way Askuvie was hit are stealthy. You won't recognize them or see them coming.

They want you to think it's the work of thugs. The neighbour may be playing a role to cover the truth though. Unintentionally. He's just a bigot with bluster."

My puzzled expression prompted Sandy to divulge more, "So here's where I come in. The group that I'm talking about could have coordinated the whole thing. Think of the top-notch athletes you've watched - how they use their opponents' bodies to win advantage or transfer their weight in a minimal way to drop a thousandth of a second in a race..."

"Like you," I said.

She laughed. "I'm not an athlete. Think of the most convincing speakers who shift your understanding or opinion very slightly through a story; not those orators with big arguments. Think of a scene in Nature like watching a sunset or an approaching storm: a moment that without explanation, you changed your mind on a topic because of the natural drama you saw and felt - a complete sensory experience - it actually changed your mind. You didn't make a voluntary switch. That's how they operate. You don't see them, you don't hear them, they simply change your perception by tweaking the environment or the 'players' around you."

"Not really the way governments work. Or the police for that matter," I laughed.

"I know that it's uncanny. But I'm the evidence that there is more going on...'Than meets the eye, Horatio.' There's a growing awareness that if we want more harmony in our world, we have to tap into things that we know little about."

"Is it working from both sides."

"Good question. Askuvie might have contacted you so that you can play a role which may merely be reporting on the story to me or others; or it may be that you are meant to slightly swell the gourd, but don't expect some startling revelation."

"What brings you to that conclusion? I can't even speak with my colleagues at the hospital about this."

"Ross, there is more of a balance in the world than first appears. There have been times in history when humanity has bungled towards utter destruction. If you listen to lots of leaders we - our species - seem to be riddled with violence."

"That's true. There's hardly ever a voice of harmony and union. Sometimes they start off talking that way, it crumbles into competition and division."

"Well, that would be a very bleak picture if it were all that drives us. There must be more."

"Where do I fit into this?"

"You must have been identified as someone with a genuinely open mind. Perhaps sending in Askuvie was a test. Ross, I don't have a full understanding of all this although I have seen glimmers of its existence - of an elusive level of leadership. Where do any of us fit into this puzzle? The whole thing is mysterious, it's intangible, when you think that you are about to make some real discovery, find a concrete fact, you slip into the picture like walking into a bank of fog or mist; you're part of it although it's constantly changing shape around you. This Askuwheteau business is the closest I've been to grasping something tangible in this realm.

"Ross, this is not about conspiracy theories…"

"I reached that conclusion."

"Good. It would be far too superficial. No. You have to get conspiracy theories out of your head to understand this. A few brilliant leaders have brought about harmony for a while. There's no grand plan for the end of history. Maybe just a path of minimum destruction.

"Anyway, I have to be going now or I'll seize up. Thanks for all the information."

"Maybe there's nothing to it. Have you thought of that? I'm going to carry on with my uncomplicated life, looking after my patients and put this whole business behind me."

Then, feeling that physical ambivalence again, I added, "On the other hand, I may be surprised and there will be more and I'll have something to share. Can I contact you if something comes up?"

She started off down the path at a slow jog and called over her shoulder, "Of course. That's my job. I'm sure that I'll see you again soon."

About a hundred metres away, she shifted into that loping stride. I was left to walk alone in the cool evening air with Sandy's comment in my ears, "There's more between heaven and earth," which exposed another aspect of her character. She had gleaned detail from my library which gave her a clue how to connect with me at a deeper level. When I reached home, I was strongly motivated to describe all that had happened that day with Sandy figuring prominently in the picture.

Chapter Fourteen

I enjoyed a good night's sleep encroached by Verne's fairy stories and Askuwheteau's revelations; however, speaking to Sandy and confiding in the USB stick had alleviated some of the anxiety of bottling up information and emotion that few would understand. The next morning I was relieved - even pleased - to see that my Inbox displayed a message from Verne. I opened it.

Hullo Mate (Some things about Verne would never change)

Since my visit to Chysauster and Penzanze, I've been walking about this Cornish peninsula to meet as many local people as possible and get more of a feel for the land. I've met some extraordinary people in this way. I'm not in a hurry and the weather is surprisingly mild and bearable for this time of the year; so pleasant that I've even been able to sleep outside on a few occasions. It saves a few pounds for one thing and I have a strong desire to be outside, unconstrained by boundaries of any kind. On the lighter side, if I take an honest look at my physical appearance right now, I may not be warmly welcomed at an English guest house. Well, I'm not that outlandish yet.

One night I found myself next to a small stone circle under a clear sky. Alone, staring at the stars these last few months, I've really started to enjoy more and more the sense of connection with the firmament - me, an infinitesimal microdot in a cosmic sphere, blinking for a split second. What does my tiny flash mean? Will it be eternally extinguished or does it flash again somewhere else? That is not to be answered now or soon, but Cador and my sojourn in Chysauster have definitely highlighted those questions.

I think that experience has altered my identity. I have given up my ambition to own land around the globe in exchange for a single spot at Chysauster. Cador told me that Chysauster land is inalienable. I haven't given up, but I am walking around with my eyes open for available land in this area that will give me the same feeling of belonging that I felt at Chysauster. The amazing thing is that by spending so much time outdoors, it's as if I'm actually learning from the land: lessons about myself. I still feel inexplicably compelled on my journey without a specific destination.

The day after my night in the stone circle I walked on and, following the path through a spinney, entered an open field and what turned out to be the start of a totally new adventure.

In the corner of the field stood a farmhouse made primarily of local stone so at first I didn't notice it as it blended with the surroundings. It intruded into my consciousness incrementally and, as it did so, I felt increasingly drawn to it; I will always maintain that I chose to visit that farmhouse, but I admit that the attraction was abnormally powerful. I decided to take that path as I had been walking all day. I know that I do a lot of things by instinct, rather than careful consideration – at least I can recognize that in myself now. Anyway, as I approached along the dusty path, I saw, framed in the doorway, the figure of a woman, smiling in welcome as I walked across the entire stretch of field towards the house.

Moruith, who met me on the threshold, is an old lady who lives alone in that farmhouse off the beaten track in the countryside north of Chysauster. Though not registered with any tourist association, she said that occasionally she takes in the rare overnight traveler. I was amply rewarded with a meal, her company and a repertoire of remarkable stories.

She claimed that her family has lived in that same place for centuries, though of course there's no solid proof before about 1700. Even that is a long time and she can relate many of the connections. Her legend-like stories date back to ancient

Cornwall and dispelled any fatigue that I felt from my journey when I first arrived. We sat up most of the night with delicious pastries and hot tea as she told tales of the area. It's a bit of a cheek to impose like that, but I couldn't resist the possibility of a new experience and stories. I'm open to them. Moruith was prepared to relate the local history to me and she gave no hint that I was inconveniencing her or keeping her up past her bedtime.

I have an appetite for parochial stories. When I hear them - especially told by local people - I feel like I'm listening to a unique version and given a glimpse of a universal truth at the same time: a blend of cynicism and wonder, but predominantly entertainment.

"We're all related, y'know," Moruith began, "I'll tell you a tale of a little over two hundred years ago to illustrate the point. It was a time before farms were enclosed by fences. A distant relative, John Pender, lived here in this house with his old mother. He tended the farm around the home and had learned well the art and science of farming of the time. However, as he looked around he realised that when he was gone there would be no more Penders to keep it going, if you know what I mean." I smiled in encouragement, appreciating Moruith's attempt to loosen up and relax with me. "Well, one Sunday at the local church, as he sat in the pew behind a young girl of about his own age, he noticed that he had a strong urge to speak with her after the service. Of course, as soon as he approached her, he realised she was Susan Pender, the daughter of his late father's brother who lived on the next farm a mile or two away from his own. Laws and custom were powerful even then - probably custom more so than law, so he tried to dismiss that interaction. I suppose that night and for some nights after, he couldn't rest easy, so he sought wisdom from his old mother.

Her response was evasive, 'She's got under your skin, John, but you shouldn't marry such a close Pender.' She could have said that he couldn't marry a cousin, cited laws or the accepted custom, but she kept it practical and for her son to figure it out.

"About a week later he made a journey to the nearest magistrate and changed his name to Pendle." I laughed of course, and Moruith giggled, glad that I'd picked up on the clue. "Well the rest took its natural course. There were good reasons for the decision. It kept all the land in the family and they really prospered. The family was bound together. And most of all, there were not all that many other young men and women around in the area anyway. It served the purpose: soon there were lots of little Pendles or Penders, however you want to label them, running about.

"Over the years 'Pendle' has altered its form and there are many derivations of the name all over."

I laughed, "I'll certainly look at Pendleburys and Penders in a different way now"

"Oh, all that stuff dilutes when enough water has passed under the bridge. We shouldn't be too trapped by things that have happened long ago. If we're too bothered by all the rules and details we'd never move forward. We have to focus on the gems in the story to guide us now."

"Good advice, I'll try to remember that. I am trying to figure out where my own past begins," I said with a slight shudder as I recollected Cador's narrative. "How far back can you trace this little hamlet?"

We were sitting in comfortable armchairs in the lounge surrounded by some items of dark wood furniture that may have been as old as the farmhouse. Even Moruith, with her long, thick white hair looked like she had always been part of the place. Her clear brown eyes pierced the semi-darkness of the room and she said, "I suppose there's the solid, then the shaky and, deep down, the murky," and then pondered more carefully as she asked, "It depends on what interests you... and what you are prepared to believe."

"Go with the 'murky,'" I urged, Moruith, "I've grown tired of the solid."

"I agree, I like to dwell in the murky. 'The world is too much with us; late and soon,' so I'll tell you one of the stories that goes around this place," said Moruith, tuning into my mood and at the same time revealing that she was very familiar with deeper thoughts and philosophies than you would first imagine from one dressed in such baggy brown corduroy trousers and a colourful heavy jersey. "Would you like another cuppa?"

"I'm good," I replied, then caught myself using a North Americanism, added, "No, thank you."

"To the story then. You know how many great cities have their founding myths and legends? I nodded as she continued, "Well our little hamlet has its own curious origins. Back around the time when England and Cornwall were being invaded by the Romans it is told that an older Roman who had completed his time in the Roman army, came to this valley with his family - wife and two sons. His wife was a local woman - beautiful and sensuous. He must have met her somewhere around here, but those details are lost in the murky."

(You can imagine how I reacted to that. Yet with the respect of a visitor, I kept my thoughts to myself. Also, I still don't know whether Cador's tale is real or not.) At that point, the electric lights quivered and failed.

"Don't worry, it's normal. I'm always ready for this. Candles are better than battery torches because they give a bit of warmth at the same time. You'll find a store on the shelf behind you."

We lit several candles placing them around the room, and the story took on the shape of a candle flame with flickering edges, a black outline and a warm inner glowing core. Moruith massaged the mood, "So, this happened some two thousand years ago when those travelers whom I mentioned arrived in this lush valley. There may have been others here or not and it's hard to picture the world, the landscape, as it would have been back then before so many others have changed it over the centuries. Try to put yourself in the mind of the Roman who had been in the army for twenty years or more and then for some reason or other found himself in one of the lands Rome had invaded. He might have been given a plot of land as a gift for his service to Rome and Caesar or he might have been attracted to the wilderness away from the Roman civilization." I kept my speculation to myself and let Moruith weave her own story uninterrupted. My suppositions would have spoiled the local brew.

Moruith resumed, "Anyway, the Roman was a soldier at heart and also determined to protect his family. A tented field would have been enough for him" (and again I had a glimpse of the true depth Moruith concealed), "but he wanted to give his wife more comfort and security for his two sons." Moruith's form blended into the age-old chair and other furniture; she became a disembodied voice relating arcane knowledge. My initiation began as her enchanting voice steered my imagination to connect her story with Cador's.

A mental picture developed in my mind as she continued, "So, it is told, that he built a barricade and then a shelter, finally a house of stone which would give them accommodation and defense against wild animals. There would have been wolves and possibly bears roaming around here in those days. The Roman's beautiful Cornish wife would have insisted on something solid that would last and he was an expert builder. They lived here for years, planting crops and living off all the land had to offer and then things get hazy - murky. It's not certain whether the Roman grew restless and hankered after his own home, that the call of Rome became too strong as he aged or whether he was unable to stay in the place where his older son was killed by a wild animal. Another version is that after the death of the older son they were all unable to accept the reality and in one of those fights that sometimes erupt between father and son, the younger son kills his father.

Regardless, the Roman disappeared from the scene; son and mother were left here alone and before long he made his mother pregnant. I know, shocking for us today."

I smiled innocently, assuring Moruith that I was not offended by that detail of the story.

"That's good. You have some Cornish in your blood." said Moruith, responding to my expression. It sounded almost like an invitation when she followed it with, "You'll find it more natural than you think," and continued the story, "Anyway, his mother gave birth to a daughter and they lived as a family for years. After that, the community grew in numbers. This valley has been populated ever since"

"I like that, Moruith. I suppose it gives new meaning to the old saying, 'Necessity is the Mother of Invention'. At least I'm starting to appreciate how complexity is hidden in stories around these parts. Focus on the gems. I like that."

"Verne, you are starting to feel the past like you should; the seriousness inside the dark humour. I'm sure that you also see how this story gives us permission to be more flexible when it comes to the rules for choosing partners," said Moruith with a definite gleam in her eye. "If you're not in a rush, you should stay for a while. Tomorrow some of the clan are coming around and you'll see that they're not too badly affected by the constraints of necessary selection."

I laughed. "As I said earlier, I haven't plotted my journey yet. Thank you: I'd like to stay to meet the relatives." The candles had nearly expired when the lights flickered on and we were back in the 21st century. "I am tired and should get ready for bed. Thanks for the food and the tales. I feel kind of wired and may not be able to sleep."

"Don't worry. It'll be just like home. Once you hit the sack, you'll be out like a light."

The room she gave me for the night was about fifteen feet by fifteen and, like the rest of the house, furnished simply with a comfortable bed. Moruith was right about sleeping well. However, her story and the comment about "home" reminded me strongly of my conversations with Cador. I couldn't help comparing the two stories; I also realised that I may never have experienced "home" as Moruith and Cador meant it. I definitely couldn't describe it. If you asked me to do that now, I'd tell it more in the Roman's terms, maybe Carenza's. The Roman could build a shelter, a house, bring his family into it, make it look like his home. He could create things around himself that he found familiar in appearance. Carenza nestled in her home: she didn't have to build anything different, she was part of the ground around her; she was enveloped in her home. Did the Roman carry his home inside himself? Could he sow the seeds of home wherever he went? Could Carenza be removed from the home where she was totally integrated, inseparable from the environment? Did the Roman come to a realization or belief that, though the images of his home in his building or his stories could take root, they would always be incongruous in a foreign soil? In the end, was Carenza unable to leave this area with her Roman because she had come to the same understanding and would not compromise? Once you remove people and their stories from their native soil, do they change their composition entirely to adapt and transform or does something shrivel inside? Are they and their stories forever alien invaders in a resistant landscape? If travelers return in the end to their original garden and are carefully tended, would they grow again into the form they once had and flourish, or are they changed forever? Is that the heart of Cador's concern about Carenza and her Roman? What is lost when I neatly package Moruith's story and send it to you across the ocean? If you want the full impact of the tale you will have to step out of your groove and join me here to feel the fibre of these fables against your own body.

A connection between the family in Cador's Chysauster chronicle and the one that arrived here at Moruith's farm seemed too coincidental. I dismissed it with the thought that there are probably many similar stories and legends with *characters like that inhabiting the history of this peninsula. But*

they are new to me.

As Moruith predicted, those thoughts faded and I slept like a

log.

Once again, I've rambled on long enough and should let you

get back to your real life. I will continue, as I always have, to

respond to, and blend with, whoever and whatever comes my

way.

Cheers

Verne

Chapter Fifteen

Avoidance is not the solution to a conundrum, I know,

but it was the reason that I was sitting alone in one of the

several cafeterias in the hospital in an attempt to steer clear of

my friends and colleagues. My estrangement was either

induced by my inability to resolve the contradiction of loyalty to Askuwheteau when faced with unsubstantiated opinion or that others were repelled by my taciturn mood. I was mute amongst chatty friends.

Alone in the cafeteria amid the hospital crowds, my thoughts still richochetted off those vicious opinions my colleagues had expressed in the lunchroom, condemning Askuwheteau on the day of his murder. Since then, I had developed a polite, tense tolerance of them, but their bigotry had exposed craters in our superficially harmonious society which I could not bridge. Invisible prison bars separated me from my hospital community and emphasized my sense of alienation. Compounding my sense of disloyalty to Askuvie, I was tormented by the memory of a suggestion he had made that the only way I could make a difference was to lead my own group to the negotiating table. I was hopelessly ill-equipped to perform that task. In that morose state of mind I retreated to my house as quickly as I could each day and resorted to confiding in the USB. At least the stick had to receive my opinion. It was during one of those confessions to the stick that it dawned on me that I was in mourning for my two friends: the only two who would have truly understood each other.

My thoughts drifted to that conversation with my colleagues in the cafeteria on the day that Askuwheteau was murdered. Not only had I denied my friendship with Askuwheteau, but I had also failed to back Rangseetal when he suggested that we should consider other points of view. Now I know that I could have turned the tide of the discussion right then by supporting Rangseetal.

"I think you need a friend," said Rangseetal, interrupting my guilt-ridden thoughts as he sat down on the chair next to me with his coffee. My bulky body would be visible anywhere. His turban no longer seemed conspicuous - in fact, it gave him poise. I was trapped because my own cup was full. We hadn't spoken since the games evening at my house.

I resented sympathy, but I did admire his taking the trouble to come over. I tried to greet him in response with a neutral expression. He picked up on my disposition and didn't try to alter it, which I appreciated. "Look, Ross," he said, "I know what it's like. Wearing this turban hasn't improved my relationships here in the hospital. Patients look at me with a wary eye. It's not easy being different. Either you're in love or it's something more serious." I took notice, but didn't reply. He continued, "It's your fault you know. You know, you or Verne are to blame for my wearing this damned tea-towel on my head." I smiled, almost laughed. "What can be more serious than love?" he joked again. He drank his coffee in a few quick gulps and, departing, he put his hand on my shoulder and said, "I don't know what you're going through. No rush Ross, but I do miss your friendship. And just so you know, I wouldn't give up the turban now. Not ever. So, thank you."

"Thank you," I replied, "You've made a difference."

As I walked briskly home on the cold winter evening, I phoned Sandy because I realised that she was probably the only other person who might understand my predicament and at least she was familiar with the Askuwheteau half of my confusion. There was a chance she could accept Verne's imaginings. I was disappointed: no answer, no voicemail, just an option to leave a number digitally. I ignored the offer. With time to reconsider, I wondered why I had called her. Did I see her as a fellow traveler on a similar path or cosmic trajectory? Had I simply hoped for more solace than the USB stick offered?

Chapter Sixteen

A few days off work, light snow and ice and extreme central Alberta winter temperatures, kept me cloistered at home. I spent the first day of my break completing a few chores and updated the USB. I had started preparing my dinner, turned down the music and prepared to read a promising new novel. It was a determined effort to dispel gnawing negativity.

Three intrusive, quiet, urgent knocks on my front door penetrated the barricades that I was building to exclude the real world. Obviously I was at home, so I could not ignore it. Hoping to dismiss the caller quickly, I opened the door and was startled by a visitor, dressed for the cold weather, who nimbly stepped through the entrance and deftly closed the door. Without hesitation, Sandy pushed back her hood to reveal her jet-black hair hanging loose down to her shoulders. A few touches of makeup exposed a feminine glow that she'd subdued in the past; her most noticeable feature, her eyes, sparkled intensely with excitement.

"Sorry about that. Are you OK? I saw that you called and came as soon as I could. I deliberately didn't answer the phone and walked most of the way here to throw any possible shadows off track. It's good that you didn't leave a number. There've been developments. I'll tell you once I'm out of these clothes."

"No, n..n...no, I'm fine. It's great to see you. More than I'd hoped for. Let me take your coat. What's going on? Thanks for coming round."

"Mmm, smells good, what's for supper?"

"One of my specialities. Won't you stay for some? I've prepared enough for the week and it won't be long."

"Good timing on my part. I will. Thanks. I haven't eaten since noon."

"Wonderful." Tentatively I added, "How about a glass of wine?"

To my surprise, Sandy accepted with, "Exceptional times call for exceptions to the rule. I think that I need it tonight."

We sat down in separate chairs in the lounge with wine. Sandy raised her glass and said, "What shall we toast?"

"It has to be Askuwheteau."

"Too soon. It's not resolved." Sandy bent her elbow and lowered her glass, looked straight at me and said, "Let's toast...not holding back."

I cocked my head.

Sandy narrowed her eyes, pretending to interrogate me, straightened her arm again and added, "...when we ask each other questions."

She relaxed back in the chair and asked, "You called me, so what's up?"

I explained how I'd become isolated at work and unable to talk freely to dispel the nonsense circulating about the Askuwheteau case; also my reluctance to socialise as a result; and thought better of repeating Rangseetal's comment about being in love.

"So you called me. I guess I should be flattered. But why me?"

"I realised afterwards that it was kind of selfish."

"Not at all. I'm glad you did."

"Well, you're the only person I know who knows about the investigation at all levels; and that Askuvie was not a degenerate as so many assume. Now that you're actually here I don't have the same nagging need to talk about being out of step. Because you understand, we can start the conversation at a different point. Why did you come around and not just call back? Why don't you have voicemail?"

"I changed all that in the last few days. I think that I'm being watched carefully. I'm not scared or even surprised, I don't think there's imminent danger, but in this line of work, precaution is better than regret. If my phone is monitored then any messages or return calls might be..." Sandy clenched her teeth, "...indiscreet. Anyway, I don't think that I can elude the powers that are probably watching me now and they have likely made connections between us. I am aware of the presence of some surveillance though I can't distinguish it which is weird because I can normally spot tails easily - at least I have a built-in radar that detects danger."

"Don't take chances…"

"Ross, my job is all about taking chances," Sandy replied with a sardonic laugh revealing a different side of her character.

"Well, what are the developments that you mentioned when you arrived?"

"I took everything you told me very seriously and of course noted your observation of the changes to the house and garden. What struck me more - usual crime scene stuff - there were no signs of struggle for such a gruesome murder. I'm sure that bothered you too."

"Not till you mention it now. I think that I was in too much shock at the time to observe rationally. I was rattled by Askuvie's death and the changes to the garden. If there was no struggle, was he murdered, killed, taken by surprise."

"There's too much hidden information. It's almost like a sacrifice. Like he was complicit. A willing sacrifice. At the river I said the investigation was going slowly. Now it's snail's pace.

"Extraordinary. And his were the only fingerprints about the place - oh and a few of yours outside in the garden."

"How did you get my...? I don't even want to know" I followed with a smile, realising that Sandy was even more discreet and expert than I had imagined.

"Anyway, whatever the reason for this, it led me to check more carefully on the history of the house. I discovered something extraordinary. The property has changed occupants many times, but it's never been bought or sold. Not even rented. Askuwheteau is not mentioned. There's no explanation for that, but I do know that since I made that discovery, I have sensed an eerie presence keeping an eye on my comings and goings. It's also like one of those bizarre and a bit hackneyed jokes: they know that I know that they know, that I can't report this anomaly about the land because disclosure would ruin the investigation. Basically, they simply would not let the secret go any further. They would shut me down - temporarily or even permanently if they had to."

"That's crazy indeed. Are there any other places like Askuvie's house...land?"

"No. It's out of the ordinary. Unique in fact. No legal titles, no paper trail at all. I haven't seen anything like it. It's possible that it was an accident, an oversight, but very unlikely. More likely it's an intentional omission that would take forever to unravel. The weirdest part about it is that I have been allowed to find the fact. My discovery's no accident. You can be sure of that."

"Come to think of it, Askuvie did mention once that the land had been with his people for a long time. He said that his sanctuary could not have been developed in one lifetime. But maybe he was only talking about visible things. That water source was fantastic - in the real sense of the word. Really. It's probably still there under the ground."

"I can't go digging around in the garden. But, we might be onto something here. Like you, I don't have many people to talk to about this. Only the direct contact in Ottawa and most of our relationship has been over the phone. Never face to face. It's very limited to maintain security. I sometimes think that my contact plays things down when I come up with new information. It doesn't surprise him as much as it does me.

Nothing is what it seems in this kind of work, for sure. Maybe I was feeling a bit isolated too and that's why I wanted to come around."

"You certainly do exciting work…"

Before I could finish Sandy drained her glass and stood up. Her eyes had become greyish and she forced a smile as she interrupted me to say, "I'm sorry. I should have thought about this more carefully before I came around. You know, it's part of my job to be disconnected. I should have been more considerate. It's really disrupted your life. I don't think that you're in danger, but I don't know enough. I should leave. Thanks for the information and wine."

I stood up, but stood still as she started to walk toward the front door. The pang of isolation returned in a flash and infiltrated my voice as I said, "Don't leave. I called you because I was strung out not having anyone to talk to about this. It's just as much my fault."

"You didn't know what was involved. It's better…"

It was my turn to interrupt, "I'm not worried about it.

Sandy had her coat on and had already opened the door to the dark night sky that comes early in winter. She turned and scrutinised my face. She was reading me carefully. I added, "Actually I have something else to share with you about another matter. Not connected, but also intriguing. And...the supper's really good, I guarantee it."

A second glance at the dark night and again at my face, changed her mind. "OK, but be warned," she said with a more natural smile followed by a relaxed laugh. "There's a reason that we are both experiencing similar emotions at the same time. Maybe we're just part of that endless human chess game that I was telling you about. Or maybe there's something else?"

I said, "There really is something else," to deflect Sandy's innuendo, "I have a friend named Verne who is travelling around England, Cornwall..."

"Verne, a traveler?" she said stifling a laugh.

"True, I'd never thought of that side."

"I've always wanted to visit Cornwall. The land of knights."

"True again. Anyway, he lived in our city for a while and left suddenly. He's written me some baffling emails over the last few months. They glide beneath the surface of common reality...a bit like shadows. You're the only person I know who might appreciate them through the kind of work you do. At least you wouldn't automatically dismiss them as ridiculous."

Sandy slipped off her coat, "OK, I could read them and make up my own mind."

I have a bit of preparation left in the kitchen. It'll give you about half an hour to read the emails. How about it? And, how about another glass of wine?"

Smiling, she handed me her coat, "Right, no seduction, though. Where's the computer?"

"Of course not. In the alcove around the corner."

With relief, I showed Sandy to the computer, opened the email folder and left her to it while I attended to the food in the kitchen with more care than usual. After about twenty minutes of silence from Sandy, I was enjoying the final minutes of cooking and Leonard Cohen's "Hallelujah" lulled me into a reflection of how his lyrics wove with the mood and captured all the mystery of our experience of the moment.

Then I suffered a jolt of reality that passed with extraordinary ease: I had given a stranger, someone I hardly knew, access to my computer. It wasn't linked to my professional life or medical records, so I hadn't jeopardized hospital patients; it did contain all my personal business; nothing lurid. Sandy had merged into my life, woven into a deep level of my world after a few brief encounters and I had abandoned myself to the acceptance that even if "...it all went wrong" as Cohen sang, I would just revel in the present - contrary to my normally cautious nature.

Sandy returned to the kitchen area with a thoughtful expression on her face. "Thanks for sharing those emails with me. Verne sounds like an interesting character...isn't Leonard Cohen a blessing to humanity? ...And he just lets images glide into your subconscious...he sort of leaves them there to grow...later you ponder 'a bird on a wire' out of nowhere when you're walking down the road. Well I do. What's wrong, Ross? You look different, relaxed."

"Maybe it's the wine. All that I could come up with is that Cohen is a genius. You've nailed it. I was just enjoying the music and concentrating on the cooking," I lied and Sandy's eyes assumed their penetrating stare, searching for the truth. I semi-confessed, "Well maybe I'm happy for the first time in a long while and it's my weekend - my break," I tried to stick to the topic. "I thought that you'd find something in Verne's letters. Like the truth about Askuvie, I couldn't share them with anyone else. Many people would dismiss them as a waste of time. As absurd."

Sandy sipped her wine and kept her eyes on me.

"You know, Verne sometimes referred to his business that he ran here till he left as merely 'passing time'. I guess in some ways Askuvie and Verne work like you said about Leonard Cohen planting images that grow with time. Their aphorisms drop into my thoughts at unexpected moments."

"Oh, I'm fascinated by Verne - I'm already used to his name. Tell me about him. Is he a loner?"

"No, I'd not say that. He was a provocative friend, always engaging in conversation. Never just for the sake of speaking though. You know, not one of those who babble away to be the life and soul of the party."

"Seems like you often pick challenging friends," Sandy smiled. "I suppose, I'm asking, do you think he's imagining that stuff or did he really meet everyone he talks about?"

"Verne has a very creative mind. It's not that he hallucinates or invents things. When I first met him, I would have described him as a pragmatist. He uses his skills and charm with great success. There's another side to him. One that sees events in a totally different way to others and he puts a spin on them; he kind of starts with the shading and the shadow, then sometimes adds the detail." I explained how he had often talked about hearing voices in the sea, but now that side of his personality seemed liberated, even more receptive to Nature.

"Do you think he's a bit off-beam?"

"If I'd have read his emails cold a few weeks ago, I might have thought that. Knowing more about him, glimpsing Askuwheteau's world and the various nooks and crannies in our world that you've described, I see it all differently. I'm the one who's grown. Maybe, I'm a bit off-beam right now. Or, maybe it's just like maestro, Leonard Cohen, says, 'I couldn't feel, so I'm trying to touch.' It's me that's changed and grown closer to all these nuances that were always there. I feel as if I've inflated."

As we sat down to eat, I added, "He does seem to have flipped into a different orbit. Almost like he's out there spinning around, a bit out of touch, but sending the occasional message to us Earthlings."

Sandy chuckled as she leaned forward across the table towards me, "Well that's not totally crazy considering the stuff I've been telling you. I'd really like to meet Verne one day. He's invited you to join him in Cornwall. You should go."

"I have thought about it, but my job is more than just work, it's a responsibility. Like yours."

"Cloth napkins," said Sandy as she spread it on her lap. "Do you use them every day?"

I shook my head and watched her taste the first mouthful. In response to my raised eyebrows she said, "Delicious, thank you. It's been a long time since someone cooked for me. Anyway, don't change the subject. I also work too hard. I'm sure that you could get away for a week or two. From what you've told me it sounds like you need a break."

Sandy seemed a bit pushy for a new acquaintance. But she had already grown beyond that and I accepted the comment as genuinely motivated. "Cornwall must be a really romantic part of the world," she added, giving me a glimpse of another aspect of her personality.

"You're not just about work are you?"

"No. But on the other hand, you can't do this kind of work with bare facts. They form the basis. I try to reconstruct a picture. Not always that easy."

"I've no doubt. Tell me more about Askuwheteau's property and that ownership bit. How is it possible that no one owns the land?"

Sandy had shifted gears back into her professional persona and took me into her confidence, "I shouldn't be revealing this, but, same as you, I don't have anyone to bounce it off. As I said, I can't even get a clear read on the man I report to in Ottawa. From the records, Askuwehteau's land has never been sold. It's always been in the same name. Nothing to draw attention. On the one hand, it's as if it doesn't exist; on the other, the land is more essential than anything else because nothing can be without it - the house, Askuvie, your meetings with him. There is an address. Clearly the house is there, in solid form, but the land ownership has never changed. Before settler times. Never. It's just there."

"And the new owner? How does he come to take possession?"

"That new occupant...doesn't own the place. Madness. I know. Somehow the whole picture has changed from that overgrown garden, ramshackle house and eccentric inhabitant. It's been given a facelift. It has the air of comfortable middle class respectability. And it all happened right in front of our eyes. Everyone was watching."

"It sounds impossible. Right here in our city, our provincial capital. Our modern city. Who owns it now?"

"That's just it. No sale, no transaction. Do you ask your neighbour for proof of ownership? Of course not. So, who's to know.

"I'm not ready to bring this to anyone's attention because I don't understand the context...the implications...yet. I'm still digging. And, as I said earlier, whether you believe it or not, I wouldn't be allowed to do that one way or another - my boss in Ottawa, or something bigger than that would block the way."

"Incredible - actually unbelievable. How long before others catch on?"

"They won't. Why should anyone look? Who would think of that reality. The house itself, the building, is registered. The whole thing is a total anomaly. From what you told me of your conversations with Askuwheteau, he was pretty vague on that too.

"I've told you too much. For some reason, I feel comfortable doing that with you. That's about all I have for now. In this 'chess game', players take a long time considering their moves."

"It's too much for me. I'm just a doctor, going about my business."

"Hahaha, that's what you'd like us all to think. I'm not fooled by that big cuddly body of yours. You are so quick and I have to listen to every word you say to make sure I'm not missing anything."

"Cuddly. No one has ever called me that."

Sandy glanced at her glass of wine and said, "Sorry. Let's blame this. What about Verne, though? Do you think that he will tell you more about the meeting with Moruith's family?"

"Verne is definitely unpredictable. Honest. The most honest person you've ever met. Very successful in business; sometimes impulsive but unwavering once on a path. Almost obsessive."

"I like him more and more. I can understand obsessive," she winked at me and, starting to stand, asked the location of my washroom. I directed her past the computer she had used earlier. A few minutes later she playfully poked her head around the corner, her face glowing and eyes sparkling and said, "Sorry for looking at your screen, but Verne's next installment has arrived."

My eagerness matched hers and we walked quickly to the computer. I opened the email and Verne delivered. He hooked us from the opening lines:

Hullo Mate

A few days ago I went down a rabbit hole at Moruith's farm; radical, even for me; even after Chysauster. I have no other way of describing it. If you haven't read my other emails, this one is worth it.

Before going to bed, Moruith could not conceal her excitement when she reminded me that the next day was Winter Solstice and that the family would arrive before sunrise for ceremonies outside. She invited me to participate to gain a "More personal understanding" of her stories and added that it was an "Investment, but strictly no money."

I woke up while it was still dark after a few short but regenerating hours of sleep, dressed warmly and descended the stairs. The house was quiet so I peered outside the front door to see Moruith sitting in the darkness drinking from an earthenware mug. She waved me over and said that she was glad that I was up early to share some farm produce to ward off the chilly morning, assuring me that it was all natural and unadulterated; that it would give me energy and instil a receptive mood for the day. The unique, fruity warm beverage coursed through my being as I marveled at the cracks in the darkness lightening the eastern sky.

Moruith pointed to stones in front of us. In the faint light I could see that they were the remnants of walls about knee-high demarcating a small house. Local stones had been used in the same way as they are at Chysauster, without a cement of any kind binding them. They were not carved or shaped, but carefully selected to wedge together to form solid walls. With reverence Moruith said, "This was their first house; the foundation of our community." It was clear who she was talking about. She continued, "My line has never felt the desire to leave this place; neither do I. We are charged with the responsibility of preserving their spirit lodged in the stones which haven't moved for two thousand years."

Moruith curbed my questions with, "It's not by accident that you have turned up on the shortest day of the year. By the end of the day you will have a better idea of what you are seeking." I felt a slight shiver as I recollected the taxi driver's parting words, "By the way, Laddie, what are you looking for," when he dropped me off at Chysauster.

Moruith ignored my questions, instead she said, "The sky is clear today. We shall watch the sunrise together," followed by a glance that silenced me. Standing she said, "Let's go." As I dutifully walked with her through a dip and upwards towards a rise, her white hair was hung loosely about her shoulders and she was carrying a bundle slung over her shoulder.

When we reached the top, we stood on the rim of a sunken hollow nestled in the summit and we looked down upon a flat circular plane - a natural amphitheatre atop a Cornish hill. In the pre-dawn light I discerned a stone circle. My astonishment increased when I saw forty or more figures sitting in a circle within the circumference prescribed by the stones. I turned to Moruith to see that she had unwrapped her bundle to reveal a multi coloured cassock. As she pulled it over her head to cover her slight stature down to her ankles, her stony expression gave way to a smile as she said, "There was more colour in our world before they brought in all the rules."

There were two gaps in the circle of people below: one in the east and the other in the west of the circle. As Moruith started moving towards the east side, she said softly to me, "Take your place and forget about yesterday or tomorrow. Direct all your energy into the sunrise."

We remained there for several hours to celebrate the sun's rise to its zenith. We were more than observers: we sang hymn-like tunes as if to lift the sun in its ascension and, in return, I felt the solar energy energise my body and blood at a deep level. Despite temperatures a few degrees above zero the rays of the mid-winter sun warmed me more than I expected; and I felt energy generated from the others in the circle as we celebrated something that I always took for granted. I do believe that the sun will rise each day; we should express our gratitude for being part of cosmogenesis.

Following Moruith's instruction I was totally in the moment and completely in tune with the surroundings. The smell of the crisp winter land filled my nostrils, the solar energy warmed my skin. I didn't feel cold. All bodily functions slowed almost to a standstill for a period: breathing at hibernation rate, my heart beat occasionally to remind me that I was alive and my whole being pulsed in time with Nature's winter rhythm; the earth and all of us in the circle throbbed slowly and powerfully in unison. My mind emptied and I know that I joined in with the others in the circle as we intoned wordless tunes of worship and praise of all that exists. Those melodies seemed familiar and as the notes came from the deepest depths of my soul, my body was purged of a sludge in my veins. The sun had enjoyed its longest sleep of the year and returned to sustain all life on our half of the planet and beyond; I felt rooted in that place on earth.

The sun was at its height, when Moruith rose as a sign to the whole group: men, women and children of all ages walked in a silent procession towards Moruith's farmhouse. Behind the house was a long, rough-hewn wooden table, laden with enough loaves of bread, cheeses and cold meats to feed everyone. Four vats of the fruity brew I'd drunk with Moruith in the morning were spaced around the area and the beverage flowed freely amongst us. The mood was respectful, quiet and powerfully positive. I drank liberally of the beverage which renewed my energy, instilled resistance to the cold and suppressed my appetite, though I enjoyed a delicious sandwich.

The company was huddled in groups of two, three or four, talking quietly to each other with little laughter. I never felt excluded at any point, for, as if orchestrated, each of them broke away to introduce themselves and spend a few minutes with me supplying such information as where they live, pointing out one or two of their adult children in the crowd, or commenting on the exceptional benefits of Moruith's winter drink. 'Pender' was rooted in each of their surnames: either a pure version or something more elaborate such as 'Prendergast.' Moruith had promised that I would meet the clan.

The last, Crandell Pender, approached me. I speculated that he might be the oldest in the clan because he stood slightly bent at the waist and the others paid him special respect as he moved towards me. His bushy, tousled grey eyebrows and hair offset his sparkling, clear eyes. He welcomed me as the others had, but instead of information, he said, "Tomorrow I will give you a special message."

I checked people's faces around the room for an indication as to how to deal with the situation. Was Crandell Pender serious or should I just humour an eccentric of the community? Everyone had returned to their own conversations.

The shadows had lengthened and, as if coordinated with that final interaction, Moruith slipped the colourful cassock over her ordinary clothes which was a signal to all. Without direction, the whole clan took up position behind her and she led the way back to the stone circle. By that stage I was not a straggler; I was an integral part of the silent procession. At the site, I understood that my same place was reserved in the west of the circle. We sat observing the setting sun on the shortest day of the year. In the twilight, Moruith ended the event with a brief soft song to wish all a good night and an expectation that we would all be there again the following morning. Everyone began leaving slowly for their homes. Moruith walked around the outside of the stone circle to meet me and escort me down the path. She invited me to stay another night. How could I refuse? I was mesmerised, captivated, and all energy had ebbed from my soul so that I could hardly walk the short distance to Moruith's house. Most of all I was intrigued by Crandel Pender's promise of a message.

"You'll sleep well," she said, "Without a doubt. There'll be no stories tonight. We'll save that for another time." I knew my way to the room and, true to Moruith's word, slept without interruption for several hours.

By the time I was ready to face the day, I found Moruith outside again, but this time filled with a vibrancy. "Did you sleep well on the long night?" she asked, but without waiting for my reply, added, "As it should be. Now you know where we are going. Have some water, 'Adam's Ale' as they say. It's from the spring over there." Till then I hadn't noticed the natural source of water coming out of the earth; it was cold and more than refreshing - exhilarating.

Moruith raised her glass, smiled and said, "Happy Foundation Day. Can you feel the energy returning?" I felt rested and energetic and the walk to the stone circle was easy. The others were already there, this time simply mingling in happy conversation. As people arrived I could hear the greeting,

"Happy Foundation' Day," thrown around. Before sunrise, they assumed the same positions as the previous day. Wearing the same cassock, Moruith rose from her place and moved to the centre of the circle where she stood next to a large flat stone and began what seemed like a ritual. She prodded and stabbed the ground with a spiked stick. Then she continued to turn the hard ground with a bronze implement until she had loosened the soil even more all around the stone. She drew dried heather from a hessian bag and mumbled an incantation over it at least three times, then crushed it in her hands and spread it liberally all around the rock until she had completely covered the surrounding ground. She covered it with soil and repeated the incantation. Her actions prompted a gentle urgency from all in the circle and they broke into a spontaneous song with increasing volume.

The chanting song reached a crescendo; it was like a chorus or a prologue to what happened next, though I'm forbidden to write it down. If you do make the journey here or we meet *again, I will tell you of something wondrous. No exaggeration. I hope we have the opportunity.*

We remained in the "amphitheatre" for the morning, then proceeded in high spirits to the farmhouse where we enjoyed food and drink till well after sunset. Many told me with confidence that the omens in Moruith's demonstration foretold a fine year ahead; that rich harvests were ensured. This ceremony is not merely a commemoration or nod to the past. It is an act in the present; an essential guide in the lives of those who participate. In fact the energy in that party was extraordinary.

You may think that I mean raucous energy; it's the opposite; not extroverted, it was directed inward to the family members. They demonstrated a deep concern for each other, bonding sincerely with one another. As you know about me, I have always wanted freedom to move about the world uninhibited, unrestricted. Here I simply wanted to be in the moment: in the space and in the time. But, despite the happy hospitality they all showed me, my antenna detected faint signals of something claggy about the ground around the place. The various family members made a point of chatting with me, often starting with "I'm glad that you could be here." At the time I took their words at face value. After speaking with Crandel Pender at the end of the evening, I'm not sure.

Despite my impatience to speak with him the whole day, others in the house kept me constantly occupied so that, even when I caught sight of him, they engaged me in conversation and physically blocked my path to Pender.

Suddenly, as people were starting to leave, he was in front of me, staring directly into my eyes and without any salutation or prelude, he declared: "Journey to Zennor. That is where you will find what you are seeking and what we need. Return with it." He turned and left through the front door. None of the remaining guests reacted to his demonstration in any way. I'm sure that I need not describe my own reaction.

Later that evening alone with Moruith, she said, as if nothing untoward had happened, "So, Verne, do you feel settled with the family?"

"Curiously, yes. They're all so familiar. One thing, though, I..."

"Poor pun." she said with a smile. "If you spent time here you'd realise how distinct and different each is, but it is the similarities that bind us together; the differences that give us strength. You know, we don't have any fences between our properties, it's a huge place, almost like a small county of its own. I know you were going to talk about Old Man Pender."

"That was fairly direct. Even for me," I said.

She raised her hand and said, "He's right, Verne. He speaks for us all. How would you know what to do, if he spoke in riddles? Sometimes the direct approach is the only way to get things done. It is his prerogative and duty to deliver messages like that.

"There's not much at Zennor," said Moruith as she responded to my stunned silence, "that's why the thing you are looking for will be obvious. The only question is, will you go?" She put her hand on my shoulder and continued, "That's to decide tomorrow. Now it's bedtime."

The next morning I set out walking to Zennor. I am following a zig-zag path to get there. I think that my exposure to Moruith's Farm has induced a change in my behaviour. It is not the quickest and shortest route to Zennor, but touches on more points along the way. It gave me time to digest what I had encountered. Learning measured in speed misses the quality of the experience, especially when we are discovering ourselves. Or it may simply be that rebellious voice in my personality: I don't like being given a direct order and I'll go to great lengths to display my displeasure. Taking the roundabout route was my show of faint resistance. The weather prediction for the next few days was favourable, so I made the most of it. I have found places along the way to write *and send this email to you. I should arrive in Zennor in a few days.*

I cannot explain exactly what has happened to me at Moruith's Farm and on this journey. The zig-zag path represents a change. I have always been curious, but now I'm ready to unlearn knowledge that took much effort to acquire. I am more receptive to truths I may have previously dismissed. Chysauster and Moruith's Farm have introduced a change in my body at a molecular level, if that is possible. I am unable to tell you more as I said earlier, so if you are interested, you will have to join me in Zennor where I shall rest for a while in this strange and rocky land. The more that I learn about this world of myth and magic, the easier it is to identify my own inner landscape and that mirror I was looking into at Chysauster, now seems to be within, reflecting the rugged terrain in front of me.

Cornwall would give you some distance from your routine life - a different perspective. Moreover, I would appreciate a friend whom I can trust implicitly right now. Collecting parcels of land

no longer holds appeal and I cannot own a special spot at

Chysauster or Moruith's Farm. The recurring message that I

should be looking for something has finally got through my

thick skull. I won't leave Cornwall till I find out what that thing

is.

Regards

Verne

Sandy and I finished reading the email at about the
same time. My intuition to show Verne's emails to Sandy
proved beneficial as she was receptive to the nuances of his
stories. This account was directed at me on a far more
personal level than the earlier ones. Or, as Sandy pointed out,
he is "Inviting you over." More than that, there was a note of
desperation. We agreed that there was a similar mystery to
Verne's story that could be detected in the facts surrounding
the Askuwheteau saga.

We were enjoying each other's company, starting to delve into the aspects of Verne's tale, when we were caught off guard by an anonymous email that appeared on the monitor: "Dear Ross and Sandy, If you want to know, you have to go."

I was stunned by the arbitrariness of the message, but Sandy said, "Ross, have you ever mentioned me to anyone?"

"Never, I've been absolutely discreet. Why?

"Why? Why would we be linked together in an email? In your email?"

"Should we report this to the police?" I said, trying to make light of it.

My levity annoyed Sandy who revealed a side I hadn't seen. The calm mood of the evening was dispelled in an instant as she switched into a highly trained warrior, all senses firing at once. While listening for noises outside, her eyes scanned the room like radar, penetrating every nook and cranny: "Ross, this is real. Stay right where you are, below the window line and behind the kitchen counter. I'm going upstairs. Are the curtains closed?"

By the time I could answer, she was moving like a wild animal on attack in a crouch position up the stairs faster than most of us can sprint upright. Within seconds she returned, grabbing a notepad from the kitchen counter on the way to join me. Sitting on the floor right next to me to calm me down, she scribbled instructions: "It's deserted outside - leaving now because they expect me to - no point in playing cool. Wait here for five minutes after I've gone, then follow your normal bedtime routine with lights etc. It's spooky, but there's no danger. See you in the morning. Really sorry I've dragged you into this."

My natural protective instinct surfaced, "I can't let you..."

Mock smiling in response, placing a cautionary finger to her lips, she wrote, "Do you want to take over?" followed by, "This is my world. You can't do anything about it. Try to get some sleep." With that she moved quickly to the front door and in less than thirty seconds had donned her coat, boots, hat and gloves while, almost unnoticed, had switched a serious looking handgun from her coat pocket to a specially designed belt on her casual pants. That freaked me out more than anything as it contrasted with how normal Sandy had seemed a few minutes earlier. Then, overwhelmed by the whirling chaos, I followed Sandy's instructions and headed upstairs, to bed, but not to sleep. Luckily I was not scheduled at the hospital the next day.

Chapter Seventeen

I didn't expect to see Sandy sitting in my living room the next morning quietly reading through her notes. It should have been disconcerting, but it was reassuring. Her cheerful, "Hi. Doesn't look like you got much sleep last night," was a playful goad.

"How did you get inside?" I replied.

"Did you lock the front door?"

"I can't recall. Did I?"

"If you had, a puny front door lock may have been a challenge for me in junior high. But, you should take more care. You'll have all sorts of young women dropping by to have breakfast with an eligible doctor."

"Sandy, this is crazy. I'll put on the coffee. Did all that happen last night? Is this your normal life?"

"My normal on steroids. Stuff comes at me really fast and I have to put it in a picture I have of the world. It's always changing and expanding - like a balloon. I paint a picture with the hazy facts that come my way. This one is out on the edge, even for me. Coffee would be great."

"What's it all about? What can you explain?"

"I've been asking that myself - since you told me of your visit to Askuvie's - your invitation to his sanctuary."

"Why can't the world just settle down to normal?"

"Ross, for most people out there the world is going on 'normally' - just look at all your colleagues and the people on the pavement. It's just a normal winter's day. For some reason, you've been sucked into a different narrative and you're unlucky enough to have to share it with me. You can leave the story."

"How do I do that?"

"Just forget about what you've seen and heard and go back to work each day. Convince yourself it never happened. I'll leave you alone."

Alone wasn't what I had in mind; I wanted Sandy to stick around, but couldn't bring myself to say it out loud. Instead, I chose a different way of expressing it and, as I poured the coffee, said, "I'm starting to understand Askuwheteau's warning about his revealing knowledge to me. What about you?"

"As I said, whatever is going on is more intense than ever. This time, I'm not the investigator; somehow I'm part of what's being investigated. I'm part of the story. What I do know is that I am totally exposed so there's no point in trying to hide from it or even pretend that this conversation is private. As they say in the movies, 'My cover is blown!'"

I'm sure that I blanched: "In my own house."

Sandy nodded. "I have contacted my superior and will be leaving for a while mainly because I can't be effective now that I'm exposed. The option was clear: 'If you want to know, you have to go.' I know where I'd be going if it was up to me. But the message was 'Dear Ross and Sandy."

"This is crazy. Talk about topsy-turvy. Where would I go?" In response, Sandy gestured toward the computer with her head. I said, "No, no. Not Cornwall. That's even more insane. If I return to 'normal' will I still be a problem? Will I be allowed to do that?"

"As I've told you, if that's your choice, the detail will blur in your memory. You'll be left with a troubled dreamlike sense of occurrences that have passed which is not uncommon in the mistiness of modern life."

"No, no. I can't just up and leave like that? How can I simply quit my job?"

"Ross, after all the evidence you've seen, you must be aware that there is some inevitability at play here. Being a doctor is only one aspect of who you are. It could be that you are being tested; pushed to discover something about yourself that informs your work as a doctor. You're a good doctor, but what would propel you to being a great doctor; beyond doing your job as a doctor. Do you really think that your day to day work is the biggest issue?"

"It is for me. I'd become a great doctor by practicing medicine. That's how. But ...I suppose...there's something bigger. I need time. How much time do I actually have? We don't just drift into things; we choose, we control our lives, we don't just let things happen to us."

"Take your time. Not too long. These opportunities don't come to everyone - and they don't come often. I have to make arrangements. As they say in the classics, I'm going with or without you."

"Are you inviting me to travel with you?"
Sandy nodded her head with that smile that I had realised was impossible for me to resist.

"What will I tell them at work? That sort of erratic behaviour won't look good on my record."

"Tell them that you need rest. You've been showing signs of stress for a while. Your colleagues and superiors have been wondering about your recent behaviour: not taking lunches and breaks, overworking. A normal modern day disease. I'll have you see a doctor at short notice to give you the note we need to..."

"We need? ...I work with doctors - remember. It would be seen as a weakness. There are all sorts of people vying for the big jobs."

"You don't know the doctors I know. Don't worry, and careers can wait. It's better to gain a solid context of why all these things have been going on and in the end that understanding will make you more effective."

"And my new house?"

"That can wait too. Your builder is busy at the moment he'll be glad to have you off his back knowing that he has work for the future. Besides, it's winter and new construction can only begin when the ground thaws."

Sandy challenged my conventional stereotype of women (which I thought was progressive to start with) by taking control of the situation, outlining the options in a practical way and dismissing my indecision with "You're inventing roadblocks. Make a decision." There was no denying, I was also grappling with my perception of her as a woman and her irresistible physical attraction. It was tangible: like rubber bands binding us, stretched to the full, about to snap us together. The more they were extended, the greater the tension; the closer together we came, the more a magnetic force took over. That would partly explain why I was so keen to share information with her about Askuvie and Verne. Her proposal to travel together was a declaration that my feelings were not one-sided. Even her cajoling me to decide was like an invitation.

"Right, make the arrangements." I chose, but immediately second-guessed myself. "I must be crazy. I should just retreat to that 'mistiness of modern life.' What am I doing? Where are we going, Sandy?"

"Cornwall of course. Can you think of another place that calls us more urgently right now? For an outsized brilliant doctor, you're sometimes pretty blind. The dithering is over. C'mon, it'll be fun."

"So, we're going from one crazy situation into another - one that sounds even weirder. Why don't we just go to a holiday resort somewhere to get a good rest? Mexico: R&R: Isn't that what I'm supposed to need right now?"

"Don't be boring. We're looking down Verne's rabbit hole. Let's just dive in. Besides, do you really think that we'd be allowed to evade the question and ignore the direction we've been given? 'If you want to know, you have to go!' Do you think it's a question? Was it related to what's happening here or what we want to know about your friend, Verne?"

"Maybe I really do just need to take it easy for a while so that I can return to my work and career. I've worked my whole life to get to this point."

"You've moved outside of that rut in the last few weeks. You've had glimpses of a different world from the perimeter of your normal. It's time to take a bigger step. Besides, if you do go back to medicine in the future, you'll be a lot more useful to your patients with your experience. And..." she laughed, "..your whole life is yet to come. Honestly!"

"OK. It could be healthy to really get away and out of the normal. Normal: what the hell is that anyway? It used to be a joke. You know, there's something that I haven't told you. I'm also a recorder."

Sandy looked at me for more information. I explained briefly about the stick that had stemmed from the game of "Genesis" and how I'd been recording things that had been happening.

"Have you written about me?" she asked.

I answered with a smile and we agreed to defer the conversation till we had time.

"What should I do in the planning?"

"Just get your business sorted out as best you can in the next few days. I'll send you the name of the doctor and time of your appointment. If you go into work avoid details. You don't have to explain. Make sure that your passport is ready and house secured till we return. And contact Verne to let him know that you're on your way to meet him. Find out where he'll be over the next two weeks."

"How long will we be away?" Sandy's look told me to stop asking questions like that, "Right, I'll just set things up so that I can deal with them from outside the country if necessary. What about your business?"

"I'm always ready to travel. I'll email you the arrangements in the next two days. Next stop London."

Sandy left in her usual swift way, pausing to hug me and, with a confident smile, to reassure me that she had things under control, adding: "Don't worry, Ross, it's going to be fine," then with a laugh and, "What can go wrong?," she was out the door and I pondered the quiet vacuum she left behind.

I returned to the kitchen, made another cup of coffee and walked to the living room which was once my sanctuary, to mull things over. Staring outside at the grey sky, I wondered whether I really wanted to escape from modern life; perhaps I was more suited to that 'mistiness' that veiled the reality we mostly avoid by not confronting the questions that are central to our existence. Why shouldn't I just retreat into the world that I had worked so hard to create for myself, and deserved, through my good fortune and diligence? I didn't want to be running away. Then guilt sneaked in regarding my patients:

How would the hospital cope with the situation in the ward? Humbly, I realised that it would not be such a dilemma for them: an older colleague had reluctantly announced his retirement quietly to a select few and would probably cherish the chance to delay hanging up his stethoscope. I knew that he hadn't made any plans and was really worried about how he was going to occupy his time in retirement. The guilt faded and I focused on my own dilemmas. Was this an escape route or a path of discovery? I was placing my future in the hands of someone I had recently met. I wondered whether I was actually going through a breakdown of some sorts, one which could be averted by just returning to my normal routine.

I picked up my mobile phone to call Sandy to renege, but it was out of power and the charger was not in its usual place on my desk next to my computer. Instead I noticed Verne's USB. That gave me a focus and I decided to attack the task of recording the confusion of the last twenty four hours. I started with the effect of Sandy in my life: her amazing athletic ability, her smile and the confidence she inspired in me. Within a few sentences, I realised that I would be boarding that plane with her and I moved on to describe the recent events with more clarity of mind. It didn't take as long as I'd expected. I also made a conscious decision not to get rattled and calmly check places where my charger could be. I would need my phone to make arrangements with the hospital and my builder. I soon discovered the cord in the last power socket I'd used to charge my phone. With restored confidence I flipped through my passport and attended to other business.

Within three days, I was ready to depart on an adventure, having negotiated my work situation (with the help of Sandy's doctor) and private business with relative ease: credit cards covered, insurance adequate and passport's expiry date two years away.

True to her word, Sandy emailed me the departure details within forty eight hours. She'd secured a flight five days from the time of our decision to travel. So there I was, heading out to foreign country with a woman I'd only met about a month earlier to connect with a friend whose sanity I questioned; who, at the very least, I judged to have chosen an obscure path that was leading him into a morass more complex than my own current situation.

I'd be dim or dishonest to deny that Sandy had captivated me; that she'd charmed.me into following a course that I would normally have considered rash or hasty. She was another friend who (like Verne and Askuwheteau) opened a slit to let new light into my routine world. She was the catalyst: without her insights Askuwheteau's death would become another significant event in my memory and I would have declined Verne's invitation to Cornwall. She had changed my perspective: what I might have considered a scrambled escape had become a purposeful, essential adventure. I was even prepared to label the trip "a Quest." I packed Verne's USB in my hand luggage.

Following Sandy's directions, I met her at the airport at midday. We went through the baggage check and the clerk spoke in friendly terms, "Thank you, Dawn. Have a great trip."

"Dawn. Please don't tell me you're travelling on a false passport?" I said in a whisper once we were a discreet distance from the checkpoint.

She laughed, "You've got a lot to learn about me." Showing me the front page of her passport, she declared with a twinkle in her eye, "I'd never break the law. No point in that."

Heading towards customs, I prodded, "Dawn, I haven't heard that name much: it does fit. Why don't your friends use it?"

"Sandy evolved. I always thought the name 'Dawn' belonged to another era - my parents' generation."

At the end of the connecting tunnel facing the doorway to the plane, I felt a wave of panic. I was about to board a plane with a new friend, not even knowing her real name till now. My face must have displayed my panic because Dawn grabbed my arm in a firm, powerful grip and, without showing any physical effort on her face, moved my two hundred and twenty pound frame toward the exit and said in a completely reassuring tone, "It's going to be OK. You know there is no real choice. We have to go to find out."

Chapter Eighteen

After we stashed our hand luggage and squeezed into the economy-sized seats I said, "Dawn. I'm already finding out stuff: Dawn, I like that name, it runs off the tongue. Pronouncing it has little to do with the tongue; the name opens your mouth and maybe also possibilities. So, what have we got to find out?"

"Ross, we've been forced to see the world differently. It's a reality that is normally out of bounds for people like us."

The takeoff pushed me back into my seat, I stared out the window at the farmers' fields and said, "I'm leaving my comfortable circle. Where are we going to land?"

"We're going to Cornwall to meet up with Verne. It's as if Askuwheteau knew it would happen. At least you'll be able to look back at this circle with a different perspective. Maybe there will even be some intersections."

I nodded and placed complete trust in Dawn Sanderson. Her confidence and presence had enabled me to absorb the recent shocks and step over a boundary of fear into a less predictable world. I was starting to feel comfortable with her comments and unable to settle into the confines of my seat when she added, "If we're going to make a habit of traveling together we should splash out on first class. These seats aren't designed for us. By the way, why didn't you tell me about the computer stick earlier?"

I started to speak, but she interrupted with, "I know. You thought it was just part of a game. It doesn't matter now. I'm exhausted; I need a nap." She pushed up the armrest between our seats, laid her head on my shoulder and fell asleep in a few seconds. I was left to contemplate an appealing vision of traveling together in the future and resolved to enjoy every minute of the present with her warm head on my shoulder and the smell of her jetblack hair in my nostrils. Between short sleeps and Dawn's penetrating conversation, the trip to London was an easy one despite the lack of legroom. If we had been tossed together by some powerful force beyond my understanding, I resigned myself to the situation.

Chapter Nineteen

There's always a Shakespeare performance in London and of course the Broadway productions. We agreed that our recent experiences nudged us to see something on the fringe - so that's where we went. We saw a play loosely based on *The Tempest,* with Prospero as a defeated female leader of a modern state, bringing all sorts of innuendo to the magic still underlying the plot, but really missing Shakespeare's core. Dawn was even more frustrated and shot off, "If you aren't satisfied with the original by someone as great as Shakespeare, you should just write your own piece and not take the shears to a work of art." It was interesting to discover that, deep down, we are both traditionalists. Dawn's makeup contains a dab of the conventional; I've got more than a generous cupful. Those measures leavened and spiced our conversation.

Dawn had booked us as far as London because it's easy to travel from there to most parts of the UK. A night in a London hotel would give us a chance to rest after the long flight before journeying on to Zennor to meet Verne. She had reserved two adjacent rooms at one of those older style hotels, converted from once fashionable houses of the wealthy. We checked into our separate rooms before the play. After a few minutes Dawn walked in to inspect mine because she wanted to "make sure that, as 'tour organiser,' I was satisfied with the arrangements." She joked about the security, alluding to the recent disturbance in my house and then tried the interleading door between our rooms. It was locked. "Are you safe from me?" she grinned.

"Should I take precautions?" I replied.

She pretended to examine the keyhole, looked up and, with a very serious expression, said, "Junior high level again."

I hugged her, thanked her for making all the arrangements and for coaxing me out of my rut into this adventure. She dismissed my gratitude saying that we could talk about those things later. She added, "We should skedaddle, so we're not late for the performance and have time to pick up a sandwich." All worked out smoothly and even the questionable play gave us more common ground. Riding the London Underground home, Dawn said something about "Any port in a storm," and winked as she slipped her thumb inside the waistline of my jeans. "Better check that door tonight," she added and we both laughed.

Exhausted, we retreated to our rooms for the night. I'd hardly been asleep when I was woken by a gentle click and a creaking hinge. In the darkness I saw Dawn enter the room and move towards the bed. "Just checking to see that they haven't stolen you away," she said. I snapped on the light to see her wearing a long t-shirt that looked a lot like one of mine that I'd packed for the trip. It was pointless asking how she'd got hold of it, so I just shook my head. She folded back a section of the blanket and giggled, "You wear real pyjamas? I've got a lot of work to do." She slipped between the sheets and snuggled up to me. "If they come for us, they'll have to take us both."

"What a relief," I replied.

Chapter Twenty

After the long flight in cramped seats, the physical restrictions of coach travel presented a daunting prospect, so we took the train to St. Ives - Verne had mentioned the exceptional seafood there in one of his emails. On the train we sat on the same side of the table because it would be easier to chat and we both prefer facing the engine. Though less than fully rested from a night in a London hotel, it wasn't easy to doze between snacks and Dawn's eager questions about Verne. Despite the South England January weather, it was uplifting to be leaving the metropolitan area for regions of the British Isles neither of us had explored.

After lunch in St. Ives we caught the double-decker bus to Zennor. We were the only passengers braving the upper level and we felt the wintry weather that clutched the rugged landscape bite into us. However, from that vantage point above the hedgerows we enjoyed an expansive view of the fields and the coastline. The hedgerows frequently scraped either side of the bus as the expert driver steered us along the extremely narrow winding road. If we had traveled that route by car or even chosen to sit on the lower deck of the bus, our view would have been limited to the wall of hawthorne and blackthorne. Thousands of miles of hedgerow divide fields and roads throughout Cornwall. A stone wall is at the core of the foliage which provides habitation for diverse fauna. From the elevated position we could appreciate that we traveled into Zennor through surrounding fields and uncultivated land; if we had been below, it would have seemed as if we entered a tunnel as we left St. Ives and popped out at the other end in Zennor: two perspectives of arriving at a new destination.

Someone who looked like Verne was waiting patiently in the cold when the bus halted at a bus stop on the road skirting Zennor. We were the only passengers to alight; Zennor doesn't host many winter visitors.

"How did you know that we would arrive today, Verne? And what's with the hair - long hair?" I asked him

"Bit of a hunch and some calculation. I took the departure date from your last email. Tried to get inside your head. I know you like to travel in straight lines so I guessed the train to St. Ives to taste their famous seafood. Not difficult and a bit lucky. If you didn't arrive today, I would have waited for you tomorrow. There are not many buses each day and it's a short walk anywhere in the hamlet." Pointing, he said, "As you can see, four quiet roads converge on the church and pub standing opposite each other. There, you've been introduced to Zennor."

"I don't recall giving you travel dates. I was waiting for your reply. More importantly, this is Dawn Sanderson, or Sandy. She is ok with either."

"Aah, you mentioned you would be travelling with a friend."

"Great to meet you at last, Verne."

"Dawn has read your emails and back home, we've had a few crazy moments in the last few weeks. We've got some stories for you. But what about your hair hanging over your collar? The blond is a surprise - and is that a fleck of ginger?"

"All natural. I blend in better this way," he laughed. "What are these exploits that have pushed Doc Ross, the Predictable, off kilter? I can't wait to hear, but you'd better get settled first. I'll try not to bore you with my stories."

Verne explained that he'd come to an agreement with the local taverner and rented comfortable 'digs' at the pub which he appreciated after roughing it since leaving our city. He recommended a guest house visible up the road, a five minute walk from the centre of the village. We estimated that two hours would give us time to organise everything and recharge before meeting for storytime and good pub food.

"Zennor's small. You won't need a map. Isn't it liberating to be able to see the two-storey church turret from anywhere hereabouts - even when you stand in the village?"

We nodded. Dawn dug her hands into her pockets and stared at the group of houses and said, "It's minute. How many people live here? Two hundred?"

Verne laughed as he added, "Small, indeed. Fewer than that, Dawn. But I have found unimaginable treasures in the tiniest places. That's for later over a pint." He headed down the road towards the pub and we walked with our luggage to the guest house.

"He's exotic," said Dawn. "Matches his name. Straight out of a movie. I can't wait to hear his stories."

I simply nodded in acknowledgement as we covered the ground to the guest house within two minutes. We reserved a single room from the cheerful hostess who offered us an open-ended stay as she didn't have any reservations pending

I was relieved when Dawn admitted that she was a bit weary from the journey and I welcomed her suggestion of "A quick snack and a power nap" which restored our energy. As agreed, within two hours we headed down the road to the Tinners Arms Pub to meet Verne. I had to deliberately slow our pace because Dawn could hardly contain her excitement. When I said, "Why does the pub's name sound so familiar?" she replied:

"Think of your name.

I frowned and Dawn replied, "Mar...Tin...Dale. Maybe there's nothing to it. C'mon. Why are you dragging your feet? Do you think that Verne'll talk openly with me there?"

"Verne's flexible and gregarious. He will be absolutely fine with it. Prepare for a long night, so slow down. He tells stories so that others can feed into them and you may feel that he leaves you circling around in the world of the story he's created. Then later you come to your own conclusions when you least expect it."

Dawn nodded her understanding as I opened the pub door to step into an antique fireside atmosphere. Verne was standing at the bar with a pint of beer on the counter chatting with the barman. Four or five patrons sat at tables around the room in quiet conversation. We had entered a hideaway of solid permanence where the people's faces changed, but the characters remained the same and all through the centuries the inn's wood-paneled and stone walls absorbed the yarns. Verne turned to welcome us and introduce Alf, the publican, whose family had owned the Tinners Arms for generations.

"Glad you could join us here," said Alf, "Verne, you'll probably want to take your companions to your rooms. Let me know if there's anything you need. We'll chat again soon."

Verne led us through corridors into a suite of rooms: a lounge area with an adjoining kitchenette. A dining table took up part of the living room. Doorways signposted two bedrooms and a bathroom. Verne's signature was inscribed on the premises as much as it had been on his townhouse - no more, no less. Three items that accompanied him everywhere he went: his well-traveled backpack settled in a corner, his versatile coat hugged one of the armchairs and his thoroughly thumbed anthology of Hans Christian Andersen's *Fairy Tales and Other Stories* occupied a spot on the table. I never asked him why he was so attached to that book; either the stories gave birth to an ethereal side of his nature or at least nurtured it along the way.

"Welcome to my abode. Take off your coats and make yourselves comfortable. Alf insisted that I should have these quarters so that I'd feel more like a local," Verne said as he moved in front of a painting hanging on the wall. It was by some unknown artist of the area completed several centuries earlier depicting a character in a scene showing that the room we now occupied was once part of the pub. At a quick glance, the character sitting on a bench in the foreground resembled Verne or it was merely a familiar facial expression that reflected a similarity. True to form, Verne had acquired something special - rooms that Alf had not advertised, but kept for family who were always welcome.

Showing his pleasure at seeing us again with a firm handshake followed by Roman-like clasp below my right elbow, he ushered us towards comfortable lounge chairs. His smile took over his whole face as he stood with his back to a wood fire holding a bottle of wine.

His vitality prompted me to say, "You're always in good shape, but I've never seen you this fit, Verne, it's hard to describe… the picture of health…that's you right now."

"I have been walking miles each day for weeks now. I feel completely in tune with everything. It's extraordinary. We have a lot to talk about. This wine is from Moruith's Farm and I think it's going to surprise you."

He was right. Combined with some locally baked bread, the first sip or two delighted and nourished at the same time almost as if it contained the warmth of summer to counter the winter weather. "There's a local surprise in the oven right now. But first, cheers, bottoms up and all that. Let's take a seat here in the comfortable chairs."

"What is this remarkable beverage, Verne? It really does flow through your veins."

"Good. It will help you to accept my story. It's made of local produce from Moruith's Farm; the brew is a family secret."

"What happened when you left the Farm?" I asked as Dawn and I reclined in the comfortable upholstery of the lounge chairs.

Verne sat erect on a pouffe with the painting of the figure on the wooden pub bench as a backdrop. He was ready to tell his story. Following his usual pattern, he faced us, locking us with his eyes, expecting his audience to make mental adjustments to accommodate his tale. He tosses out a few pieces of information to entice his listeners, but then they have to earn more by commenting or questioning as it evolves; they have to prove that they're worthy of the complete yarn. I knew that Dawn had intuited the process.

"I haven't left the Farm," he began with a nod in response to my question followed by a pause as he corrected his seated position and noted our raised eyebrows, "Moruith's Farm has become my inner landscape so my footsteps never leave its fields. When you watch something as violent as the explosion of an atomic bomb on a screen with the sound muted, you know that there's been a complete violation of Nature and nothing could survive anywhere near the mushroom cloud despite the silence. The imagined roar in your ears is louder than anything that could be captured by the most modern technology and the conceived smell of destruction and dust fills your nostrils. You don't have to be physically at the explosion to be certain that you and everything around it would die or be altered forever. I underwent a change of that magnitude at Moruith's Farm when I saw the midwinter sunrise and took part in the celebration and the demonstration that followed. In contrast to the destructive force of an atomic explosion, the sunrise on that day injected me with the constructive power of the universe. I am transformed."

Our attentive expressions gave Verne the signal to continue. "I headed towards the coast on foot. The sun was sparkling on the sea which was particularly blue for that time of the year. I've spent a lot of time around oceans, but I've never seen such a crystal radiance shimmering on its surface;

the shining light gleamed off the waves in golden patterns. The sea sent me a message that it was going to offer up the fulfillment that I am seeking. I would not have been able to interpret those marine signals before my mutation at Moruith's Farm; my search became more focused because of what I learned there.

"I'm going to share the event at the farm with you in full, but first you have to understand my transformation. I am liberated from my quest for land around the world. I'm free in a way I never imagined possible. Do you recall I wrote about emerging from a cocoon in the morning after sleeping at Chysauster? I think it started then, but my passage through Moruith's Farm was a metamorphosis. I know now that chasing after land never offered freedom. In fact that pursuit was the exact opposite. I've found freedom within something. Can you believe that?

Verne earnestly searched our faces for signs that we were in sync with him. Dawn smiled as I dug into my jeans pocket to extract Verne's USB stick as I said, "More than you expect. This may surprise you."

"You brought it." Verne beamed.

Dawn explained how I had recorded everything that had happened in detail and included a synopsis of the mystery surrounding Askuwheteau. All the while Verne nodded his understanding with no hint of surprise until Dawn asked, "Did you leave it on the couch on purpose or did it... creep out of your pocket that night?"

Verne's eyes widened slightly and a hint of a smile of appreciation of Dawn's insight played around the corners of his mouth as he answered, "A bit of both. Of course, by then, I knew that Ross was the Chronicler."

"Dawn's an expert on traditional structures and how they are embedded in our world today. Did you know that the stick instructed me to keep a record of things that happened in my life?" I asked.

"Not that it would be you, Ross. I made some predictions to myself about who of us would take on different roles before we played 'Genesis.' I didn't know. On reflection, these changes in my identity might have begun back then.

Anyway, the dinner smells like it has gone through enough of a change. Let's fill our glasses and eat."

We sat at the table, Verne raised his glass and said, "Here's to discovering the weird."

They both laughed when I said, "Normal is weird enough for me."

Dawn looked at Verne and said, "Have we passed the test? Are we ready for the next installment?"

Chapter Twenty One

Verne responded with a question: "Do you believe that seemingly inanimate objects can conceal themselves and stay hidden if they don't want to be found?"

"Sometimes it seems that way - especially when I'm looking for something that I've put in a safe place. A few days ago I was looking for my phone charger - my cell was out of power - and I wanted to phone Dawn to cancel this trip, but I couldn't find it because I'd left it in the socket I'd used last. At the time I thought that it was a temporary blip of memory. By the time I found it, my anxiety had passed." Dawn looked at me quizzically, words being unnecessary. "The crazy thought snuck into my mind at the time that with all the bizarre things that had happened, I was being manipulated by things around me in a direction that I wouldn't normally choose. I didn't lose sleep about it. But now that you mention it..."

Verne nodded, taking in what I had intended as a light aside and dismissal of his question. He rose to check on the dinner in the kitchen. After a pause that was longer than expected, he commented. "I suppose you think that was a coincidence?"

"Of course. What else could it be?"

Verne shrugged, "Good question. I do know that 'coincidence' is too shallow an explanation at times.

"As I said, the Farm is inside me and I see things differently from before that visit. The particles of my being have been rearranged to integrate with Nature hereabouts at the deepest level, at a cellular level. I cannot divorce myself from this soil, this ground and all that is around this place without a physical wrench."

"Can we stay with the normal for now?" I said.

Verne removed the food from the oven, carried it to the dining area and placed three large pies on the table.

"Looks interesting, Verne," I said.

"You don't know what they are, do you Dr. Martindale," said Dawn with a sparkle in her eyes, clearly sharing a joke with Verne at my expense.

"They're pies," I said.

Both of them laughed and Dawn picked up her knife, tapped the pastry firmly and said, "Do you think they'll survive being thrown down the mine, Verne?"

I was no longer surprised by Dawn's store of knowledge, but Verne surveyed her extensively and quickly with his eyes. A smile broke out on his face as he said, "A real treasure in a small place. I told you. You are perceptive, Dawn."

He winked at Dawn, turned towards me and said, "Let's toast to finding treasures." The two of them couldn't help laughing again at my confusion.

Dawn explained, "These are called Cornish Pasties, Ross. The tin miners' wives hereabouts took them to their husbands at lunchtime and the joke is that they had to be able to survive being tossed down the mine shaft."

"Alf's wife - you know Alf the taverner - she showed me how to make them in the traditional style. It's a recipe and method passed down in her family for generations. It's a complete meal inside pastry. And there's only one way to test them," said Verne as he placed one on each of our plates, picked up his knife and cut into the pie in front of him.

The aroma of meat and potatoes filled the air and I said, "This smells normal enough for me."

"And so it is, Ross, but I've had to dig deeper. I wouldn't have believed it before Moruith's Farm opened my mind to a depth of Nature that is only visible under certain conditions. It's always there, but to discern it, everything has to align. We are part of Nature, so why wouldn't we be able to hear its voice, see its signs and understand its messages? Do we fear Nature because it threatens us with ultimate removal from what we know? Do we shove Nature into the background? Try to set ourselves apart from its awesome power and baleful embrace? You know, like energy - it doesn't disappear - it transforms from one form to another, from kinetic to potential energy; on occasion it goes nuclear. We give Energy and Nature names to make it comfortable for ourselves: Mother Nature, the Natural world. We are only another element of Nature. Do we also just change our form: birth, maturation, death? Humans like to be hopeful.

"When I reached the sea that day and sat on the cliff, I heard the song of the sea. Distinctly. I've heard it before as an attraction, something pulling me away from the shore, even stories for those who pause to listen. This was different; as the reflected hues turned from gold to various shades of red and the ocean music played a tranquil tune in my head I understood that I was in my particular place. Most of the time for us that music of the spheres is so attenuated we don't even hear a whisper. That day it was at full volume. I could decipher the message glittering off the white spray of the waves and repeated in the sound of the waves crashing on the shore. It promised me that "A treasure was waiting close by and that I should not be afraid to take it."

Verne seduced us into his story. He infused what we consider normal with a vibrancy and a novelty that shifted the picture in its standard frame. He introduced the abnormal with new perspectives that blended with ordinary vision until we were immersed in another world that blurred reality and fantasy.

I did resist a little, by saying, "Verne, it's good to find a special place. Now all you need is your special person. Promised? Aren't you taking this a bit far? Another bottle of this good stuff might help me swallow the story?"

We had started eating slowly. Verne walked over to the kitchen to fetch a bottle to replenish our drinks and said, "I wouldn't have been able to see in this way without my transformation at Moruith's Farm. Physical sight is expanded by what we learn. If you let the learning guide you instead of trying to consume knowledge, you may find that insight blends with eyesight. I wouldn't have come this way unless Old Man Pender had directed me. And, yes, maybe my anticipation conjured a vision. But I believe it was my experience at

Moruith's that altered my vision, deepened my perception, even transformed my being. Anyway, it was pivotal."

"This food is delicious, Verne," I interrupted his flow.

"I've never tasted anything this good," echoed Dawn. "Somehow the vegetables and meat seem to blend together to improve each other."

"Thanks. It's not that difficult."

Dawn leaned forward towards Verne and said, "But I want to hear more about the Farm."

"OK. Back to your phone and charger, Ross. I know where you plug it in; you probably walked past that charge cord a couple of times before you saw it. Why? You think that it's just you being careless. Could there be more to it? I know you're not convinced, but just accept for now, for the story, that you simply would never be able to find Moruith's Farm unless those who live there intended it. You could say that I chanced upon it, but I now believe that all concerned wanted me to find it. Dawn...Ross...it's not marked on the map, but I spent several days there. I don't know exactly how long I was there. I thought that I was keeping track, but now I'm no longer sure."

"Come on, Verne, it's only a farm. It won't be on the map"

"With modern technology we can find anything. In this case, it doesn't show up. I've tried using my computer - various programmes. It's not on paper maps and the infallible source - the locals - they've never heard of the place."

"Well, what of it? Maybe it's a different name, maybe marked as something else."

"You're right. It's open country. Ross, as far as everyone is concerned, Moruith's Farm doesn't exist. Would you like to know what really happened at the Farm?"

Dawn helped us by saying, "Ross, you have to let go of those rigid borders in your mind if you want to understand new realms. Remember Askuvie's place. Not so different. I couldn't find Askuwheteau's land either." She placed both hands firmly on the table and lifted slightly off her seat. Total engagement and excitement inflamed her eyes as she said, "Of course we want to know everything that took place there, Verne."

Relaxing back in her chair, she added, "Verne, if we have time tonight, we will tell you what happened to us back on the prairies. I've a feeling there's going to be a strong similarity. It's all on the stick if we don't get to it."

Verne raised his eyebrows slightly in response. I said, "Askuwheteau is a long story. We've traveled thousands of miles to hear what happened at the Farm. I won't interrupt again."

Verne nodded gently several times to Dawn, acknowledging her intervention and that they were on the same wavelength when it came to handling their pedestrian, less imaginative companion. He continued, "As I told you in the email, when I arrived at the stone circle on the farm, people formed a second circle within the ring of stones and my place in the west was vacant. All were essential participants in what followed; as a group they had a role to play, especially on the second day. They were like a Greek chorus, commenting on the plot and even moving the action forward.

"And now I must be careful how I describe the part I dared not write. Every year on the day after the winter solstice, the family convenes to reenact the founding of the community and reaffirm their right to the land. Their claim is absolute. It's not a vague notion or even a flimsy piece of paper. Their claim is based on the bones and dust of their ancestors buried on the spot, generation after generation, century following century, eon capping eon. They will not leave the Farm; they cannot because they are biologically attached to the ground, their ancestors and the past."

I turned towards Dawn to see whether I could detect on her face the disbelief I was feeling. Instead she said softly, "How did you get so close, Verne? How could you be part of it?"

"I believe that I was brought there. Like I said, you cannot find the place even if you try. I am part of it and I'm on a mission, sent to find something irreplaceable. The ocean encoded my destiny in its molecules, and announced it to me."

"The universal fire," whispered Dawn, "Askuwheteau was rooted in the same way as those at Moruith's."

My face must have betrayed my skepticism, because Verne became more emphatic. "Ross, I knew that you'd find this difficult," he said, "But soften those borders of your mind and let the story take over." We'd finished eating and rose to return to the easy chairs with Verne perched erect on the pouffe. He continued, "We were all seated in the circle and Moruith began by tapping her hands on the ground. All followed her lead and it intensified. It was easy for me to join in like this." Verne began beating the sides of the pouffe with regularity to draw Dawn and me into the scene. Dawn picked up on the beat with both hands on the arms of her chair. Awkwardly, I joined the rhythm. And, nodding his head in time with the beat, Verne said, "The chant, the prayer, the request began. The group, the chorus, made things happen. It went like this. 'Restore our souls with the truth of the past, the present, the future. Show the truth. Show the truth. Show the truth. Heal our weary souls.' There were more words repeated over and over and they seemed familiar though they were sung in what I think was a Celtic sounding language. After about ten minutes of singing and chanting, there was movement around the stones behind us." Verne rested his hands as a signal to Dawn and me and said, "Sitting in the circle, we called on our patriarchs and matriarchs to return to restore our faith in a show of the true story."

Verne paused to let his words penetrate, took a sip of his wine, and continued, "On the opposite side of the circle, figures appeared from the shadows of the stones. Perhaps they were actors coming from behind the stones, but in a way, those shapes seemed to morph out of the rocks, summoned by the chorus.

"They moved to the centre of the circle and began to reenact the one true version of the establishment of the community. It was an enactment of the story that Moruith told me the night that I arrived at the farmhouse. It started with the arrival of the family in the valley, but it seemed as if it was happening right there and then for the first time; that they weren't actors, but the first generation, the founders themselves, conducting their lives in front of us."

Verne broke the tension by sitting back and asking, "You'll probably think that I've lost my mind when I say that I may have been the only one in the circle who made the connection with Chysauster - Carenza, her Roman and her sons. However, that knowledge may be why I've been given the special task. What do you think?"

Dawn detected a twitch on the side of my mouth and, before I could spoil things, she said, "Verne, we haven't traveled all this way to judge you. It's fascinating. Don't stop."

Reassured, Verne continued, "A Passion play is the closest thing you'd have seen to anything like this. The actors assume the nature, the character and being of the original founders. Each year the players are carefully selected by Moruith and one other unnamed person. Once they are chosen, they retreat from the community to live apart for a whole year in preparation for the performance. They spend the year as a small, separate group, in a modified excommunication, but not in solitude, because they have each other's company. It's a sort of rite of passage. The actors know that they will make the sacrifice of exclusion for a year when it is their turn. It's not a penalty or persecution; it's to keep the balance, I'm told.

"By the end of the year, all members of the Farm community are desperate to see the reenactment again and how the selected actors have grown into the characters. That shared emotion may be partly what generates the tangible energy for the play in the stone circle.

"The energy took us beyond the level and intensity of a Passion Play. It's about the past, but it felt like it was happening for the first time, like it was immediate. And, without exaggeration, the players seemed like the real people in the story, not actors; that what was happening in front of our eyes was the event. We were transported in time, not just in our minds, but bodily, with every sense.

"They adhere to a set unwritten script that has been passed from generation to generation. Children start to learn the story that I saw played out from the time they first see the enactment; they learn by absorption, not a conscious rote learning, but even when they are very young, they know it by heart.

"The story started with a journey of the young family through the Cornish countryside in a time which predated the history of the area written by those who lived here. (We've got a Roman version). When the family reached the site of

Moruith's Farm, the sun broke through the clouds to illuminate a crop of berries, mushrooms and a water supply to show that this was the precise place where they should settle and remain - 'for all time.' The chorus in the circle softly intoned a song of praise and gratitude that the journey had come to an end and that it would give rise to a new community which would forever recognise the event. In the song they promised to mark the day of arrival each year on the day following winter solstice. That day is chosen because it is at that precise moment that the earth pivots and there is a chance for us to reunite with Nature in a deep and profound way. I didn't know the words of the song, but the tune was familiar.

"In what seemed like a whirl of snowflakes, a new figure appeared from the rocks. If I had been closer, I could have been sure, but from where I was sitting, I could have sworn it was Cador, you know, from Chysauster."

"Unforgettable. I'd like to hear more about that too," I said.

"Later. Some of his story at Chysauster bothers me now because he spoke as if he never left the place and he didn't know what had happened to Carenza. Now, I can't quite trust Cador. Of course I can't be sure that either Carenza and the founder of Moruith's are one and the same or it was Cador at Moruith's. I think Cador was telling me enough so that I'd make my own connections. And, I still don't know if Cador was a guide or player-actor." Verne took a sip from his glass to refresh and continued, "Back to the play. That new figure brought warnings and a prophecy that all could not continue in the same way because the Roman, the father figure, was tainted by the stain of human blood from his past. This paradise was to be free from the blight of blood - human blood shed in anger - and had to remain so for its continued existence. The Cador-like figure ended with a command that seemed to contradict his warning: he insisted that the only time human blood should be deliberately spilled at Moruith's was on a particular day to keep the order of things. I don't understand what he meant yet.

The next scenes were fraught with indecision and discord until the father made the unilateral decision to leave -

a fate more severe than death - to leave his family - for them to continue to live in a paradise that he had founded.

The next part of the play or enactment was very confusing. In a blur of figures, the mother and eldest son became increasingly affectionate until they seemed to merge into one in a carnal scene with the most balletic movements you have ever witnessed. Have you seen "Pas de Deux" by Norman McLaren? You're Canadian - you must have…"

I shook my head while Dawn nodded in understanding.

"You must as soon as possible, Ross. McLaren drew each frame on the celluloid. It's one of Canada's greatest contributions to the art world. Well if you watch that and then imagine seeing it in real, three-D format with live dancers in front of you, you'll have an inkling of an idea of what I'm talking about. In fact, when you see the striated effect of McLaren's film, you'll understand what that whole event looked like for me. Ethereal, but possible.

In a brilliant artistic performance of love-making, son and mother embraced and became totally intertwined. Our natural response is to condemn incestuous sex. No, it was magnificent. In fact it was an apotheosis of the two characters as the chorus, our circle, rejoiced in the consecration of their founders' relationship. The community drew strength from the reenactment. The community at Moruith's Farm is based upon a principle of open-fields: no fences, no barriers are allowed between any members of the family; yet the whole thing is contained within wider boundaries. They're all entitled to the full expanse of the land on the Farm; it's exclusive and inclusive at the same time. They're free, but only as long as they follow the established rules, practicing rituals and blood rites within the agreed upon boundaries. Their own law is effective within the confines of Moruith's Farm. There, I experienced freedom and felt authentic. It's not that kind of freedom about having given up all worldly possessions."

I laughed, "Verne, all your worldly possessions are in that one bag over there - and plots of land dotted around the world. No one travels lighter than you.

"Ross, it's biological and beyond...like there is something very precious to lose. Their freedom is a treasure; it's guarded, almost worshipped and constantly rekindled through things like the regeneration play I described. It's not freedom for everyone, but it is for me and that's one reason that I find it distressing not to be able to find the Farm again." A smile flashed across Verne's face and he developed an idea as he spoke, "Maybe. Yes, maybe... If I find the thing that is missing...whatever it is...I'll be able to go back to the Farm."

"Verne, that goes against all science and philosophy. It can only lead to disaster. As a species, we are meant to integrate with others. You're talking about pure inbreeding."

"You're only staring at one piece. You have to look at the whole thing. If you meet them, you would see that they are just as normal as anyone else you've met. There's some way that they bring in enough difference to strengthen the lineage...the core. I don't know what it is. This foundation story is fundamental to them keeping possession of their land and the laws that govern their lives. They have never given up any of their land to another tribe, group, clan or authority. The land remains in their hands; they practice their specific customs found nowhere else. At the end of the play, the figure that reminded me of Cador closed it with a call to 'Keep the Balance for all time and celebrate equilibrium on the right day'.

"The weirdest part of the whole thing took place at the party afterwards. I hoped to meet the actors, especially the one I thought could have been Cador. They weren't there. I asked various family members and they claimed that the actors never attended this function even though their roles were over. Everyone insisted on the same thing - that it would break the magic, refute the charm, perhaps even interfere with good fortune for the coming year."

"There's not much unusual about that. We still have quaint customs around theatre even in this century," I interjected.

"Agreed. So I asked about people who had played the parts in previous years because I wanted to hear how they experienced the role and what it feels like to take on a different character, identity, for such a long time in preparation."

"And…"

"And everyone I asked said that they couldn't remember. Claimed that many had. I asked whether they had played the roles and, you guessed it."

"None of them had."

"Correct.

"I can't answer your next questions. They're probably the same as mine. Anyway, towards the end of the performance of the play things took an even stranger turn. The chorus around the actors began a clapping, chanting and rhythmic beat, faster and faster and as they gained in volume and speed. There was a light dusting of snow on the ground and in the centre it started to melt and the ground itself glowed orange like the sun. As I said, the light plays tricks. Then Moruith approached me and led me to the centre and incorporated me with the son and mother. The chorus hushed and Moruith gave me direction: she had me repeat a pledge to seek, discover and return a missing element - reunite to ensure the continuance of the Farm."

"That sounds outrageously weird, Verne. You can't take it seriously."

"With what I've felt and seen since arriving in England, and Cornwall in particular, I can't distinguish any more. I certainly don't dismiss things like that easily. Especially when Pender gave me explicit instructions at the party."

Dawn broke her silence to say, "Ross and I have had some similar uncanny experiences recently. The long story is on the USB stick and we couldn't start that now. I want to think about all you've told us."

I spoke my mind: "All I can say is that this whole business doesn't sound very inclusive. It's an amazing story of course and what an adventure. You were privileged to see it - be part of it. The only reason that you are prepared to accept it, though, is that you were included. It's like a cult. You said that it can't be found. It's dangerous, Verne."

"Not if you're part of it."

"How can a community that tries to exist without interacting with any other part of the world be normal, good?" But I moderated at a nudge from Dawn, "I'll have to think about it. Perhaps in the morning - or later today - it's well past midnight - things will be clearer. I'm just very skeptical and I hope that you aren't considering going back there."

"Not likely. I can't work out what I would 'bring back' as Moruith instructed. Besides, as I said, I wouldn't be able to find the place again. It has crossed my mind that some of those experiences took place partly in my imagination."

Dawn replied, "It's not simply your fantasy, Verne. You may be recreating it now, but I think the basis is sound. Practically, though, how do they keep this place to themselves? It's in the middle of England. It's not a desert or forest."

"That's baffling for sure, Dawn. As I said, it's invisible or just unrecorded, unregistered."

"We've seen that before, Verne," Dawn turned to me for confirmation, "There has to be absolute cooperation to keep a low profile. But how is that done?"

Verne was ready with an answer: "A lot of it has to do with Moruith: she holds everyone together and she did say to me that the time for head on confrontation passed a long time ago - that it's better to work in less direct ways. Moruith draws on a truth or strength that has survived for so long that no challenge is new; as she interacts with the others she dispenses that power and wisdom. She did it with me from the moment I stepped through her doorway."

I admit that I hadn't overcome my suspicion or skepticism (or my science training kicked in), so I asked, "Why would anyone, people, do that in the first place? What's to be gained by avoiding the convenience of modern life? What's there to be afraid of?"

"Depends what you're looking for, Ross," replied Dawn, "It's not a fear. There's an intelligence, a wisdom that's been lost in the modern era. Maybe not entirely lost. It's trite to call it an alternative lifestyle. No, it's more like a different approach to land ownership. But to live that way they have to stay completely low profile. Is there something similar to the way Askuwheteau saw the world? Was he killed because he became too visible? Something like that. What's the cost of being out of time? How do they keep the balance you were talking about, Verne?"

"This is all too unsettling," I conceded, "Perhaps you're both looking for more than necessary. It's just some whacko group that wants attention."

"Ross, by now you should be more open.You've seen things that defy superficial explanation. They're avoiding attention. What bothers me comes out of something you said, Verne. Is there a price to pay for being out of time with modernity? How do they keep the balance they mentioned? Why are these shadows flickering now? And why are we being given glimpses of them?"

"Way too tough, Dawn, but I have lost my obsession with owning land all over the world," replied Verne. "Anyway, on Sunday we should go to the local church to get a sense of how the modern people of Zennor and hereabouts relate to their spiritual world"

"Church. That's not something you normally do. Why now?" I asked.

With a shrug, he said, "The stones, circles, the Farm, church: they're all mixed together here. Perhaps it's where the patterns and rules we still live by really come from. At least church is the one icon that we can understand a bit better than the others. We can only try."

A bit flippantly I probed, "What about Cador? You haven't told us whether he is an actor or a character tripping around in your imagination. I'm almost scared to hear the answer."

"You are persistent, Ross," Verne laughed somewhat nervously, I thought. He stood up from the pouffe and said, "He pops up unexpectedly. I wouldn't be surprised if he was waiting at the door right now. Perhaps we'll meet him at the church on Sunday. Let's leave that one for now; it's a good time to call it a night."

Dawn and I stood up, pulled on our coats and Verne escorted us to his private entrance. "Sleep well" he said, "Perhaps we can figure it out together."

Chapter Twenty Two

Walking back to our B & B, Dawn broke the silence. "Verne has interesting eyes: they sparkle with old wisdom. His eyes add an essential nuance to his story; a slight narrowing provides a cue when to believe him and when not. What a story, though."

Dawn was thoughtful. Then, almost debating with herself, said, "If he has come across an outlandish cult, it's way out on the spectrum of unusual - on the one hand. But on the other...those who live at Moruith's Farm might believe that their community is founded on a history that could have happened. I don't know Verne well yet so it's hard to say whether he is giving meaning to something because he wants to find it, or he's accurately recounting things that really happened in front of his eyes. One thing's certain, he has a special genius for bringing the abstract to life. It's like a power that flows through him."

I nodded, "Undoubtedly. He has exceptional potential in so many areas. He can be the most pragmatic person you have ever met. It shows in his business track record. On the other hand, as you know from the game he invented, he has artistic flair - like a special connection with the mystical world. I guess you'd figured that out for yourself."

Sandy tilted her head in reply.

"I think he may be struggling with those two sides of his personality. I'll head over there first thing tomorrow and ask him about his personal conflict. That may help. I am a bit worried about him. He is on the crazy spectrum. You can't ignore that."

"We're all on that continuum. He's in a different spot from most of us. He's also so marvelously grounded that he can play around and test his own beliefs. Practical and artistic aren't necessarily divorced from each other. But you should satisfy yourself.

"I've worked with groups outside mainstream modern culture - cults - sometimes with Indigenous groups. I've read about all those groups and often got in close, but not as close as Verne did at Moruith's Farm. I've infiltrated cults - mind-blowing stuff. I only visited Indigenous groups by invitation. I don't understand any of them like an insider, but one thing I've noticed is that even while they're out of the mainstream they are still part of modern life. They're peripheral, not severed from it."

"There are things I have to learn about you. But, anyway…"

Dawn continued, "Yes, Verne's account sounds more like the Indigenous side of things…I was thinking…no, that would be impossible. In the middle of England?"

"By now we know, nothing's impossible, maybe improbable. What are you thinking?" I asked.

"Well, what if there is a group - with ancient ties - that has kept strictly to itself over hundreds…thousands of years…classifications like 'Indigenous'… 'tribal'…some words not so acceptable today come to mind…?" Dawn was searching for a way to express her thoughts while my own were tumbling around. With a slight shake of her head, she mused, "What if this is an extreme form of Celtic resurrection? Or something that's never been extinguished? The dedication of those at Moruith's is beyond an interest in an ancient language or ritual. Their passion and fight to keep an ancient practice alive, springs from a conviction that there is a special knowledge… Ross, you must see the similarity with what we experienced through Askuwheteau. Wherever you go on the planet, there's always something in the history of any particular place that fits into the category of 'Indigenous' though it may be denied."

"You're right. That's absurd in today's world."

"More absurd than Askuvie's backyard? More absurd than the latest discoveries in science that are often scuttled by big bucks interest groups?"

Dawn had a way of shocking me out of my complacency, "I think that we have to start with Verne. I'll talk with him in the morning about his psychological state."

"You do that. See if you can put him into one of your neat boxes - a psychological category. Good luck."

"You always spin me around to look at my own thoughts and ideas more carefully. I'll give it a try anyway. It's late. Let's get some real sleep."

Chapter Twenty Three

When I returned from my early morning chat with Verne, Dawn was sitting next to the window in the sunshine with English muffins and coffee on the table. The host had allowed her to bring breakfast to the room as there were no other guests in the house. Recently showered, her fresh scent filled the room and her glossy black hair falling over her athletic shoulders filled me with a joy that was hard to describe. All I could do was smile and say, "Morning Dawn, looks like you've got our hostess where you want her." It had nothing to do with my depth of feeling for this wonderful person with whom I was sharing such mysterious encounters. My comment belied my admiration for her brilliant interpretations about the Askuwheteau affair and Verne's exploits; it concealed my appreciation for her ability to enable me to overcome my physical and social awkwardness; and avoided mention of that warmth I felt when in physical contact with her. I wanted to say something much more flattering and affectionate, but as Dawn had said in London, "She had a lot of work to do," and that included getting me to express my emotions.

In response she said, "Just enjoy it. You need something substantial to keep that beautiful, bulky body of yours on the move." She changed topics, "It's Saturday, but I have an urge to walk to the church today to see the 'dead centre' of town," and with a pause, "I know, an old one, but very true in such a small place as this."

"Witty works every time. Who knows what treasure we'll find there?"

I relished each mouthful of the best breakfast I've ever tasted because of the splendid view from the upstairs window, or sharing the food with Dawn.

As we set out around noon, there were signs that winter was losing its grip over the landscape. The late winter sun had already melted the dusting of snow on our path and the trickling sound was an accompaniment to the shining evidence of melting on little pools of water off our path. It struck me how extraordinary it was how my life had suddenly taken a drastic change and was accompanied by happiness. The two-storey church stood proudly dominating the hamlet and the single road led in one direction. Our destination was clear; we could not get lost.

"Dawn, how could we have imagined that two successful city slickers who didn't know each other a few weeks ago would leave their comfortable North American homes and be walking together in the ancient Celtic countryside. This is the place that inspired some of the best stories we heard growing up?"

"I've wondered about it too and I'm happy and content about it."

"What a relief to hear you say so - it's mutual," I said, hoping for more than 'happy and content.'

"I was always busy, ridiculously, overwhelmingly busy, but I feel like a gap, a void, in my life has been filled."

"Work swamped everything. I understand what you are saying. Now there is time to look around at the world with more appreciation. That happiness has a lot to do with you, Dawn. All this would be meaningless without you."

That special, radiant smile spread over Dawn's face, then clouded over as she said, "Happiness can just as easily be removed. Is the happiness about us being together or being in this spot in the world?"

"Depends who you ask," I hesitated, looked firmly at the church turret and continued, "Verne may say that it's the 'particular place'. My answer would be different."

Her special smile returned and she said, "How did your conversation go with him this morning?"

I saw that she was genuine and not trying to prove a point so I said, "He is uneasy, though he claims he is where he is supposed to be. OK, you were right. He's not on the edge in the sense that he's suicidal or about to fall into some sort of dark pit of craziness."

"I didn't think so."

"He did say that he was glad to be rid of his land ownership obsession, but he felt adrift without a goal. He knows that he can't buy land at Chysauster and Moruith's Farm is elusive - he's not sure whether he can ever be part of that community. He's trying to fill a void in his life like you just said about yourself. He explained it more vividly with better word choice. It's his journey. Not mine."

"His artistic tendency feeds his practical nature." Dawn couldn't resist a dig, saying, "So, is he paranoid or schizoid?"

"No, he's fine. Let's just take him as part of the landscape."

"Agreed. On the other hand, I've been thinking about the deeper aspects of Verne's tales. Funny, that now we are here, I can't get Askuwheteau out of my mind. He was also connected to the land, like Verne thinks he is here - and at Moruith's farm."

"And does that connection give stability beyond relationships with people?" I answered. "You always hear, 'Home is where the heart is' thrown around. It was originally 'Hearth'. I don't know why it changed, but 'Home' should have a depth to it. You can't just carry the "Hearth" around with you like you can your "Heart," although we live in this mobile age. 'Hearth' has more stability, but less portability."

"It's a sad piece of our time. It's both as you say: 'Heart' and 'Hearth,' I suppose you can carry your hearth in your heart. You have to rebuild the hearth wherever you land. Home is more, as you say - and like Verne has talked about - it's not just the place. The people fit into the picture. It's also the food, the memories and the stories that are part of any place. Those myths and legends explain a place; stories coming out of a place take hundreds, thousands of years to develop and you can't just make them up; they have to be part of the soil, the vegetation, the air. And they sound more authentic when you hear them in their place of origin. Yes, as Verne says, when you can see the particles."

We walked in silence for a few paces watching for icy patches or divots in the road. Dawn lifted her head and said, "The church seems so big. The pods of snow in the fields and the robin or two give me the feeling that I'm in a story from my childhood. Like a CS Lewis story or something like that."

"The church turret reminds me of a rook on a chessboard," I added.

At the edge of the church property Dawn concluded, "I've never been here, but there's something comforting about the whole scene. We're a long way from home. Why does it all feel so familiar?"

"Don't get too carried away," I said. "I'll think that you've caught something from Verne."

Dawn chuckled, but continued, "You can 'call' a place 'Home.' Doing that may bring hope and comfort, but if we keep analysing the word and the concept, there's far more to it."

"I'll think about it. Too deep for a short walk. I guess everything's a short walk in Zennor. Funny that the first stone we should see is … you don't know Verne's last name, that's it," I said, pointing to the stone in the entrance.

"I didn't, but the one next to it is the same name, and those other two. It must have been a family thing. And over there, the same name. Everywhere you look the same last name - or versions of it. Speaking of 'Home.' There must be twenty."

"At least," came another voice from the side of the church. "The same surname - as they say here - that's not counting the variations."

Till then we hadn't noticed Verne standing in the shadow of the church's wall. He was clearly overcome with the magnitude of the situation in a little country churchyard.

"That's only the last 300 years. Those are just the marked graves - with stones above the ground. This one here died in 1743. He missed American Independence and the French Revolution. There'll be many more beneath the surface. It is overwhelming. I feel like they're trying to tell me something important. This must be why Old Man Pender told me to visit Zennor. He and Moruith said it would be obvious."

"Hi Verne. You blend in well. We could've mistaken you for part of the old building," I said.

More sympathetically, Dawn picked up on his mood, "Hullo, Verne, you gave us a lot to think about last night. Wasn't easy to fall asleep." With a wave of her hand, she added, "A dead cert, if you ask me."

Verne laughed, "Well, it certainly takes away that edge of trying to fit in, but I'm not sure if I want to slip into mine right away. On the other hand, yes, I suppose it's a pretty clear statement that I belong here and it is carved in stone."

We laughed. Then, Verne, voicing his own reflections, expressed doubt about whether he could adapt to a place which was so isolated as he was far more accustomed to modern cities and larger numbers of people.

He added, "But, as I've said before, I feel as if I've reached a resting place - not altogether ready for extreme downtime," he said, pointing toward the graves. "I still have a desire and energy to be exploring opportunities and maximising the time I have to find out new things. That urgency is more focused in a good way. When I discover something new it brings deeper understanding. It's different. I don't have to collect things - land - in the same way. I can just let it all pass through me." Without rebuke, she said, "Verne, you should simply enjoy your time here, not resist it."

"I would if this comfort wasn't cloying at the same time. It's as if I'm being dragged down by the nature of the place; sucked into a hole or bog that cuts off my oxygen, snuffed out, soggy. At the same time, I'm happy."

"You'll get over it. Maybe the cold weather has something to do with your mood. Just don't get stuck in one of those ruts yet," said Dawn, pointing towards the graves.

"No, outside weather never bothers me. I'm not self-destructive. Don't worry about that."

Moving out of earshot of their conversation, I meandered through the graves and came upon a large, light coloured stone monument, higher than my head, marking one of the graves. It might have once been ornate, but it was so old that the engraving had disappeared; the corrugations on the surface, once words, were illegible and could not even be deciphered with the most up to date methods. We would never know who lay beneath this pretentious attempt by some ancient mortal to mark his or her grave. The stone was faceless, like the remains of the human underneath who would be forever anonymous unless there was some old church record of his life.

Inexplicably, my thoughts flashed to Askuwheteau who, like this memorial stone, had been defaced by his attackers. In his death he too was faceless. I wondered whether removal of his facial features eliminated his identity and whether the stories that he had told me in his sanctuary would be lost forever. Staring at that nameless edifice, it struck me that the stories we hear and tell, grow and swell as the authors acquire anonymity; that there were countless humans with their stories beneath the ground where I stood. It was not tragic or even sad; it was a revelation that we can only tell our stories today because of the magical tales that our forefathers have left us. Their yarns and endeavours have endowed us - layer upon corporeal layer - with the ability to tell stories and leave something to our own descendents. Even the art of using the format of a story is an ancient inheritance. We have the opportunity to forge our own link in the unbroken chain of narration so that all who participate become immortalised. Would we recognise those storybook characters if they were to come to life in some new form or other? That ancient gravestone prized my mind open to give Verne's stories more traction.

Verne called, interrupting my thoughts. When I reached my friends, Dawn was at the church door, testing the large knob, "C'mon, Verne, let's see if there are any more of your people inside." She laughed, "They may be more communicative."

Dawn swung the unlocked door open and we followed her inside the small country church where the tranquil, spiritual atmosphere was palpable. The afternoon sun shining through a stained glass window with only two figures and few colours in the design created a pool of light on the opposite side of the nave. And there she was. We halted to take in a wonder of Nature sitting in pensive meditation on an old wooden bench in an alcove off the main seating. An exquisite woman sat in the pool of sunshine. If the greatest artist of all time had painted this figure he would have not been able to capture its perfection. She 'beggar'd all description' is the only way I can put it.

Dawn and I glanced at Verne. He was still transfixed and his body quivered. The incarnation of dreams, glowing in the sunlight, rose from the bench. She crossed the nave adorned with a golden aura of sunshine that spread to Verne's body. He was enchanted from that moment; and so was she. If I were more imaginative, I would say that invisible hands impelled them toward each other. As they drew closer their bodies radiated something that seemed to pull them together; they vibrated as an irresistible magnetic force surged between them. Their eyes spoke to each other in a way that can never be translated into language and their silhouettes formed the complementary contours of a two-piece puzzle.

From ten metres away, amazed (and with respect), Dawn and I witnessed the union. The two remained in profile with the sunlight endorsing every move. Slowly and deliberately Verne reached into his backpack, withdrew his hand, and offered an outstretched palm. She stared intently at his open hand. Then she looked up and their eyes locked again as she reached into his hand, picked up something and lifted her own to her ear. Verne gazed at her for a few moments, then nodded approval. She was holding his earring; she lowered her hand from her ear and returned the jewelry to Verne's hand. They were mere inches apart and he held the earring between their faces. As he looked directly into her eyes, he whispered words of a sentence that we couldn't distinguish except for his last word, "pledge," which made her glow even more brightly - if that was possible. With ritual care, he affixed the earring to her ear nearest us.

She turned to face us, realising that there were others in the church, and it was then that we saw the whole picture.

The radiance of her face was bracketed by matching earrings. Hand in hand they approached us, moving out of the sunshine into the shadow in the church, with the solar glow blessing their union. Months of planning a ceremony couldn't have equaled the spontaneous splendour of the moment, ordained by Nature, that took place in front of us.

"Kensa, meet my friends, Ross and Dawn."

The couple were dazzling; Verne spoke those words with such ease and normalcy that we simply focused on the visible detail. I said, "Your earrings look like an absolute match. Verne didn't show us the one he found. Do you mind if I look closer?"

Kensa removed them from her ears and placed them in Verne's hand. He pointed at them and said, "Look closely. They're a matching pair for sure. There are identical markings on the inside, perhaps, the signature of the artist."

Dawn had a special interest in ancient jewelry and when she examined them more closely, she said, "It's rare to find ornamental jewelry like this here in Britain like Verne did.

They were definitely made in exactly the same forge. Where did you get yours, Kensa?"

"I've had it forever"

"Do you know where Verne found his?"

"In the Old Place, I suspect. I was never sure where I'd left it."

Verne confirmed, "It was stuck in a crevice next to a doorway."

Dawn pursued her earlier line of thought, "Jewelry like this would more likely surface in Italy...places where Romans lived more settled lives...not just conquerors. This would likely be a gift from a Roman to a special person."

"Well, it probably was," smiled Kensa. "Verne just gave it to me. You must have traveled a lot, Dawn. I admire those who explore that way. I've spent all my time in this land, though I've heard about some other areas."

"I haven't actually traveled that much; I want to, but I have studied Classical Antiquity as an interest and those earrings are at least two thousand years old.

"Talking about old things, what is that bench with interesting carvings you were sitting on, Kensa? It looks really old." Dawn pointed to a roughly-hewn seat with some figures decorating the lower parts which stood apart from the pews as if set in place for someone in particular.

"My chair." She laughed, "if you read the information on the signage you'll see that some call it the 'Mermaid's Chair.' The carvings are about four hundred years old and not very flattering of mermaids."

"It's not bad for that long ago here in the countryside," I said.

"I'm not talking about the art. It's the content that bothers me," Kensa replied. "Why would anyone carve a mermaid with a mirror and a comb? Why would they think that a mermaid would spend so much time preening herself?"

I shook my head.

"Anyway, I come in here when there is no-one else around to reflect and wait. You caught me by surprise and I am glad that you did – I think."

Kensa's voice tumbled like no other, redolent of waves gently breaking rhythmically on a sandy beach, producing a sense of seductive calm; it was a voice to be felt not merely heard. She continued, "I don't have any wish or whim to leave this land. I'm part of it; the rocks, the stones, the sand and sea are all part of me. We are one. That's the wonder of living in the same place as your ancestors as long as anyone can remember or further back than recorded time." When Kensa smiled I sensed the freshness of a new spring, a raw energy and the wisdom of the ages: beguiling. She was asking for her words to be taken at face value when she concluded, "You become your ancestors."

This might have been the only encounter where I have seen Dawn visibly, genuinely, accept everything someone said without question. It was clear that Kensa completely enthralled her in that initial meeting. Dawn replied, "Sometimes I would like to have that comfort. But it's not to be. I can only imagine what you are talking about." She added, "What are you waiting for?"

"I think my waiting is over," she smiled and said, "Welcome to my home. I am excited to hear of your travels and impressions and how they can benefit this land. Verne has said that we will dine together tonight."

Chapter Twenty Four

Dawn and I strolled back towards our guest house to rest for the evening. She broke our silence with, "Of all the weird stuff that we have been through these past weeks, what happened back there was the weirdest of the lot. I mean, it wasn't hidden, subversive or shadowy like Askuwheteau's death or that computer message at your place. It was right in front of our faces. Normal: two people meeting. But impossible. How could they just respond to each other without any warning, any introduction? It's crazy. And the two earrings. What are the chances?

"Agreed. The odds must be billions to one. Trillions. I wonder whether they are actually a pair or there are several like that around?"

"I know enough about ancient jewelry to recognize authenticity and an artist's unique work. They are an absolute match. It's beyond mind boggling. It's not even trillions to one; it's the only chance in the whole world out of infinitesimal numbers. It's like zero chance. And Kensa seemed to know where she had left it. That doesn't increase the odds of the two coming together; it just makes the whole thing more mysterious. Last night we were talking about objects concealing themselves? Well, this is almost the opposite of that."

"I've never seen you so thrown. It happened. Right there. Yet, for Verne and Kensa it seemed normal."

"They didn't falter. It was as if it was meant to happen for them; as if they expected it. Kind of preordained. That's why I say that it's totally out there. Like beyond fiction."

"Kensa is really something. I can understand Verne's attraction," I said, trying to rationalise the whole business.

"Haha, you're right there. You were taken with her yourself. I've never met someone so sensual."

I felt an awkward twinge of guilt that Dawn might have been annoyed in some way and I tried to dilute my comment by saying, "What I mean is there is something unusual about her...she is attractive..."

"Ross, she's phenomenal. I was attracted to her, physically and that's not normal for me. You don't have to pretend or make excuses. She is radically beautiful. Don't worry. I'm just razzing you."

I laughed, "Thanks. Let's face it, she's exceptional. I wonder if it's even a good thing for Verne"

"Come now, Ross. He also scores high points and once you penetrate that crusty layer he wraps around himself, there's something mystical about him too. And 'mystical' is just a starting point when you try to describe Kensa."

"Mystical is right. She seems to be ethereal - of another world. I paused, considering whether to share my thoughts, "There is lots of really old stuff around here. Something came to me when I was walking around the cemetery alone. You could call it an insight... about how we are instructed by our past." I continued to explain to Dawn how the idea came to me in the cemetery that stories from our culture come to us almost directly from our ancestors and we reinvent them for our consumption and that of our children.

Dawn was fascinated and staring into my eyes picked up on the theme: "Do you think that, if the characters kept coming back, we'd recognise them? What if there's more to those characters than just make believe; and way back - in the distant past - someone actually met them and told stories about them? Would we know one if it just popped up right in front of us now?"

"That's what I asked myself."

"Ross, when Kensa stood in the sunshine in the church in all her magnificence and spoke to us, she was exactly how I have imagined Carenza."

"Oh my god. That's exactly what I thought, but I was too afraid to say it."

"I was reminded of Cador's description of Carenza and when the church door opened, I thought that I smelled the sea air, but now I wonder...."

We stood still, staring at each other for a few seconds. Dawn shook her head and continued, "And Kensa's comments about the Mermaid's Chair? It was like she was personally offended by the image?"

I had been nodding in agreement with everything that Dawn said as we carried on walking back to the guest house. I added, "Dawn, you're my anchor in reality. If you weren't here, I would dismiss this stuff, ignore it, or think that I was losing my mind. Sharing it makes all the difference. The big question for me in all this is, are we being exposed to some different kind of world? Like Verne said in his emails, he couldn't share the stuff with anyone because they'd think he was crazy. Imagine if it were just one of us seeing all this."

Dawn answered, "I'm starting to wonder about certain people like Askuvie, or even Verne, whether they inhabit a different plane and that they've intersected our world for a brief moment? They're almost too rarefied for our world and vulnerable at the same time. They're strong, indestructible, but also so fragile."

"I know. Sometimes I wonder whether they only exist because I give them life. I realise that sounds odd. But what proof is there that they exist, live as you or I see them, or that they are there at all? But you and I see the same things."

"We do see Verne interacting with people around him. Did you catch Kensa's words?" said Dawn. Did she say, 'Welcome home' or 'welcome to my home'?"

"Either way, it's unusual. I'll be listening carefully tonight. She does put things in a quirky way - like the stuff about her chair. And, talking about reaction, you seemed very accepting of everything she said. That's not like you."

"Yes, I couldn't catch it. Honestly, I was overawed, like being in the presence of someone, something other than human, a power or grace in human form. She seemed to have an understanding that came from a deep impenetrable core."

Dawn returned to something more easy to describe: "I thought you and I connected quickly, but that was like a fairy story. I suppose we are in one of the lands of fairies."

"In an instant is right. They didn't seem to be taken by surprise - just propelled together and totally unresisting. And when he introduced us, it was as if she was the old friend...intimate friend, and we were new on the scene. It was as if they'd known each other forever."

"It's all too much," I said. "I need a rest because tonight should be interesting."

Chapter Twenty Five

When we arrived at the pub I was surprised to see Verne moving easily amongst the dozen or so local customers like some civic benefactor, doling out favours and encouragement. He could have been mistaken for an established community leader - like the mayor - joking with the locals who depended upon his beneficence and advice to solve their problems. He was completely at home. He greeted us warmly and went over to pay for his beer, but Alf dismissed his offer with a grin, a wave of his hand and a "Goodnight and all the best to the misses. Enjoy your home cooked meal."

Glancing at Dawn, she wrinkled her brow and whispered, "Kensa's already playing hostess?"

"And he's sharing advice with everyone. He normally withholds his opinion till he knows people well."

We followed Verne through the familiar passage to his rooms as he cheerily told us how both he and Kensa were looking forward to our company that night. He conceded that it was a bit disconcerting how "Those fellows in the pub take my suggestions so seriously and even act upon them."

Kensa had heard us coming down the hallway and was waiting at the door. Framed by the doorway with the electric light behind her, she was as radiant as we had seen her in the church. She greeted us warmly and nestled up to Verne with the comfort of an old, favourite pillow, more characteristic of couples who have been together for fifty years. After a few comments about Zennor, the guest house and the weather, as Verne was pouring wine from the same stock that he had the previous night, I made a light-hearted comment that he must have a "full store of Moruith's wine."

Dawn had regained her nimble reactions and, turning to Kensa, enquired, "Have you ever been to Moruith's Farm?"

"I know it. Moruith's is a place that few can see or visit. You could pass right through it without realising that you are in that particular place. It has a long history and some True Brits live there."

Dawn replied, "I know that I'm an outsider, but isn't that expression, 'True Brits,' a bit out of date now - off limits: politically incorrect, and all that?"

We laughed, but Verne caught up on Kensa's tone, "Why's that? Those values are still important: hard work and loyalty to the land, the kind of British spirit Churchill kindled in 'Never Surrender!'."

"For those at Moruith's, sentiments like that are as old as the stones themselves," added Kensa. "As you know, they've never submitted to government rules to fence their property, but they've also never given up any of their land to another group of any sorts, not Romans, not Saxons, Vikings, Normans nor any other pillagers. They keep the fire alive."

Verne was nodding in agreement and smiled at our reaction and the skepticism evident on our faces. Dawn spoke quietly as she asked, "I know that throughout English history, groups were able to avoid the invaders in one way or another. But how did one group evade all those different conquerors?"

Kensa faced us directly without the hint of a smile and said, "Only the bravest hearts can keep the freedom that they've won. Moruith, or any leader at the Farm, would never expect someone to give it to them."

Still speaking quietly and glancing at me, then avoiding eye contact with any of us, Dawn said, "OK, but Verne says he can't find it on maps. And now Kensa, you said that you could walk right through there without realising it. How is that possible?"

Kensa laughed, "Maps are just drawings; ways that people use to try to control how we think about a place. People find them helpful, but they merely layer over the reality. You won't find Moruith's by using maps."

Dawn continued: "We know the power of the British government. You can't stand up against Whitehall."

Kensa enlightened us: "Artful leadership and connection. They live by ancient codes. King Arthur didn't invent the bonds of loyalty and allegiance; he simply resuscitated something that lay dormant for hundreds of years. For a while those values were more widespread. Robin Hood and his Merry Men - and women - ruled the forest. The people at Moruith's are content to work within their boundaries; they don't seek to expand their power or possess what others have."

"But there are no boundaries. They're not marked on the maps?" said Dawn, casting her eyes down at the floor, "You talk of legendary people - not real..."

"The boundaries are clear for those who accept Moruith's and live by the code," said Kensa with a smile. Then she lifted her chin, thrust back her shoulders and in a slightly louder voice said, "They're as real as Verne or me; maybe even you or Ross, for that matter. You choose." That part of the topic was closed.

I turned to the other aspect of the discussion and asked, "If Moruith's the leader now, have there been others in the past who have wanted more? What if they were attacked?"

Verne placed his hand on my shoulder and guided me towards a lounge chair with the words, "So many questions,

Ross. They can't be attacked if no one knows they're there and they don't want to expand; no thoughts of conquest..

"Let's all sit down and enjoy the wine. Moruith has the understanding of the ancients. She leads or rules according to whatever the occasion demands with subtle skill, never revealing the reality of the place to the wider world."

Dawn's more direct question revealed her greater understanding, but once again, with absolute reverence, "Is she from ancient stock?"

Kensa, now seated and more relaxed, nodded and said, "She's from ancient stock." With a gesture as if holding something in her hand, added, "Or is ancient stock. There's not much difference for the people at Moruith's."

Verne chipped in, "When I was there, none of the family questioned her authority. It was as if they knew what she was going to do or say before she acted or spoke. There was absolutely no division or subversive undercurrent even when there was ample opportunity at the parties or one on one conversations. Astounding."

Kensa elaborated, "And, it is sincere; it works both ways. People are free to act however they want to or say whatever they think. Though it's leadership through a lineage, it's also by consensus: the family consent to her authority. It's not a formal election, but more powerful. Moruith allows questions and discussion in a civilised way that guarantees respect."

"I enjoyed that profound respect while I was there."

"If you were treated with the same respect, it is because they considered you to be of the family. You would never have seen the ceremonies otherwise. Respect is in their blood and governs their relationships with each other; their attachment to the land. Some of us feel grafted into this part of the peninsula; it gets under our skin, penetrates the roots of our hair, it's joined to our bones. We're mortally inseparable from the stones, the earth and the surrounding sea. We're integral to it all and it makes us immortal."

Verne stood up with the bottle in his hand to refill our glasses and in front of Kensa, he looked at her quizzically and said, "It's strange, Kensa, but you are remarkably like the character I saw playing the mother's role at Moruith's farm. Is that possible? Is it one of the things that make me feel that I've known you for so long?"

Kensa answered, "Those who look carefully notice all kinds of connections in these parts. Links between people are only visible to a few."

"I should try to return to the Farm. You've reminded me of Moruith's words."

"If she gave instructions you should follow them. You will not be able to rest till you do. That's her power. Like the land, she gets under your skin."

Unable to contain my concern, I blurted out: "Verne, I have to warn you. Firstly, you said that you wouldn't be able to find the farm again; that it's not on the map. And the whole thing still sounds like a cult to me."

"No it's not," said Kensa, "It's far more complex and unifying. True ownership and kinship with land is not gained through pieces of paper or fancy rituals; it is by pledge and allegiance demonstrated through custody over time… if rituals emerge, they are expressions of gratitude. You'll walk right past the place if they want you to."

Dawn and I looked at each other knowingly and said, "Askuwheteau."

"That's exactly it," Verne added, "I've skimmed through the USB stick. But you haven't seen Moruith's and you probably won't."

Kensa seemed to glow from the comfort of her arm chair when she added, "The greatest rulers, especially monarchs, are sensitive to minute signs that are imperceptible to most people. Wars are won by understanding the deepest flow; the world below the surface. The clash of arms, the bombs and the bullets are a screen for the hidden victories and defeats. We are so often fooled by a brash show of strength. In the old days the brilliant leaders settled matters before the blood flowed because their motive was for the good of their people. Moruith still operates like that."

"We're open to that. I'd like to know more," said Dawn.

"Only to a point," said Verne. "We leave the magic behind with our childhood and spend so much effort looking for explanations instead of just wallowing in the mystery of the legends like King Arthur or Merlin. People dismiss them because they can't attach a money value."

"You have a vivid imagination, Verne. I know that my views are based on scientific principles."

"Not everything can be explained neatly. In Chysauster and at Moruith's Farm, the people are the priority in all ways; the stated purpose for the existence of the place and all they do. At Chysauster, even the souls of the past are accommodated in the stones. Those inhabitants won't give up their home at any price."

"It's hard to understand, Verne," I said. "How's that different from anywhere else?"

"They work for the community."

"I've always thought that the best we can hope for is not to work against each other. Isn't some competition healthy?"

Kensa remained seated, raised her palms upward with her fingers relaxed and spread and with a smile, said, "While you're here, the best you can do is immerse yourselves in the Cornish landscape and listen to the stories with all your senses. When you do return to the 'real world', you will take some Cornish enchantment with you."

Dawn spoke quietly for both of us, "Ironically, Verne, Kensa, we're actually receptive to these things. We've had some experiences that have profoundly altered our perception. Not to the same extent you have."

I added, "We don't intend to be critical. We respect everything you and Kensa have said. It's outside my understanding, but Askuvie did talk about similar stuff, so it's not entirely new to me, or Dawn."

Verne stood up, walked over to me and clasped my hand in that same grasp of my elbow with his other hand and said, "Ross, I haven't thanked you for coming over when I asked. I don't know what else prompted your journey, but thank you. And now I have three friends whom I can trust with these stories. I am lucky."

We were all taken aback and silent for a few seconds before he said, "The only word for my transformation is an epiphany and I cannot resist the yearning to return to Moruith's Farm. Kensa is determined to go with me; she is no stranger there and together we have a better chance of finding the path. The second earring might be the thing that I am supposed to take back with me. If we are able to find our way, we know that we'll be welcomed.

"We're going to stay around in these parts too," I said, "as we have no pressing need to return right now. We have the luxury to determine our own itinerary."

The tone of the conversation subsided into an excitement of travel and enjoyment of the food Kensa and Verne had prepared. They had worked wonders with local vegetables such as potatoes and turnips. Kensa claimed that using storage places in properly designed pantries in the house and not in the fridge ensured that they retained their flavour and goodness throughout winter. The meal was strong evidence that she was correct.

As we ate, Verne and Kensa described some of the most important places to visit around Cornwall that would give us a sense of the history and culture of the myth-soaked land. It was going to be difficult to select from such a long list. The rest of the evening continued in that calmer mood and we ended by agreeing to meet in the church vestibule the following morning which was Sunday.

Dawn and I jogged the short distance back to our guest house and we were soon lying in bed reflecting upon the conversation. We realised that if it hadn't been for our earlier experiences with Askuwheteau and the email messages, we may have dismissed Verne and Kensa as either crazy or drunk and laughed about their descriptions of mystical Cornwall.

Instead, Dawn began with a practical suggestion that, "On Monday we should go and find some maps and brochures of Cornwall so we can plot a route." Turning her head to watch my reaction, she said, "But that will only let us scratch our way along the surface of the places. How will we be able to enter those deeper layers Kensa spoke about tonight? Do we really want to go deeper or are we going to take a holiday from that as well?"

I closed my eyes, took a deep breath and said, "They're not going to let us in. Even if they would, I'm not ready to dive in yet - or ever. I'll just wait to hear more from our friends when they get back from Moruith's Farm. They seem at home in fairyland. Zennor is far enough down the rabbit hole for me. Going to Moruith's would be more like joining a scuba diving expedition to Atlantis."

"Ross, that's what Kensa meant." Dawn sat bolt upright in the bed, stared down at me and said, "You're a genius, Doctor Martindale. There are places, like Atlantis, that may be there, but first you have to believe that they exist before you can find them. There are others. People all over the world do that kind of thing - sometimes kind of jokingly. I can tell you that indigenous people of many countries call places that have a special meaning for them by different names; and those names present a different reality for those who use them."

Dawn flopped down in the bed and stared at the ceiling and continued, "Back in Canada, places have Indigenous names as well as those plastered over them. Names define what places mean for different people: Derry or Londonderry. A few people even call England, 'Albion'. But that raises all sorts of other issues. That's why Kensa can talk about 'True Brits.' Moruith's Farm sounds like the middle of nowhere, or fairyland. It could well be there, but it's not for us. We wouldn't know that we had walked into the area because we're not invited."

"Glad to hear it," I said, "I decline all invitations to that place."

"I don't mind taking a real break either. Let's just be tourists for a few days. Verne's and Kensa's report of their next visit to Moruith's will be enough for me." After a pause, Dawn added, "I never thought that I'd say a thing like that." She pushed her athletic body right up next to my bulk and, with her full smile, said, "And I never thought I'd feel like I've got everything I want." She chuckled and repeated something she had said some days earlier, "Any port in a storm," and added more softly, "Permission to dock my craft, Doctor?"

Chapter Twenty Six

A brisk walk to the church was not enough exercise to counter the cold of the bleak Sunday morning weather. Verne and Kensa arrived right on our heels and we all scurried inside the church together with other congregants arriving for the morning service. Less than two minutes after finding seats in a pew on the side nearest "Kensa's Chair," a round-faced, dark-haired, younger than middle-aged vicar entered the church and moved amongst his parishioners, greeting them by name with a charming smile and a cheery word. He was average height, a little chubby and wore a faded black suit. The villagers returned his greetings warmly using his first name. He scanned the pews and made a direct line towards us. I was surprised (but shouldn't have been), when he addressed Verne by name and asked him to introduce us.

After giving us each a firm handshake and personal word of welcome, he walked towards the pulpit, raised his voice to address the whole congregation, maintaining an informal tone as he said, "A full house today, I see. Is it because we are all feeling righteous this morning, or is it out of interest for the extra souls in our midst?" Everyone laughed and, addressing us by our names, "Welcome to our parish. In your honour I am going to change the first hymn to one of our favourites with the opening line 'Who would true valour see...' and you will notice that we use Bunyan's original lyrics here -

even if he was a bit of a radical in his day." With a chuckle the minister (and I can't recall his name) continued that he was sure that the parishioners would, "Overcome their curiosity and bear in mind one of the alleged inspirations the hymn, and give the 'strangers' a typical Cornish welcome after the service." Everyone laughed again and turned to us in greeting.

As the organ sounded the first few bars of the familiar tune, the congregation rose to their feet. Several cleared their throats and the happy faces showed their eagerness to participate in the first hymn of the service. They raised their voices together for the first line and then came a startling surprise: the notes of the richest tenor voice I have heard in close proximity filled the church. We all turned to see Verne with his face tilted slightly upward, his long ginger-flecked blonde hair shining in the sunlight, singing with apparent ease. The rest of the congregation, including the vicar, softened their voices so that we could listen to Verne at the same time.

Dawn and I were equally astounded, but we noticed that Kensa was unflustered; in fact, she was singing softly next to Verne and her only reaction was that she leaned even closer to him - if that was possible. Her voice, redolent of the sound of the sea, tumbled in perfect pitch, her indistinguishable words, providing a gentle harmony to Verne's lead: it was as if they had rehearsed or at least performed a duet together in the past.

At the end of the first stanza Verne turned, swept his eyes over the whole congregation, raised his right hand like the conductor of a choir and the whole congregation responded in full volume to join in the chorus. Verne's powerful voice remained clearly audible, supported by Kensa as she intoned the harmony at his side.

At the end of that first hymn, the congregants sat down, slightly pink-cheeked and invigorated as if they'd just finished their morning exercise. The vicar was delighted by the enthusiastic participation and picked up on the theme of "Pilgrim." He urged the parishioners to think about migrants and pilgrims with equal respect as they were all children of God and drew some parallels from Biblical times that I can't recall with accuracy. His message was clear.

After the service, the congregants needed no reminder to spoil us with a special Cornish tea. At the reception the locals complimented Verne on his singing which led to light-hearted references to the folk-history of the church and that there's often more truth in "them myths that we'd like to owe." They cautioned Kensa not to be ensnared by Verne's voice and warned him that his mellifluous instrument could awaken the spirit of the nymph who used to sit in the "Mermaid's Chair." And that it already had. Dawn and I laughed along, agreeing that they were both in grave danger.

Near noon we left the small church and had a chance to talk with Verne and Kensa alone as we walked towards Verne's lodgings. When Dawn and I expressed our admiration for Verne's singing he became silent for a few moments and his brow crinkled in thought. He said that, surprisingly, the hymn came back to him from his school days and the atmosphere in the church probably inspired him. Kensa added one of her mysterious comments that the "Power of the voice comes from the song itself. Those songs or hymns have been in this land for a long time and they were only written down in the last few hundred years. As you travel through the land, you become attuned to them, they take over your voice and soul" and she left it at that as if we should be able to understand.

Kensa's remark dispelled Verne's puzzled expression. His face lit up as he smiled and said, "That was it. That's why I knew the tune. That was the tune they sang in the circle at Moruith's. The words were different, but it didn't seem to matter." Kensa shrugged and gave a single sideways nod of her head to the left as if Verne had confirmed her point.

When we reached the private door to Verne's rooms at the pub, he and Kensa that they would head back to Moruith's Farm that day. We made a pact to meet in Zennor two weeks from then.

Dawn said, "We are going to take your advice and explore this area as much as possible. We'll be taking buses and cabs - walking around is too demanding for us right now. One small act of rebellion though: we've decided that we're going to keep our cell phones turned off as we have since we arrived in England."

Verne replied with a wink, "I've lost my charger and Kensa doesn't have a phone. We'll have to rely on being here simultaneously two weeks from now."

"I've never had one," said Kensa, "I think that it'd just be a nuisance - another unnecessary item. I'm keen to be at Moruith's again too. What I really appreciate about the Farm is intimacy with Nature. There, buildings like this one, don't screen the vibrancy of Nature. Ceremonies inside the circle bring us into direct communication with the land and help us to regenerate by drawing on the power of the earth and stones that are there. The basics haven't changed. At the Old Place the stones used for the houses were unchanged, unchipped. When the Romans arrived there, it was the stones that kept the unity; protected the inhabitants at critical moments."

Dawn voiced the thought in my mind, "We haven't been to what you call 'The Old Place', I presume Chysauster. But how do you know those details, Kensa?"

"We keep telling it through the ages; it's a truth only evident to a few who experienced 'the exchange'. That truth was carried to Moruith's Farm and it keeps the Farm sacred. It has never been penetrated because of the union, the bond, with the land and the stones. Those who lost faith had to leave. They may return to the Farm, and can, when they've resolved their conflicts; when their receptivity is restored."

We stood facing each other outside the door in the bare winter garden. Verne stared into the distance as he said, "Ross, do you remember that conversation about 'freedom' outside your house after we'd played 'Genesis?'"

I nodded my recollection and Verne continued, "Back then, freedom for me was being independent; being able to come and go anywhere in the world I chose by owning land, a 'home', in various spots. That's just superficial possession, economic independence; it's not freedom. That way I'm still dependent upon the rules someone else has imposed; that kind of ownership is only possible if everyone agrees to those rules. I see freedom differently now. I have to be able to stay in one place and be totally comfortable to act in ways that match my framework of thought and I believe that I've found freedom and 'home' with Kensa, and at Moruith's. That is one big reason why Kensa and I have to return to the Farm together.

Kensa had been thoughtful and seemed to echo our exchange of ideas when she said, "If people would stay in one place, not exactly one spot, but one landscape, for a long time, they'd begin to take in a wisdom that Verne is starting to feel. You might find an essential truth if you join sight and imagination. And dispel the illusion that we can know all. At Moruith's we can give up the quest for all knowledge."

I had been listening carefully to both of them and, despite their bright shining eyes and expression of optimism, I said, "How do you know that you'll even find Moruith's again? You said yourselves that it is not up to you."

"We feel deep down that we're ready," said Verne. "But it will be a test. If we are worthy, it will be easy and our values will line up with those of the community. Within the boundaries of Moruith's we will be free. We can't do any more to prepare ourselves. Now, all we can do is put ourselves in the spot and then it's up to something beyond our control."

Dawn and I glanced at each other with special understanding that they, and perhaps we, were on a course that was only partially of our own choosing. But I wasn't ready to give up my choice in any situation.

Verne and Kensa were ready to leave immediately - that part of Verne's personality was unchanged, yet he seemed less encumbered than ever. They had no need to go inside his lodgings. He stood slightly more erect as if he had shed a load and, with a lightness in his step, it was as if he glided across the ground. Kensa was uncluttered; she carried nothing in excess; she was complete in herself, with the natural elements visible in her physical makeup: sky, sea, leaves and soil. Perhaps Verne was carrying her possessions in his backpack, but even that looked a lot less bulky than before. As the two figures walked along the path away from Zennor, they represented a new level of traveling light: freely embracing their destiny.

The world around had slipped out of the coldest time of the year and was showing signs of regeneration. Verne and Kensa traveled along the rocky pathway, blending with the surroundings. All the snow had melted and the stems and branches of the trees had a greener tinge.

My awareness of the environment had deepened since leaving the all-consuming occupation of a doctor's routine and, for whatever reason, I had grown more responsive to seasonal changes in the landscape with all my senses. Detecting the rise in the outside temperature, I could feel my expanded arteries carrying more blood around my body. Grey squirrels were scurrying everywhere and we even caught sight of porcupines and the rare red squirrel. Birds sang with excitement as they frolicked in the air, laden with a pervasive scent of compost and regeneration. Dawn winked and said, "Those birds don't need any lessons, do they?" We snuggled together on a nearby rock, cast our eyes down to our paper map and started to plot our course through Cornwall. Dawn placed her hand on the paper and said, "This map will show us the route to all the special places in Cornwall with their history. That's enough for now."

Chapter Twenty Seven

The prospect of two romantic weeks with Dawn Sanderson exploring the sites of Cornwall was special enough for me - never mind the "layers or history." But Dawn was insistent that we inject our trip with purpose; that we should try to detect the magic of Cornwall and whether we felt connected with the history of the place. We chose Chysauster to start our quest to understand ourselves better because it was the oldest and closest on our list; Verne's and Kensa's stories of the "Old Place" had bestowed it with a spirit that made it personal.

As we walked around the restored village we saw Chysauster through Verne's eyes, which was not the same as using our own imagination. We imposed his framework on Chysauster to give meaning to the landscape. The history was fascinating and it was fun to sit on the outer wall and imagine the Romans advancing up the slope while beautiful Carenza dashed for cover in the fogou. We scrutinised the doorway where Verne had discovered Kensa's earring. Both of these locations sparked further questions in our minds about connections between Carenza and Kensa. Of course, we knew that they couldn't possibly be one and the same person, but we agreed that, to enrich our trip, we'd let the child part of our personalities take over, and pretend that Kensa was a reincarnation of the legendary Carenza. We laughed about catching the virus of Romanticism, but concluded that, while the history seemed familiar, neither of us felt a direct, physical connection to Verne's ancestors and Cador stayed in hiding. We decided to move on to Tintagel Castle.

Our first first sight of the impregnable fortress, perched on the rocks in such a way to make it defensible by a small number of skilled soldiers against whole armies of the day, stirred our blood. My mind swirled with images of horsemen charging around the area and I half expected Merlin to appear on the battlements raging against the elements and portents of gloom. The birthplace of King Arthur, the fortress of Uther Pendragon, an entrenched setting for the stories of *The Knights of the Round Table* or *The Sword in the Stone,* taunted my imagination.

As we entered the castle, Dawn said, "I can almost hear the characters, but not as clearly as Verne and Kensa do. Those two are still a conduit into the past for me." Three hours exploring the castle passed easily. Sometimes we took on roles of the characters who were familiar to us from the stories heard in childhood; the characters fitted us very comfortably even though it was years since I had thought about them. As we conjured up a scene between Arthur and Gueneviere, Dawn said, "Do you think that we have a sprinkling of magic powder on our shoulders? Is this the magic of Cornwall?"

At Tintagel we gave ourselves permission to play. Early in our journey we had decided to treat the trip as a break from our normal lives; at Tintagel we paid homage to the "spontaneous" and gave it the authority to take over the next few days of our lives. We spent ten days visiting key tourist sites, walking on the deserted beaches and growing increasingly comfortable in each other's company.

Penzance was our last stop before returning to Zennor. The day before we were scheduled to meet Verne and Kensa, Dawn shook me awake and announced that her "spontaneous wish" for the day was to visit the Minack Theatre.

Performances weren't scheduled for another month in the outdoor arena, but visitors were welcome to tour the venue. There weren't many other sightseers that cloudy, blustery day when we sat huddled together on the stone seats four rows from the stage. On a bright sunny day with a sparkling blue sea as a backdrop, the stage and stone architecture could be considered a Greek amphitheatre. That day, the enormous swells on the grey ocean in front of us presented a bleak picture.

Dawn drew herself closer to me as if to pass on some secret information. With a sweeping movement of her hand that took in the sea in front of us, asked, "Ross, what sea are we looking at?"

"The North Sea, of course," I answered. Then thought for a few seconds. I could feel Dawn's eyes fixed on my face as I stared intensely at the sea hoping for some sort of revelation. "Or is it the English Channel?"

I turned towards Dawn's smiling face as she said, "Both. And recently people gave it another name: 'The Celtic

Sea.' It lies further west, I think, but it's all one. When I say 'recently,' I mean the last half century or so."

"Really. I think that I know where you're going with this."

"I bet you do. Atlantis, The Celtic Sea...Moruith's Farm."

We sat in silence for a few minutes absorbing how that information bolstered our hypothesis. Dawn interrupted our thoughts with, "However you interpret this whole thing we're in, we should pay tribute to Rowena Cade who turned her vision of this outdoor theatre into a reality - single handed. She hauled everything up here herself. All built with local stone and stuff brought up from the beach. Now it's a perfect spot for Shakespeare's plays. You should watch one."

Dawn bounded down the four or five tiers of seating to take her place on the stage and, with her back to me, facing the sea, hunched over, she paused to gather her thoughts. She turned towards me with an absolutely serious expression on her face and recited:

"I pray thee, gentle mortal, sing again!
Mine ear is much enamoured of thy note.
So is mine eye enthralled to thy shape,
And thy fair virtue's force, perforce doth move me
On the first view to say, to swear, I love thee."

I recognised Titania's words from *A Midsummer Night's Dream* and did my best to respond in character. Hesitatingly at first:

"Methinks…." I looked to Dawn for a prompt.

She provided it, "…you should have little reason for that."

"I've got it," I chuckled as the words came back to me:

"Methinks, mistress, you should have little reason
for that. And yet, to say the truth, reason and love keep
little company together nowadays - the more the pity
that some honest neighbours will not make them friends
- Nay, I can gleek upon occasion"

Dawn continued, "Thou art wise as thou art beautiful."

That was too much of an exaggeration and I said "You can't be serious, Inspector Sanderson. I may be an ass, but I know what my body looks like."

We burst into laughter and I realised that Dawn had helped me to take myself less seriously over the last few weeks. But our flirting with Shakespeare did lead to a far more important conversation involving the naming of secret places and the thin line between magic and the real world.

Shakespeare had worked magic on us, but we were still actors on the stage. Verne and Kensa were the story of the place in the hilltop amphitheatre at Moruith's Farm. Dawn asked the all important question about them: do 'reason and love keep little company together' with them? We were eager to hear the latest installment of the modern story directly from Verne and Kensa.

Chapter Twenty Eight

As we approached Zennor cemetery from the east we saw Verne and Kensa seated next to a gravestone, silhouetted against the setting sun which had paused on the horizon to accentuate the distinction between night and day, light and dark. Their pliant bodies bent over something between them which could have been a picnic and, though they were attentive to each other, they threw glances at their immediate surroundings, turning their heads as if following moving objects. Verne and Kensa were central to the picture.

"What a photo op," said Dawn.

"Agreed. But I feel like I'm intruding on something."

"A photograph wouldn't include the mood. It would have to be a painting. Maybe one of those old school film negatives could capture the weird otherworldliness," Dawn whispered, "They look enchanting with a hint of the sinister. And what's that movement around them?"

"Are there others with them? There's no colour; it's just black and white for me. I can't tell shapes apart clearly. I think my eyes are playing tricks on me with the sun behind them."

We were speaking very softly to each other which is probably why they weren't aware of our approach until we were mere metres away. Up close the illusion dissolved. Full colour returned to our friends in flesh and blood in contrast to the magical negative photographic image we had seen from a distance. They were a normal couple enjoying the evening and the warmer season. The two of them were as physically attractive as ever, but they both had dark shadows under their unblinking eyes.

They stood to greet us and Verne said, "Spring is definitely showing; it comes a bit earlier in Cornwall. Have you noticed the buds on the trees and bushes?" and, laying his hand on a gravestone, "The sun has been warming these headstones today."

My curiosity got the better of me and I asked, "Were there others around here a few minutes ago?"

"Only our children," answered Kensa, sweeping her hand around in a broad gesture and laughing dismissively and, when we were clearly confused, said, "Just a poor joke." Then added, "Do you know how old this church building is? It goes back to the invasion time - about 1000 years ago. But there was a church with a cemetery built here about four hundred years before that."

"That's a lot of ashes and dust," said Dawn, "It's humbling, isn't it."

Kensa continued, "This spot was chosen because it has been sacred forever, not just when the first church was built. The bones of our ancestors are the foundation of the foundation."

Verne rubbed his foot on the soil in the same way he had outside my front door weeks earlier, smiled at me knowing that I had made the connection, and said, "We do know what's underneath here. We're on sacred land."

Dawn said, "It's great to see you two again. This place could be home to a lot of ghosts. As we walked towards the cemetery it looked like there were figures racing around the two of you. I think that's what Ross was talking about."

"Graveyards can be such distorting places, but they're home for many," said Kensa.

Verne winked and chuckled, indicating to us that Kensa's words should be taken as a joke, but added, "So, what's more important, the land that contains the bodies of our ancestors or this building next to it? If the land is already sacred, why do we have to mark it with the church to bring people here to honour the ancestors? Then we start coming to this place because of the building and forget why it's built right here and the dead who should be remembered. C'mon," he lightened up with an attempt at a joke, "Let's undertake to celebrate our reunion."

"We have lots to be thankful for," added Kensa. "We have been reunited and we were reaffirmed at Moruith's.

Although, in the end we could not stay. Our home is elsewhere."

Verne set his jaw, fixed us with haunted eyes and said, "I have made a painful sacrifice to be with Kensa. I used to acquire land because I thought that I was buying freedom. Back at Chysauster I learned that if I bought the right piece of land, it might offer the freedom I sought. At Moruith's I discovered that that was all wrong. It was self-deception; avoidance of the inevitable and in the end I had to make a choice. At Moruith's I had to choose and I chose to be with Kensa."

Dawn and I were staring at him with incredulity right then, unable to respond so he tried to help us by saying, "Ross, you know how you used to say that I was born with a backpack on my shoulders? Well, you weren't far off the mark. I was always ready to carry on my journey. I just didn't know where it was going at that point. I have discovered that I can't be settled on one piece of land and be free at the same time. For some people, having their spot gives them freedom. It's the opposite for me. As Kensa said, 'Our home is elsewhere,' and that means our freedom is also somewhere else."

"I never thought that I'd say this, Verne, but you said that you'd found where you belong: at Moruith's. Surely it's best if you stay there to be part of it. Part of the story of the Farm."

Verne's and Kensa's jutting jaws and rigid shoulders sent a clear message; Dawn's silence showed that she was also aware of their intransigence. Right then our two friends seemed larger than life and I felt slightly daunteded in their presence for some reason. Even Kensa looked at Verne with respect as he uttered extraordinary words:

"The clash and tension in my life came to an end at Moruith's yesterday. But it was at the cost of a huge sacrifice. And now there is no turning back. I am completely connected to Kensa."

Kensa astounded us as she added, "Once again….There is a Spring storm brewing. Sometimes they are let in through an open portal. You can tell from the intensity."

"Where did you get that from?" asked Dawn staring up at the clear sky, "Did you just make that up?"

"You shouldn't question Kensa too deeply," said Verne, "She is saturated with the ancient wisdom of this area."

"I only know this part of the world well; other lands may be similar or totally different."

Verne ended the conversation with an invitation to, "Join us for dinner tonight and we'll tell you what we can about Moruith's Farm."

Verne and Kensa turned in the direction of the pub; Dawn and I walked towards our guest house to check in with our host. After a few paces, Dawn confirmed my observations about Verne's and Kensa's haggard countenances and the haunted expression in their eyes; that they tried to dismiss our questions with weak jokes. I said that they reminded me of my traumatised hospital patients who had lost touch with reality.

Dawn replied, "It's the same in my line of work. Our friends look damaged. They were trying to avoid something. But don't get into that whole deranged thing again." I managed a smile and Dawn continued, "And Kensa comes up with the most unorthodox things. They're so out of context, so random. And her choice of words sort of fit, but jar. When she said we're 'reunited' I didn't know whether she meant the two of them or all of us. Then she spoke about them being 'reaffirmed' as if we should understand."

"Did you notice that when Verne said he had been joined to Kensa, she added, 'Once again,' before going off on a tangent about the weather?"

Dawn nodded and said, "It's cold, but there's no hint of a cloud in the sky right now. Well, Ross Martindale, we knew we were going down a rabbit hole, but even if we'd rather not find out everything that happened at Moruith's, I've a feeling that we're going to be sitting at the Mad Hatter's Tea Party tonight."

Chapter Twenty Nine

We agreed on a plan for our date at the pub: experience had taught us both that there is little to be gained by contradicting or challenging people who are traumatised; Verne and Kensa were showing definite signs of stress. Dawn had also inferred from our conversation with them that, though they were shaken, they had grown in conviction; that they were not to be edged off their trajectory. Professional insight warned us to anticipat various twists and turns during the evening. However, I was derailed the instant we entered Verne's living room.

I glanced up at the painting incorporating the Verne-like character hanging in the same spot as it had on our earlier visit. I blurted out my surprise that last time I'd missed the female figure now occupying the middle ground.

"Typical of Cornish women," suggested Kensa. "They're at the heart of our story, yet never get enough credit, though it's usually about them in the end." She moved a step or two closer to the painting and with reverential, slow nods, added, "She comes and goes. English women are a lot like her. They are powerful; not the ones who want to be in the limelight, but those summoned to be leaders. Think of our queens: Boudicca, Elizabeth, then and now. They're irrepressible, incontestable and have total integrity; ready to sacrifice when the need arises. If you ever meet one, you will know. Moruith has those qualities."

Sticking to our plan to conciliate Verne and Kensa, I said, "Last time I was probably so focused on the man on the bench that I missed the woman. She's kind of ethereal. At the same time very strong… powerful."

Dawn's response, "Kensa, you seem refreshed. You too, Verne. Did you take a nap this afternoon?" was her signal to me to listen carefully and be ready to change our tack if necessary.

Verne replied that they had not slept, but the chance to spend an hour together was enough for them to "Recharge in preparation for the transformation." That last word caught my attention and I noticed that the haggard, haunted look had left their faces, leaving the spirit of resolution accentuated in their eyes and jaw-lines. Verne added, "We are ready to tell you the story, but we should eat first. The food can't wait." As he filled our glasses with Moruith's wine, he said, "Cheers. Drink up."

During the meal they asked us about our trip around the peninsula and were amused by our games at Tintagel and

Dawn's acting at the Minack Theatre. They hardly interrupted except to show pleasure that we had been able to visit most of the places they had recommended. Verne refilled our glasses a few times as we ate. At the end of the meal he said, "Let's top up our glasses - you'll need it - and move over to the more comfortable chairs so we can tell you our story of the Farm."

We eased back into the padded cushions of the four lounge chairs. Verne took a sip from his glass and said, "We found the Farm easily enough. A narrow track directly to Moruith's farmhouse opened up in front of us as we walked, but I did glance over my shoulder a few times to see the bushes blown by a zephyr, closing the path behind us; a dusting of early spring snow erased evidence of our passage. A disconcerting feeling overcame me that we were leaving the modern world behind and entering a realm where the pace and values were different from those I understood. It crossed my mind that we may not easily find our way back.

"I thought that we were approaching the farm from the opposite direction I had on my first visit, but in the same way as then, we passed through a spinney to see the farmhouse in the distance. The building darkened in my view in the same way it had before. I found the vanishing path and the emergent farmhouse disturbing. However, Moruith dispelled my unease by meeting us at the door of her farmhouse in the same way she did the last time. She greeted us both with equal warmth and the words, You found it. Then with a slight hesitation and glancing at Kensa she repeated her words, You finally found it, and, at the same time, she reached up to stroke Kensa's ear.

"Verne brought it to me in Zennor, Kensa clarified. Moruith expressed her pleasure by saying, It is as it should be and I presume that you will be staying for the 'Day of Balance' to fulfil our pledge. It wasn't a question.

"I recalled the Cador-like character's words in the play on my previous visit which stressed the obligations attached to the 'Day of Balance' and that it was essential for the community to consecrate the day. Moruith confirmed my thought and emphasised that it was vital to mark the day without a single omission to maintain the order of life and receive the promise of restoration.

"Moruith directed us to our room - the one that I had occupied on my last visit. The furniture was unchanged and Kensa said that it was exactly as she remembered it. She even pointed out the section of the wall built with stone from the remains of the old house outside. When Kensa and I were alone I asked her about the 'Day of Balance' which she told me is not held annually or with regularity."

As if choreographed, Verne took a sip of wine and Kensa cut in: "The 'Day of Balance' is proclaimed when elements in Nature, like a super moon, align. Verne has told you about Cador - he met him at the Old Place for the first time. Well, it's true that Cador has collected deep knowledge about our land over the years and sometimes shares it, but he prefers to let us learn through participation, using all our senses. He doesn't act in a vacuum. Cador meets with others to confer and they reach decisions and he brings the benefits of that collective knowledge to the rest of us. So, Cador will select the dates for important days because he, and those like him, can discern Natural rhythms that are invisible to the rest of us. Those ordained with the task of selecting the dates may spend weeks together to ensure the accuracy of their selection. We all know - those of us who have spent time talking with Moruith - that she couldn't keep everything in place alone, without Cador. He advises Moruith, and even decides on ceremony, but never steps into her area of rule over the family.

"I've participated in the 'Day of Balance' several times and it always starts the same way, but I can never remember how it ends for some reason. In fact even this time, the end is already murky. But Cador is always there."

"I thought that he was an actor-guide, just having fun," I said and turned to Verne for verification.

Verne just shook his head and said, "Your glass is empty. Let's top it up.

"We were at the Farm for almost two weeks, waiting for the ceremony. Moruith ladled abundant hospitality on us and, again, I had the feeling that my feet were being sucked into swampy ground. I lolled in an internal glow of being immersed in my true home, tainted with a desperate panic that I would never be able to extricate myself from the clod. A foreboding that I would not be able to meet expectations set by the clan, grew inside me as the days passed. That premonition intensified because each evening we visited a different member of the family and we were welcomed as special guests, given the place of honour at the table, and asked to open each meal in any way of our choosing. Sometimes I said a few words about being grateful for the food and the company. As long as I included a mention of the 'Day of Balance' all were happy. At Old Man Pender's home Kensa and I even sang 'Amazing Grace' together."

Kensa laughed and said, "Crandell hasn't changed though. He grumbled that he'd prefer us to use the original words to the song. He can't seem to get used to the new ways of singing."

Before we could ask for clarification, Verne quickly continued, "Kensa was much more comfortable with all that. I had a greater and greater fear that I'd be unable to pull my feet out of that mud; that I would be seduced into accepting whatever it was that the community expected of me or us. Perhaps it was some action or value they admired that I didn't know about.

"Apart from our visits to the nearby farmhouses to meet members of the clan, Moruith kept us in isolation at her farmhouse during the day. She made sure that we were well fed and rested in preparation for the 'Day of Balance' and what she called 'our prominence.' We did have lots of time to explore the remnants of the original house she showed me on my first visit. We spent time meditating on those walls."

Kensa smiled with a faraway look in her eyes, "That house brings back memories. The Roman was immensely strong and a skilled builder. He built that house entirely on his own. It was impregnable. No wild animals - or unwelcome humans for that matter - could ever get inside. The family was completely protected by it. Besides, the Roman was a match for ten men. Even though it was in the middle of nowhere, it had all the comforts of any house of the time."

Dawn stared at Kensa and asked, "How do you know that? Where is it recorded?"

Verne brought us back to his story, refusing to be sidetracked, "It isn't. That's why we're telling it to you. Moruith explained how important it had been to use a few of the stones from the original house in the walls of the present farmhouse such as the ones Kensa pointed out in our room. That way the past is built into the present, but we have to work hard to see it.

"Anyway, the morning of the 'Day of Balance' arrived and we started with a hearty breakfast. Moruith insisted that we drink a bottle of her mead as it was customary on that day. She explained that it was different from the beverage she had served on my first visit and that it would bring a calm to counter the excitement of the 'Day of Balance' - especially for us in 'our prominence.' We drank two bottles of it at lunch and another two in the evening with an early supper.

"Darkness fell. We proceeded up the slope to the stone circle where all the clan were seated as before, but this time there were no open spaces in the circle. Moruith led us both to the centre. With a clear and powerful voice she announced to all that events would recur and that we had returned as promised. She delivered a blessing and incantation that stressed balance, renewal and regeneration. Yes, it was slightly uncomfortable being the centre of attention, but we both welcomed the spiritual gift and covenant. Moruith placed us on either side of the stone block in the centre of the circle."

Verne was struggling with his emotions and we thought that he was overcome with his immense love for Kensa. She took over, "When Moruith declared that our reunion was inevitable and that it recurred indefinitely we were both flooded with a sense of *deja vu*; we were - we talked about that afterwards - we were consumed by the power of attraction for each other. Moruith clasped our hands and raised them above our heads as she tilted hers upward, facing the full moon. Her song increased in volume until she lowered our hands and joined them together with words including 'inevitable' and 'forever.' Then she turned back to the moon calling on it to give us the strength to perform our obligation that can be done by no other. The arena was bathed in lunar light: the incandescent moon gleaming at full power, bore witness to the proceedings and I was filled with foreboding. We had no warning of what was to come. Moruith continued that our presence that day had brought an added dignity to 'Balance Day' (it had been shortened) and that we would have the supreme privilege of confirming the promise. We felt like we were being physically drawn inside each other - literally merging."

Verne was able to continue: "The ceremony assumed a sinister tone because each time Moruith mentioned 'The Day of Balance,' 'Balance Day' or just the word 'Balance,' those in the circle chanted 'Balance,' once, twice or several times. It was numbing to say the least. More than that, our bodies were being invaded by a dark, thunderous energy, an irresistible force pulling us away from the centre into the circle of people. It might have been the effect of Moruith's wine, or the power of the chant from the circle, but it felt as if we were levitating. Then came the first real surprise: Moruith bowed towards us and, in what sounded like an invocation, a blessing, or even a song of praise; she addressed us as 'Mother and Father' and thanked us for abundance in the past.

"Dawn, Ross, I can see from your faces that you are as astounded as we were. Of course it was a shock and I had no inkling of what gifts I had bestowed on the community. Like blood, the chant from the circle pulsated through me, but burst out through my pores; my heartbeat synchronised with the chant and I transformed into something beyond my physical being; I absorbed the power to conduct any act required of me. The chanting intensified and Moruith continued her address; I morphed into one of the actors - or real people - playing a role yet unscripted. We seemed to slide into a different reality. I had adopted an ancient identity, like Cador or those other actors in the plays, and I was destined to follow a predetermined, unwritten script. At the same time an icy fear gripped me that it wasn't an act; that something had swollen inside me and my true identity was emerging. The praise and adulation from the circle was my birthright. My blood urged me to merge with Moruith and all those family members in the circle; my spirit or soul or conscience, or call it whatever you like, screamed at me to rise above the tribal beat. It was agony - a violent physical and mental tension at rupture point.

I was on the verge of yielding my identity to the call of the clan."

Kensa took over as Verne was clearly overwrought: "Moruith's words wrapped us in a cloak of adoration, setting us aloof, but not separate from the drumming and chanting in the circle. We were godlike figures, dominating the ceremony. I heard the sounds of a baby gurgling and cooing coming from outside the circle."

Instead of smiling, Kensa's face crumpled near tears and Verne had recovered sufficiently to pick up on the story, "Like my last visit, it was a play and a revival; an enactment and a real event all at once. This time I was in it. My apprehension intensified as two figures entered the circle carrying a baby in a wicker basket and bore it directly to the centre, placing it on a wooden platform in front of us. The circle began a beautiful, harmonious tune that announced the arrival of the infant. Again the tune was familiar, but I couldn't distinguish the words; it was low and soothing as if Nature had orchestrated its elements into a song praising the innocence of the baby. The song and the scene were a relief and a contrast to the earlier throbbing chant from the circle. It was a gentle song of welcome for the baby in a basket; a baby who was totally trusting and content, smiling and making baby noises - you know, one of those ideal painting scenes and images.

"Moruith approached Kensa and me with the same veneration she had displayed earlier. Again she held our hands and raised them above our heads, but this time she joined them while they were elevated. The gentle song in the circle changed suddenly to a wild chant and the innocent baby was in danger. With a swift, smooth, sweeping movement, Moruith drew a gleaming dagger from a leather belt around her waist and snapped it into my hand which was encased by Kensa's. Moruith said …" at that point he couldn't repeat them and Kensa took over.

Kensa braced herself to speak Moruith's words: "'You are forever duty bound to keep the balance in our land. Excess will kill the land and all its bounty. Balance is necessary for the land to sustain those who belong. It is your right to return and stay, if you first fulfil your obligation. It is your destiny to choose which path you wish to follow."

Kensa choked and Verne, with halting sentences continued, "It was obvious what Moruith was expecting from me... and Kensa. Moruith was like a statue of ice, but she commanded, with passion in her words: 'If you do not perform what is preordained you will be exiled like your forefathers. You belong here. But you have to keep the balance. If you do not, your freedom to remain will be revoked.' We were being commanded to kill an innocent baby, to stab it, impale it like sacrificing a lamb to some invisible ideal."

Verne's unseeing eyes darkened even more and, as if struck down by some giant hand, he dropped to his knees, shaking on the ground. Kensa managed to gain control of her convulsing body and whispered, "It wasn't always that way. There was no incest. Carenza's son never mated with his mother. Never. The story's changed. It's perverted. It's a horrible lie and they all believe it. They know the Farm has to stay a secret because it's unnatural. Carenza was unblemished."

Dawn and I were stunned, barely breathing, terrified of what was to come.

Kensa dropped to her knees on the floor next to Verne and with a deep, rasping voice emanating from the depths of her soul, whispered what she may have intended to be a secret, "They're all mine. All of them. Because I am the origin. I cannot live with that."

Verne pulled himself up onto the pouffe between their chairs and continued: "The chant became a roar and throbbed through my arteries, urging me to plunge the knife into the tiny form in front of me. I could feel the incredible strength of Kensa's grip, promising to guide my hand to do what was right. I stared into Moruith's face which was unchanged from that of our gentle, kind host and priestess, but her white hair intensified the blank stare of her black eyes and the smile hovering around her mouth, set in a frozen expression as she uttered the words, 'This is ever the Nature of things. You are ordained and obligated to keep the balance.'

"A voice of conscience was shouting from the back of my head to throw the dagger to the ground and run. It was screaming that I am not free to take human life; the life of a defenseless, pure baby. My body felt ripped apart between the urge to respond to the chanting, restrained by everything I believed to be inhuman. I trusted Kensa to do what was right and I plunged the knife down. I couldn't look; I just felt the knife crashing through the wicker of the basket and slamming into the wooden board as the chanting rose to a crescendo. I couldn't hear anything above the cacophony of voices.

"Moruith had ordered us to slaughter innocence and Cador was suddenly standing next to her. It was his show and he was terrifying. The people in the circle were chanting at fever pitch, without any reservation, their bodies shaking with emotion. They were completely under the spell of the stone circle, ready to obey Cador and Moruith. Murder of that magnitude Is the essence of evil. They seemed oblivious of the crime, consumed with the ritual They're all implicated. We're all implicated wherever we live. It's not just one thoughtless man or woman killing one baby. You can't avoid the guilt and the shame. You are part of it. You can't push it aside. You have to wrestle against it. At Moruith's, it isn't just infanticide. Slaughtering the innocent isn't symbolic. It's essential for those at Moruith's. They want one person to make the sacrifice. But who is being sacrificed: the innocent infant or the knife wielder's soul? It represents a whirlwind of slaughter, a turbulence that rocks the universe. All rules are bent and twisted, stretched and torn. Cador, Moruith, the ceremony, ritual and the power of the past demand it. All at the Farm truly believe that everything will collapse without the sacrifice. For them it is essential to justify everything they do. They wanted us to do it because we had morphed into the original parents."

Tears streamed down Kensa's and Verne's faces, their eyes hollow and black with an indescribable emotion. I had leaned across the arms of our chairs to edge closer to Dawn as the tension mounted. Like me, she was hardly breathing. Her waxen colour and grim, fixed expression revealed that she shared my terror and apprehension. I stammered, "Is that where it ended?"

Verne shook his head, "Driving the knife down was a release. I couldn't bring myself to look at it. Our 'prominence,' was over.

Kensa, now calm, but with sadness etched into her face, said, "They are wrong. And parents who point out their children's errors are pushed aside if they threaten the new order of things.

"Carenza and the Roman left a strong community. There was no lust between Carenza and her son. Both boys found their own mates. We could not condone and perpetuate the error at Moruith's Farm, but we are damned and banned because we refused to carry out the sacrifice. The life of the Farm is based on false records. The whole family or community used to make the decisions. Now, what Moruith says is the law. I don't know when that changed. Killing the baby has nothing to do with limiting numbers. It's about reinforcing Moruith's rule and Cador's custom."

Verne was still tense and continued, "At one moment we were the most venerated people in the ceremony and in an instant we were shunned, scorned parents, pushed outside the circle. Those in the circle resumed the chant slowly at first, then faster and accompanied by a deafening drumming of hands on the ground till it felt like an earth tremor. Do you remember that I told you about the glow on the ground in the centre of the circle when I was there the first time?" I nodded. "Ross, Dawn…," Verne stared at us with haunted eyes and I thought that he would not be able to continue, but he did in what was barely more than a hoarse whisper as if to avoid anyone else hearing, "From outside the circle, we could see the moonlight shining brightly on the centre and on the object lying there. It was the same stone Moruith had stood next to in the circle on my first visit, but I then it was only a stone. This time I realised it was a hearthstone; a large flat stone - ageless - but clearly marked by thousands of fires. It might have been there all the time, but I hadn't noticed it before that moment.

"I was drawn towards it by a powerful force. This was what had been sucking me down, clutching at my feet, holding me. A hearthstone was the centre of everything that I have discovered in Cornwall. It is the centre of my home. But it is not for Kensa and me. Those in the circle raised their hands in the air in adulation and worshipped the stone with all their being. They were worshiping a stone object. It was the core of all they believe, the source of their entry into the world. Who can defy the vision of the soul-maker and resist its demands? We were exiled. Moments before we represented the stem of the community, but we would not conform and we were condemned..

"Kensa kept her presence of mind. She tugged at my hand and we slipped away unnoticed. We resisted the urge to run and walked as fast as we could away from the Farm until we reached Zennor where you saw us this afternoon.

Kensa added quietly, "We were rejected from what we thought was our home, our community. We were expelled because we defied the central belief. We are in exile because we exposed the lie."

In a pain-filled, louder voice, Verne said, "The revulsion rose up inside me. I can still taste it. We are powerless to alter it. " Then he bellowed, "I reject them. We reject them."

As if the energy and anger had drained from his body in that shout, he spoke more quietly, "We haven't slept for more than twenty four hours, but the exhaustion has left my body. The war between my body and mind or soul that started when I held the knife in the circle is over - especially now that we've told the story. We have decided and we are at peace."

Verne reached out to Kensa and they embraced. Verne spoke more calmly, "I'm sorry, you could never have seen this coming. It's almost impossible to live with this knowledge."

Kensa added to her earlier statement, "You are the only outsiders to have any inkling of the existence of the Farm. It doesn't matter because you can never find it. No one will ever believe you anyway, and there is absolutely no evidence, so we risk nothing by telling you. What you do know now, is that the Farm is a place on earth where spiritual forces vie for dominance at crucial moments; when the faith of the few is tested to the extreme."

We did not respond, but our expressions may have reflected our confusion, even lack of acceptance. She continued, "You have to remember - to understand in your head and your bones - that our people have been invaded and conquered many times. Some groups like Moruith's have survived intact. They know that obscurity, invisibility, is their only real protection. They've guarded their covenant for centuries. Two little people are not going to overturn their haven and their custom. Even we can't correct their fundamental error or choice. They made it somewhere in the past. It's best you forget about the reality and only take the Cornish magic back with you."

Verne and Kensa never disclosed any further detail of the ceremony at Moruith's or their role in it, but Verne ended the evening with an explanation that, "Our scars are healing. I thought that I'd found home. That may be it, but I can't live inside that boundary. Every stone, every blade of grass and even that hearthstone is mine; I'm entitled to it and it's all part of me. Now I have to let it all go. I reject that security. I reject that evil. I could not live and act according to the norms of that fatal flaw. I would be spiritually paralysed. My freedom lies with Kensa wherever it leads."

His voice strong again and the determination back in his eyes was an indication that he had settled down, but Kensa's eyes held a faraway expression. The message in hers blended with Verne's words; the two were in mournful harmony.

They had been restored to relative peace; we, on the other hand, were distraught and disintegrated, and did not know how to leave Verne's rooms. Kensa helped, saying, "You should get along before that storm hits; it's going to be a cracker.'

"I don't think I'll ever sleep again," I muttered as I pulled on my coat, "I wouldn't believe that story from anyone else in the world; I'd dismiss it as a hallucination or that Indiana Jones has come to life."

"It's nothing like that," Kensa spoke softly, "They're simply protecting their land and we have our role to play in it. Moruith's Farm has to be kept apart and out of view of the authorities. Outsiders, officials, the government would never stand for it. Neither Moruith nor Cador nor any of them will ever allow any outsider to discover it. The clan members know that would be the end of their custom and way of life. I have decided that I will return to my natural home very soon. I'm out of my element and at some point we all have to reconcile ourselves to our limitations."

Chapter Thirty

Dawn and I walked along the path to our guesthouse, hardly looking at each other, unable to voice our thoughts. Finally Dawn ventured, "If things were dark and unnatural with Askuvie, what the hell is this? It's not possible. Not in our world today."

"Hell. It's hell in the middle of what Verne thought was heaven. They took us to the end of a path of no-return and we were staring down into a nightmare. How can Verne and Kensa recover? Just hearing about it is more than I can handle. Imagine having been there. Imagine holding the knife. How did they withstand the force of evil, urging them to kill the baby?"

Dawn shook her head to indicate that she couldn't grasp the situation. She grappled with the fragments: "If they had done it, they would be murderers. But that it happens here in England. We're not in the middle of nowhere. We're in the heart of civilization. What the hell is that place?"

"They seem to believe, or at least those at Moruith's believe, that killing - murdering - the baby was a necessary sacrifice."

Dawn walked more slowly and said, "They were there and they made a choice not to kill the baby. Now they're exiled because the baby lives. The clan must exile their 'parents' because that is the only way that they can justify their own existence and way of life. They all believe that they are the distant progeny of the incestuous act between mother and son. If they are to sustain Moruith's version of how the Farm was founded the parents or the symbolic figures must leave."

I reminded Dawn that, "Kensa was adamant that it was false. That there was no incest in the foundation of the community. How could she know that with such certainty?"

"It's weird. Eerie. Who is Kensa? Whatever. Where does that leave Verne and Kensa? They are exiled, discarded by their own family. They are homeless, destined to wander the earth in search of a new hearth. They can never find a home of equal quality for them because they have been cast out by their clan. That is the source of their anguish. The only way out of it was to sacrifice the baby. Then they could have stayed. The myth remained intact whatever they chose."

"That's the brilliance of the deception, whether it's Moruith's or an earlier leader of the community," I said as we reached the guest house pathway.

Dawn stopped and said, "I can't explain it, but for some reason Askuwheteau has popped into my mind. His death seemed arbitrary for most people; a violent act in our modern world. We know that there was more to it; maybe someone or a group of people considered it essential."

"Askuwheteau, Verne and Kensa had to make choices involving freedom. Askuwheteau chose to stay on his land on his own terms even though it meant death. What will be the consequences for Verne and Kensa? Their story isn't over and it feels like they've dragged us into a world of make believe."

Dawn hesitated at the door, looked up at the night stars and said with a slight smile on her face, "Cold, but not a cloud in the sky, not a breath of wind. Where is Kensa's storm? She said some pretty weird things tonight about the painting and other stuff, not to mention how she justified the existence of the Farm despite the truth. And Verne - there was something different about him too... as if he had taken on some of Kensa's glow. I can't explain it. Maybe they're not of our time. They both intimated that they were the parents or at least that the acting role had swamped, even replaced, their own identities during the ritual. You know, Doctor Martindale, maybe I'm starting to go with your diagnosis of crazy. But are we the crazy ones to see these things?"

"I wish it was that easy," I said as I opened the door and we stepped inside. We went upstairs to our room, but didn't sleep much that night.

Early in the morning the wind began to howl, rattling the windows. It was freaky that Kensa could have predicted such a violent storm without any apparent signs, so we decided that it was safest to stay in bed till forced out.

Before daylight, what sounded like the wind shaking the windows, turned out to be gravel thrown against the panes. I got out of bed to check and saw Verne and Kensa standing below the window beckoning us. We went outside to find them in a buoyant mood, revelling in the wild weather though the rain had stopped. Kensa told us in her peculiar way of phrasing things that "We shall go to witness the power of the ocean; it's in an angry mood today, for sure. You'll be amazed."

She dismissed our questions about forecasting weather, saying that, "More than the stones and the land, the wind and the sea are 'My Story,' they're part of me and I know when they're restless and heaving with the promise of a spectacle. The spirit of the waves is at full volume now. Can you hear them calling me? It's the voice of my true home."

We invited them inside while we went upstairs to dress for the weather. Dawn raised her eyebrows at me which told me that she was also questioning our friends' sanity. When we came downstairs, wrapped up and ready to go, Verne was adjusting the front pocket of his backpack. Straightening, he seemed slightly taller and his body shone with a radiance much like Kensa's when we first met her in the church. In response to my comment that he looked a lot better than the previous night, he answered that he felt wonderful and was ready for anything. He added, "My soul is at peace and in control."

Kensa was shining with happiness and had untied her long wavy hair. When Dawn remarked how she could almost feel the powerful smell of the sea in her nostrils, Kensa said, "Don't you just love the freedom of a storm? There's nothing more liberating than letting the wind and rain whirl through your hair." Remarkably the haunted, haggard look had been replaced with an optimism of anticipation that vibrated in their voices. It wasn't merely what they were saying; the vigour and enthusiasm that they generated shocked and inspired us at the same time.

The contrast between us was dramatic. Dawn and I, two cowed humans, crawled along the path towards the edge of a precipitous cliff, led by two spirits, liberated by the power of the storm, danced on the wind. Verne and Kensa were fearless and defiant in the face of the ferocious energy unleashed by the gods to remind us puny creatures of our frailty.

At the vantage point of the cliff face, Dawn and I crept within a few meters of the edge. My eyes narrowed against the ferocious wind and spray, I caught a glimpse of a world inaccessible to humans. Giant rollers crashed in from the Atlantic while the wind howled across the peninsula and clouds billowed above. Kensa ordered us to feel the full might of the storm on the cliff top, so we relented and inched further forward to peer down at a tiny strip of sand remaining of the swamped local beach fully exposed to Nature in crescendo.

Two hundred feet above the mayhem of waves, Dawn and I lay flat on the ground with our heads over the edge of the cliff and dug our toes into the turf in a pathetic attempt to secure ourselves against the tempest. In contrast, Verne and Kensa stood fearlessly inches from the edge and welcomed the savage barrage of Nature. They implored it to purge all impurities from their cluttered souls.

Madness? What had taken over their minds at that moment? Their reckless actions were understandable after their trauma. Hours before, their hearts had been ripped from their bodies and laid bare on the altar of union and sacrifice. Then their deep confidence in the security of their sacred home had been shattered. Dawn and I cringed in our vulnerability; they offered their bodies to the storm with extravagant gestures, spreading their arms wide and inviting the elements to seize them.

Kensa drew our attention to a greyish object on the beach, half submerged by the foamy water washing around it. We all stared at it for a few seconds until we realised that it was a large fish: a shark or a dolphin. Kensa called out, "Oh no, that's …" and the rest of her words were lost in the wind. She was propelled into action and found an obscured path down the cliff side which only a native of the area could know. She hurtled down it, leaping like a mountain animal. As if connected to her by an invisible cord, Verne followed with an agility even Olympic athletes would envy.

"Let's go and help them?" I screamed into Dawn's ear.

"Hold on," Dawn yelled, "Wait. See what happens. We might have to run for help." Her natural, sensible response, not just her training and professional skill returned in a moment of crisis. But neither of us would risk descending the cliff, let alone at the speed our friends had negotiated the hidden path.

A curtain of sea spray partly obscured the scene we observed from the cliff, two to three hundred meters away. A dolphin was stranded in the shallow water. Kensa reached the beached mammal first and bent over to put her mouth close to its glistening skin near its head. Seconds later, Verne was next to her and helped her to point it out to sea. It seemed as if the dolphin was listening to Dawn's direction and was helping them with undulating movements in inches of water making it possible to return to its environment; they could never have budged the large dolphin without its cooperation. Then, when it was comfortable in deeper water, it paused for a moment, glanced backward and gestured with its tail as if to summon the human couple.

"They saved it. How? A miracle," I shouted as I moved into a kneeling position.

"They're heroes," said Dawn. "Like superheroes. How did they even get there?"

Instinctively, we held onto each other and carried on shouting, "Did I imagine that Kensa called the dolphin by a name? I couldn't hear it."

"I thought I heard her say a name. It was drowned out by the wind."

"What are they doing now? They're going out onto the rocks. That's reckless."

"Reckless. It's wild. Madness. They don't care about themselves. Do they want to die?"

Our screams urging them back to the beach were futile: Verne and Kensa were disconnected from us by distance and, though far below, they were elevated to thespian proportions; to a size that matched the storm. They would have ignored our warning screams even if they had heard them. They were resolute. They disappeared from sight behind a large rock, and when they reappeared, we were hushed into silent wonderment. The pair had joined hands, united precariously on an outcrop of rock, facing the wild winds and surging waves. The two were human in every way, but larger than life and their clothes seemed torn to shreds, as if stretched to partially cover their enlarged bodies.

We stared into the heart of the storm. The wild waves and the screaming wind were the incarnation of the force of total annihilation. It threatened to obliterate everything in its path. And we had a full view of Verne's and Kensa's intimacy as they welcomed implacable, violent Nature. Verne's radiance equaled Kensa's. And they seemed indestructible.

Nature, in all its glory, bulged with the unbridled power, beauty and depth of our world. A hole opened in the clouds as if to unleash a blast to whip the waves into even greater fury. The clouds and the sea spray coalesced in a murky brew and then cleared partially for us to see the two mortals. The tempestuous sea formed a backdrop for the drama of their intimacy: an open profession of absolute love for each other and, simultaneously, a communion with Nature. It was a show of smooth flowing movements in shades of light and dark, similar to the one we witnessed in the churchyard, but this time only Verne and Kensa featured. At times they merged into one, then split in an erotic dance while the sea spray, as if by design, cast a veil of privacy over the carnal parts of the scene. We witnessed Nature and humanity in harmony.

A master choreographer was at work: the dolphin they had saved earlier from certain death, surfed the swells in the background, trying to reconnect with its human saviours. A wave, larger than any other, loomed over them; the dolphin hovered in the foam-tipped swell till the very last second and, with a deft movement of its tail, flicked the two into the boiling ocean before curving out to sea. All went quiet for a few seconds as the wind paused before resuming its howl.

We were jolted out of our trance, but remained in stunned silence. Shouting was pointless and there was no one around to help anyway. We were too far away to do anything. No one could survive in that sea. They were gone.

Moments later Dawn grabbed my arm, pointed with her free hand and yelled in my ear, "Look at that."

About two hundred meters out to sea, beyond the breakers, Verne and Kensa surged out of the water as if propelled by an unseen hand. The dolphin swam ahead between the peaks and valleys of the swells, guiding the united couple towards the horizon with the sun glinting through the billowing clouds.

"Am I imagining it, Dawn? Did Verne just throw away his backpack?" I screamed.

"Unmistakably. And is Kensa wearing a long green skirt down to her ankles?"

Chapter Thirty One

We were witnesses and obliged to report the event to the local constable. We knew that we couldn't describe the details of Kensa's interaction with the dolphin on the beach and Verne's and Kensa's open profession of love with credibility, let alone the image of them surfacing. However, we didn't anticipate the constable's resistance to a report of our two friends' drowning. The village constable chuckled and said, "I saw you two arriving at the pub last night. How many did you have, then? No one would go down onto the beach and the rocks in a storm like the one that just came through.

Besides, we'd have to get proof that those two were actually here in Zennor before we start putting people on the job."

The pub was the best place to start to gather proof, so we headed over there to chat with Alf. He allowed us to look through his register and neither Verne's nor Kensa's names appeared. He responded to our questions about letting special guests stay in the quarters behind the pub with a blank stare. He also laughed and, with a similar dismissal to that of the constable, said, "Blimey, you two must have woken up with fat heads this morning. I saw you leaving and was half inclined to see you home myself. Did you miss that storm this morning?"

There was no point in asking to check the rooms because the taverner would have displayed ignorance of such premises. Besides, Verne was carrying his backpack, presumably containing all his possessions and Kensa had arrived in Zennor empty handed. We were exhausted and decided to return to the guest house to consider how to proceed.

Inside we found that our host had gone out. We flopped down in chairs in the common room off the entrance. Dawn began: "You know, Ross, at no stage were Verne and Kensa panicking. It was as if nothing was unexpected for them. Last night they were distraught when they told us about the 'Day of Balance', but by this morning they were resigned, calm, even radiant. Do you remember that Verne said something about being ready for anything?"

I nodded, "It was like the dolphin was escorting them somewhere. Kensa said stuff about going back to 'her element'. The paradox between Verne's itchy feet and his quest for land are reconciled. He chose freedom without boundaries - land, the Farm, the clan. He chose to go with Kensa."

"I think they had just seen too much. They couldn't stay in this world. It was a release. Not a drowning at all. Who would believe all this? Are we losing it, Ross? What happened at the pub last night? Are we trying to avoid the truth of their death? Was it suicide?"

I replied, "This is simply too much - even for you, Dawn. I looked at her and said, "It's been long enough. We should head back to reality where we might be able to make sense of all of this. Verne and Kensa must have existed outside of our own minds: physically, tangibly. We hugged them, shook hands. What I do know now is that we can't dismiss it, forget about it; we have to tell this story to others. I should turn on my cell phone and find an available flight home."

I walked upstairs to our room and plugged in my phone. After a few minutes, I checked to make sure that it was charging and there was a solitary message on the screen. My astonished silence attracted Dawn's attention.

"What's up? She called, "Is it working?"

"Define working. Here, read for yourself," I said to Dawn who had rounded the corner, filling the doorway with her fists clenched and a quizzical look on her face that I attributed to my words.

The message was short and to the point: "Now you know what's possible, are you ready to enter a new story? Askuvie."

Then I grasped the meaning of Dawn's expression. She opened her hands to expose the contents lying in her palms and whispered, "These were on the table next to the bookcase downstairs." Kensa's earrings glistened in one palm and, in the other, the unmistakable "Genesis" USB stick.

The text message, the earrings and the USB stick crunched together in my consciousness; the events of the past months erupted in one mighty explosion in my mind. I looked up at Dawn with a new understanding that our thoughts were transmitted in ways that made words redundant.

Dawn and I are forever bound through our richest experiences and a shared knowledge that our true existence would forever be beneath the veneer of daily life. We had slipped through a chink in the boundary of our world that rarely opens, alone, but together, into plausible unreality. We had been tossed mercilessly by the events of the past months with the most extraordinary friends, witnessing their travail in their search for harmonious freedom only to be left gaping at the final scene of Kensa and Verne mingling with the spray of the tumultuous sea as they effortlessly surfed on the dolphin's wake into a realm where we could not follow.

Their choices had been whittled away; they could not survive in this world where they were confronted by stark alternatives. Verne's transformation began with the game of "Genesis" and gathered speed till he was enticed by the dithyrambic beat of Moruith's clan on his first visit to the Farm. On his second visit, he suffered the torture of being torn apart as his reason clashed with his own blood and passion. What we witnessed on the rocks was his transfiguration that enabled his departure from a world that imposed limits on his itchy feet and his soul, seeking freedom.

Our only option was to turn around and to re-enter our aleatoric world of ambiguities and less permeable barriers where we could justify our existence - together if we were fortunate - trapped in an ocean of social sanction. I have recorded the flash of time that brought us into contact with these characters and I will try to convert it into a chronicle of events. The real genius, or maturity, is to give the characters their independence to mingle with the sea spray like Verne and Kensa. Dawn and I will strive to retain the wisdom that they discovered and shared as we carry on our enriched lives as we tell and retell their swelling story flecked with truth.

Epilogue

It's been more than a year since "The Cabal" sat around my table playing "Genesis." Now back in my new home, meditating in the study, I visualize Verne with his shaven head, explaining the rules of what was simply a board game. That Friday evening, over a year ago, marked the start of a sequence of events that ended months later when Dawn and I returned, smuggling deceptively normal goods through customs - unchallenged. The customs official didn't even glance at the national treasures decorating Dawn's ears. We considered surrendering them, but their personal value outweighed any significance they would have as a museum exhibit. Kensa probably never visited a museum. Besides, they were made to be worn and Kensa left them as a gift to Dawn who hasn't removed them since she first put them on. They seem grafted into Dawn's ears as if they have never been anywhere else. I've been reluctant to mention my observation to Dawn for fear of summoning Kensa's spirit.

That customs official ignored Verne's USB stick stashed in my hand luggage though it contained subversive information: a record of Verne's exploits and struggle. I presumed that, with the topsy-turvy period of my life over, I would be released from the obligation to record events. I was wrong.

Dawn's thirty four week pregnant stomach hardly inhibits her athletic stride as she enters the room with a cup of tea. She places it on the desk next to Verne's USB stick and asks, "Is it finished?" She smiles and adds, "Need some inspiration?" as she sets "Genesis" on the desk right in front of me.

"Perfect timing," I say, "The chronicle is finished."

Dawn's smile captivates me, as always, and she asks, "Does it satisfy all the voices…Verne's, Cador's Moruith's and Askuvie's?"

"Even those under the ground in Zennor's cemetery. I have fulfilled my commitment to tell it to those on their way," I say as I stroke Dawn's stomach. "It's our testimony. Do you think the chronicle can survive on its own in public? Or should I keep it private, like a diary."

"You haven't actually told the story to anyone until you cut it loose. Verne's legacy is trapped in the stick. 'Genesis' won't let you off the hook till the next generation can hear the story."

"I suppose Verne or 'Genesis' wanted me to be a witness."

"Your chronicle is like this baby inside. You will have to cut the cord, like we will when this baby's born. They'll both grow to independence."

"That's what Verne discovered: everything, including the chronicle, has to be independent to be able to choose freedom. Then it'll expand and change in its own way."

"Even in ways you may not like." Dawn pauses for a few seconds as she picks up the USB and twirls it between her fingers and says, "Verne and Askuvie would remind us that one can't always fit in...but that we should try to most of the time."

Dawn strokes her stomach with one hand, sits down in the chair next to me, puts her other hand on mine and says, "Let's hope both our creations have a touch of Cornish magic."

I squeeze her hand, lean back in the chair and gaze out the window as I say, "Months ago, Verne asked me if he was irresponsible to want complete freedom. His hunt for land didn't give him that freedom. He thought he'd found the freedom of home at Moruith's Farm, but he was repulsed by the horror. Was he chasing an illusion of freedom - something unattainable?"

Dawn's smile broadens into the one she reserves for me, and says, "Verne and Kensa broke free from this world. Now they live on their own terms."

"What about us? I'm still rooted in science. But I have more faith in mystery and magic now because we walked with fairyland characters for a while. I know that I have to escape with them every now and then."

"We have to find compatibility with those around us here to live in harmony if we want our descendents to prosper in this land."

With a chuckle, she continues, "The game was in one of the boxes from our move. Jeff's house is exactly what he promised you. Now we have to fill it with spirit. It's time to invite friends to sit around our hearth."

Verne and Askuwheteau converge in my mind, "We have to delve into the strength of the stories beneath the living land. This house and this piece of ground is our home till we become part of the story of the soil, the rocks and the water, and that will take a long time."

"How will we know when we are part of the story, Ross?"

I laugh and pretend to admonish Dawn with a wag of my finger and say, "I know you're testing me with the question I asked Askuwheteau. All we can do is live life with honour so that our descendents will have something solid they can build on."

"And we must keep a cold, clear eye on our ancestors... and their deeds."

"We have to deal with the present," I wink and answer, "If it's a boy, should we call him Verne?"

"Now you're testing me, Dr. Martindale," says Dawn with a laugh. She holds my shoulders firmly and continues, "I've cut my cord with Ottawa. It's the rule: that job demands someone without baggage - no family connections."

She takes a deep breath and says, "I want to meet 'The Cabal'. I think that you are also ready for them. You won't withdraw now."

"You're right." I nod in understanding and reply, "I'm ready to stand my ground now. I know how to acknowledge Askuwheteau and everything he represented. Verne has inspired me to engage. I'm stronger and more resourceful."

I turn to the keyboard to draft an email to "The Cabal" with the subject line, "Your Chance to Change the Rules: 'Genesis' Round II."

Printed in Great Britain
by Amazon